The Haunted Reality

True Tales of Ghosts,
Haunted Houses
&
Poltergeists Activity

By
Sharon A. Gill & Dave R. Oester,
The Ghost Hunters

A StarWest Book

Book Cover Design: Dave R. Oester
Ghost Photographs: Sharon A. Gill

Composition Software: WordPerfect 6.0a for Windows
Typesetting Software: PageMaker 5.0 for Windows
Photography Software: Photoshop 3.0.4 for Windows

Front Book Cover: The Ghost of Sellers Arts & Crafts
Back Book Cover: The Ghost of Connor Hotel

First Printing: October 1996

ISBN 0-9654405-0-8

The Ghost Hunters Gallery Web Site
http://www.aone.com/~starwest/index.html

Published by

StarWest Images
P. O. Box 976
St. Helens, OR 97051

Other Books by
Sharon A. Gill & Dave R. Oester

Twilight Visitors: Ghost Tales

To Sheri
Best Wishes
Sharon Gill
Dave Oester

Table of Contents

Introduction

The hardest aspect of writing this book was where to begin and which material to include that would give an accurate representation of that fabric of reality that is called the Spirit Realm. Many authors simply relate tales of supernatural folklore or interesting ghost stories without any insights or observation concerning the nature of the paranormal events. However, in this book, we will give our insights that we have gained from our observation and empirical study of the supernatural.

The ghost stories are true and happened to real people who had no intentions or desires to meet up with real ghosts or to find themselves living or working in haunted houses or buildings. Their first reaction normally is of disbelief and doubt. Depending upon the type of disembodied spirits present and their natural disposition toward the "living", the outcome can be generally predictable. In most cases, people will simply accept the situation and acquiesce to live with the poltergeist activity.

However, in some cases where there are a lot of negative emotions being strongly expressed or if stressful events are occurring then the situation for violent behavior is more likely. Just as some humans feed off of negative emotions, some disembodied spirits feed on the negative energy being generated by the intense emotions.

In many cases when ordinary people encounter disembodied spirits, the natural reaction is that it can't be happening to them. After all, if ghosts were real, why haven't they been taught to us in school or by our parents. It is a human reaction to fear what we do not understand and often we are quick to label something as evil simply because we do not comprehend it's nature. Death scares us because we do not know what will happen to us after we depart this life. We have stories of NDE (Near Death Experiences), but we do not know of anyone who has died and returned to life to tell all.

Some people associate death with darkness and oblivion which instills a fear of the unknown. Often our attempts to gather strength from organized religion will work well when we are in good physical and financial health. But if we suddenly find ourselves on the down side, we question the basic tenets of our belief system while we struggle in mental darkness for a ray of hope. Why? Do our organized belief systems fall short of providing us with proof of life after life? We can gather strength by understanding what happens at death. Ghost entities prove beyond a doubt that we have life after life.

What we have attempted to do in this book is to provide the basis for understanding life after life from our empirical investigations of disembodied spirits that are haunting our homes, buildings and work places. These spirits have become earthbound on this physical plane and can provide us with interesting information about life in the spirit world. This knowledge becomes the framework for building internal strength that provides the insights we need to face death, without fear.

Since not everyone has the opportunity to be ghost hunters or to explore haunted houses, we thought it would be proper to provide an example of our own investigations. We often share our insights and understandings concerning the Realm of the Dead with the people who request us to investigate their haunted homes. This sharing of insights will alleviate most of the fears felt prior to our arrival. Many people ask if we are "ghostbusters" as well as ghost hunters. Our purpose is not to cast out spirit entities, but to understand the nature of their world. We do not judge or condemn earthbound spirits simply because they exist and interface with our physical plane.

We approach each investigation with an open mind and a nonthreatening attitude toward these twilight visitors. Approaching these spirit entities in a nonthreatening manner is very important because they will mirror back non-aggressive responses in return. When we encounter the spirit entities, we respond with respect and reverence by our actions.

Our purpose is to gather information about their activities and to ascertain the reasons these spirits have become earthbound. Once we understand why the spirits are earthbound, then we can help the people involved come to a better understanding of why they remain earthbound and how best to deal with the situation.

Our field investigations of paranormal events have ranged from such simple things as ghostly scents and poltergeist pranks, to the more diverse realms of the phantom voice phenomenon or ghostly sounds. We have photographed ghostly apparitions being manifested in the physical realm by the corporal spirit entities. We will discuss the significance of capturing a disembodied spirit on film later in the book.

Often several different ghostly phenomena occur simultaneously in a given location. Seldom is there a singularity of occurrence or a single ghostly visitor that haunts a given location. We have discovered some common threads that are woven throughout the hundreds of investigations we have undertaken as we gathered ghost stories for this book and for our search for truth.

As researchers and students of the Spirit Realm, we investigate hauntings using our state-of-the-art electronic ghost detection equipment. Our black bag includes many devices used to monitor physical changes in the physical plane.

The first electronic device is a gaussmeter designed to register deviations in the electromagnetic fields. The second electronic device is a sound level meter designed to measure the intensity of audio sounds generated from below or above the human audio range. Our third device is a digital thermometer designed to measure temperature fluctuations.

Other important instruments are a tape recorder to record audio sounds for digital analysis and last, but not least, two 35mm cameras and a Polaroid camera for recording images on high speed film. Later in the book we have included chapters on the technology employed and the sources where our readers can find this technology.

Perhaps the first question most people ask regarding our paranormal investigation is, "How do you do it?" After giving it some thought, we have decided to give a typical scenario of an investigation for your benefit. The following scenario is based on a typical investigation we would conduct.

In a typical haunting, the occupants of a home might experience any of the following paranormal events in the course of their day. These events are normally minor in nature and often will go unnoticed by the occupants.

1. Creaking boards that sound like someone is walking across the floor.
2. Sounds of boxes being dropped or moved in the basement or attic.
3. Mist like apparitions may appear.
4. Items turn up missing and suddenly are returned within a few days.
5. Strange scents and odors, especially tobacco odor or a strange perfume or aftershave.
6. Electrical appliances turning on and off, such as lamps, lights or fans.
7. Low muffled voices coming from empty rooms.
8. The feeling of being watched by someone.
9. Brief peripheral glimpse of white shapes moving about.
10. Dishes or glasses sliding across counters, levitating or cups swinging on hooks.
11. Cabinet doors opening and closing on their own.
12. Objects placed in one location show up in another area of the home or building.
13. Invisible things jumping onto the bed or

couch sometimes leaving impressions
on the sheets or couch.

14. Human like apparitions that appear and
disappear in the blink of an eye.

15. Strange scratches on the skin that
appear without apparent reason.

16. A cold spot that "floats" around without
apparent explanation.

17. Physical sensation of being touched by
an invisible hand.

18.. New batteries suddenly losing their
charge after being installed.

19. Strange white streaks captured on film.

20. Strange white balls of light that appear
and disappear during an electrical
storm.

21. A child crying or a child's voice calling
out usually when no children are present.

22. Anything strange and unusual that is
happening that cannot be explained.

23. A dog or cat will react strangely to an
unseen presence.

If any of these common traits occur then there is a
good possibility that your home has spirit entities present.
A good starting point would be to keep record of the time
that these events occur and notice if they occur around the
new or full moon. We will discuss the influence of the lunar
cycle as it relates to ghostly activities later in the book. As
you begin to record the time and dates of the events, you
will see a pattern developing. We have found the patterns
to be similar in all hauntings.

Let's advance forward to an actual investigation.
Let's assume we have been contacted about a haunting
and have been asked to investigate. We will arrange a time
in the evening to visit the party requesting our help. We
request that they stay in one area of their home and let us
conduct our scans alone. We have found that when the
individual or individuals follow us around while we are
conducting our scans, it is more difficult to detect EMF

anomalies. However, once we have detected the EMF anomaly, we invite the people present to observe the readings which helps them realize that there is a non-physical presence within their home. Now we will describe the procedures we follow during an investigation.

When we arrive at a home or building where we will be conducting our investigations, we will first determine the normal background electromagnetic field energy levels. Once we have established the background level, we can eliminate all readings falling within this range for being normal and not paranormal in nature. Readings that exceed 7.0-milligauss should be ignored because its source is artificial and is being generated by some kind of electrical appliance such as fan, television, fish tanks, refrigerator, stove or electrical junction boxes.

While Dave is determining the normal EMF background levels, Sharon will load her camera's with high speed color film and checks her settings. She normally takes three camera's with her on each site. One 35-mm is loaded with high speed B&W film, another 35-mm is loaded with 400 ASA color print film. The third carmera is always a point and shoot type camera for quick response. Often she will take her Polaroid camera as a backup unit for immediate developing of prints.

If the site is a home, we start in the living room and scan with the EMF meter from floor to ceiling for any electromagnetic anomalies. We scan each room eliminating the artificial sources of EMF, hoping to find a spike or adnormal EMF signal. If an adnormal EMF anomaly is detected during the scanning phase, Sharon will immediately start snapping photographs in the immediate area of the anomaly. While she is photographing the anomaly area, Dave will scan with the thermometer to determine if there is a temperature differential within the energy anomaly as compared to the room ambient temperature. Once we have completed our investigations at a home or work place, we send off the film for developing and printing. Now lets talk about how may rolls of film we shoot during our investigations.

In any given investigation, Sharon will shoot approximately five or six rolls of film of thirty-six prints per roll. If we detect multiple anomalies then Sharon will shoot up to ten rolls of film, completely covering every inch of the home many times over. We never know if we have captured anything on film until the developed film and prints arrive from the photo lab. It is not easy to capture ghosts on film, we average about one ghostly apparition for every two hundred and fifty photographs taken.

We have assembled a collection of ghost tales under various topics, such as Lost and Confused Ghosts, Unresolved or Unfinished Business and Haunted Houses, Buildings & Places. In each of these sections, we have presented stories that illustrate the topic of the chapter. It seems that ghosts will haunt not only houses, but buildings and physical places. In the section called Insights, we will share our insights gained from our investigations of spirit entities and of life after life.

Localized folklore often represent universal notions that bridge cultural and political boundaries. Many local ghost stories will be similar to folklore tales found in other areas of the world. We have chosen a Malaysian folklore tale that will illustrate our point. This local folklore comes from a friend in Malaysia who sent this story via the Internet while we were typesetting the book. As you read the ghost story you will immediately notice that this story could easily have taken place in South Carolina, Maine, Kansas or even Oregon with just minor changes to the details. The ghost story goes as such:

This ghost story comes from reliable sources and has been confirmed to be true concerning the sweet smell of the jasmine flower. It all happened to a business executive whose car had broken down in the middle of nowhere on the north-south highway of Peninsular Malaysia, at exactly 2:00 A.M. on a Tuesday night. Due to the absence of public phone booths and his cellular phone battery was dead, he decided to walk until he came to some place to crash for the night. As he was walking, he heard footsteps behind him and he could distinctly make out the smell of jasmine flowers. Curiosity aroused, he turned back and saw the most gorgeous woman he had ever seen!

She had long silky-smooth hair and she was dressed in a pure white gown. She beckoned him over, and

13

he approached her. All of a sudden, she turned into the most hideous creature on earth. Needless to say, he fainted on the spot. He was found the next morning still unconscious and was taken to the hospital. A few weeks later, he committed suicide by jumping out the window of his ward. It has been the advice since, that whenever you travel alone at night, should you smell the scent of jasmine flowers, just keep going and don't ever look back , for once you do, you will be entranced.

The witching hour of 3 o'clock in the morning seems to be a common time for ghostly apparitions to appear in many folklore tales. From the investigations we have conducted we have found this to be true. When ghost stories are concocted around a campfire, they seem to exhibit common features such as a stranded stranger on a dark road at night that meets a beautiful woman. How often does this element appear in ghost tales? It seems that awful things happens to people as a result of meeting ghostly apparition at night that may well reflect our deathly fear of ghostly apparitions.

Whether this Malaysian ghost tale is true or not is not as important as the perceived notion that ghosts must be bad for our health or if we see a ghostly apparition something bad will happen. This notion is like what happens when a black cat walks in front of someone or not walking under ladders. Superstitions die hard even in the light of truth. Superstitions are like folklore, they seem to persist nudging the back of our minds.

"The Truth is out there" was the principle message presented on the Fox Television "X-Files" television hit show that developed almost a cult following. People want to believe that truth is really out there and that we have a right to know it. The ghost tales we will present in this book are a far cry from the Malaysian folklore of scented jasmine flowers because our stories are about real people who have experienced ghostly events in their lives and have had to come to terms with the reality of ghosts.

Find yourself a cozy chair, stoke up the fire and lean back with this book and enjoy an exciting and revealing side to the real world of ghosts.

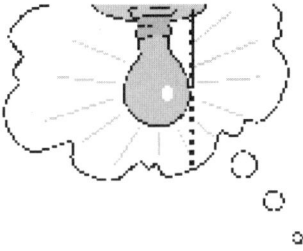

INSIGHTS

We now have a better understanding of the Spirit Realm than when we first began our research more than three years ago. Each time we investigate a paranormal event, we become further reassured as to the reality of life after death. It is not any single event that has given us hope but it is the totality of all events that become linked into an unbreakable chain of evidences. We will share with you some of the conclusions we have come to as a direct result of our research into the Spirit Realm. We know that the life force does not perish at death but continues after physical death. Our life force is an energy field; Physical death does not destroy this energy field.

We will start off with a discussion concerning the cosmology of ghosts, also known as spirit entities, departed spirits, disembodied spirits or as energy patterns. As we begin our study of the Spirit Realm, we will construct some elementary building blocks so we can apply the corollaries that are discussed herein. The first building block necessary for understanding of the Spirit Realm pertains to the First Law of Physics. This Law states matter and energy cannot be created or destroyed only transformed. This is a very important building block as it provides insights into the nature of our twilight visitors.

We know that water, H_2O, can exist in three different configurations, as a liquid, solid or gas. If we limited our contact with the liquid form of water, we would have no understanding of the potential for water to exist as steam or as ice. Now consider the analogy that the human body is like the solid form of water which is ice. At death, our body will undergo transformation as ice becomes transformed into steam. The death of the physical body empowers the metamorphic pattern known as the human spirit or soul. Thus, the spirit or soul parallels the ice to steam analogy. We still contain the essence of whom we are, only in the transformed state, without physical boundaries.

Consider the basic example of a match. The composition of a match is of various materials that yield thermo combustion. What happens when the match strikes against a hard surface? The chemicals in the head of the match ignite, venting released energies in the form of heat and light. These units of "heat" and "light" fall within the electromagnetic spectrum of energy. An ash residue becomes what the wooden stock was, yet still containing trace elements of the various chemical compounds.

Chemical agents when combined according to the right formula will generate intense heat. Some chemicals, such as potassium strips are cool to the touch but when ignited will reach very hot temperatures. Certain radio frequencies in the microwave regions of the electromagnetic spectrum will generate extreme internal heat on a cellular level of the human body. Nothing is lost in the transformation process.

Now, consider an example of a radio frequency. When we broadcast a television signal over the airwaves to our homes, then is the signal lost once we have received the broadcast? No, the original broadcasted signals are traveling at the speed of light, approximately 300,000 meters per second, into the far reaches of the Universe. We have not destroyed the signal. Our radio and television sets' capture a fraction of the signal and transform it into sound and images.

We are seeing cases where children can tap into the higher levels of their brain and increase their visual and audio range. Television shows, such as Unsolved Mysteries, Sightings, Encounters, Parnanormal Borderland and others have had children on their shows who could "see" departed spirits who have died long before the

16

children were born. The children could pick out their photographs when grouped together with other photographs of individuals. In addition, these children could also "hear" the departed spirits speak to them and in turn were able to respond to them. Some animals such as cats and dogs appear to have this higher function available to them. Just because we can't "see" or "hear" these spirit entities does not mean they do not exist.

Apparently, the ability to "see" or to "hear" the spirit entities or departed spirits lie in our innate ability to access a greater range within the electromagnetic and audio spectrum than previously thought possible. We know from our investigations that the spirit entities are able to manipulate electrical appliances, such as light switches and fans. Somehow, these spirit entities can access the control switches and bridge the gap for the electrical current to flow. In other recorded cases, a telephone will ring and when answered, telephone conversations have taken place with deceased loved ones who have "called home" to relieve fears and to console loved ones.

In many cases, these spirit entities have affected temperature changes, such as when we have experienced a narrow vertical cold spot, often running from floor to ceiling, when ghostly presences are felt or inanimate objects suddenly become hot to the touch. This sudden drop or increase in temperature is unique and impossible to explain according to our current understanding of modern science.

There are, then, four key physical manifestations or configurations for these ghostly entities:

1. The electromagnetic spectrum allows in, for example, visual images that can be seen or recorded on film. The latter are important because with a still camera or video camera there are no psychological or telepathic factors involved and the record is objective and permanent.

2. Sounds that can be heard and often picked up by various recording equipment. Again, the latter are key since the record is again objective and psychological or

telepathic factors are eliminated.

3. Physical manifestations, such as objects moving or electrical switches allowing electric current to bridge switch gaps.

4. Temperature inversion, cold or hot spots that will be very localized without any obvious causes such as drafts or external sources of heat.

The first characteristic, especially, is important since it implies that these spirit entities are a component of the electromagnetic spectrum or "energy pattern." Our physical body contains the energy pattern we call our spirit or soul. The soul or spirit conforms to the shape and size of the physical body. Consider a helium balloon for a moment. The helium gas conforms to the inner dimensions of the balloon but the helium gas is not the balloon. In the same way our soul conforms accordingly to our physical bodies. Once we puncture the balloon, the escaping helium gas assumes an entirely different shape and size. It becomes part of the surrounding atmosphere as it becomes so many parts-per-billion of the composition of the atmosphere.

This energy pattern we call our soul or spirit is one component that makes up our Universe, at least, as long as this energy pattern remains earthbound. Consider the following analogy. If we compare our Universe to the Empire State Building in New York City, the first floor would be our existence as mortals. Our spirit or soul becomes part of many energy patterns confined to the ground floor of the Empire State Building. We can't access the elevator doors to reach higher floors without a special key. We don't understand what this special key is or where we can find it while we are alive. However, upon death, we discover that the special key to unlock the elevator doors is our spirit or soul. Thus, at death, we can access the elevator doors and ascend to higher floors within the Empire State Building.

While on the first floor of the Empire State Building, we create myths and explanations for the reasons that we are here. We cultivate interpretations of life on the first floor, often seeing visions of ascended floors yet lacking the understanding to comprehend or to accept their reality. We suggest various interpretations that offer answers to our questions about the higher floors. Unfortunately, many have come to believe that once this life has come to an end on the first floor, no other floors are left to ascend. They have a mistaken belief that once the body crumbles back to the earth, all are relegated to the basement of the Empire State Building. That this becomes the end to life as we know it.

People live with the fear of death, of loneliness, unhappiness, of despair and grief when someone close to them passes on through the portals of death. Sometimes someone will die and immediately return to life filled with amazing tales of life after life. These people who have died describe bright lights and dark tunnels and are given a second chance at living. Unfortunately, most of the people living on the first floor refuse to believe, or they disregard the knowledge gained by others. Why is it easier for people to fear death than for them to rejoice at the prospect of a new life, free of the human limitations and health problems inherant in this human life? Perhaps we are afraid to believe that man is more then the sum of his earthly experiences. That there is life after life.

The photograph of the swirling energy vortex taken at Sellers Arts & Crafts is a very important part of the puzzle concerning life after life. The swirling energy vortex is casting a shadow yet when we took the photograph we observed no swirling energy vortex with the human eye. Let us consider what we can discover from this photograph. What we are seeing is pure energy! The swirling energy vortex is moving very quickly and it is stirring the air about it. In this state we find the changing density of air molecules unobservable by the human eye, yet a light striking it could not penetrate through the dense swirling energy vortex completely which resulted in the shadow cast behind it. The swirling energy vortex exists in a corporeal state but outside our human range of vision.

Thus, the spirit entity is an energy pattern that becomes a part of the universe as in the example of the helium balloon. Simple EMF gaussmeters can detect the spirit entity and by other pieces of equipment susceptible to magnetic fields and the electromagnetic spectrum, such as compasses and cameras. There may come a time in the future when the frequencies or vibrational rates effected by these energy patterns become known. When this occurs, then we can design electronic detection equipment to tune in these frequencies when ghosts are present just as someone can tune in a radio station. Until that time comes, we must rely on the basic EMF gaussmeter to detect the presences of spirit entities.

We have found that some religious groups feel consternation by our study of the paranormal world of ghosts. They will immediately judge these twilight visitors to be evil or demons. This attitude descends from their assumption that the soul is supposed to depart for an eternal resting place with God in Heaven or with Satan in Hell. The returning dead is regarded as unnatural, frightening, and demonic. The demonic spirits sole purpose is to tempt and torment people and lead them into sin, except for the Catholic Church which acknowledges that souls in purgatory might return as phantasmal or ghosts to ask for prayers from the living.

To better understand the basis for this attitude, we must turn the pages back to the dark ages of Christianity when the gods and goddesses of the pagan religions were absorbed into Christianity as the Church attempted to gain a foothold in virgin territory. The old gods and goddesses become politically incorrect and had to be portrayed as demons to the new converts. As the dark ages of Christianity evolved into the Age of Enlightenment, the old superstitions were relabeled with new names and definitions. Thus, old superstitious beliefs became merged into modern tenets of Western religion.

The original translation for the religious terms, "angel and demon" can be very enlightening. Consider the term "angel" which is translated from the Hebrew mal'akh, which originally meant "the shadow side of God." The term "demon" means "replete with wisdom" derived from the Greek term daimon, which means "divine power." Today, both terms are used by Western religions, but they are diametrically opposed to their original translation. However, if one separates religion from the study of life after life events then we have an opportunity to understand the reality of what exist in the world of the Spirit Realm that is void of bias and personal belief system which tend to color the outcome of the study.

Among religious groups, if we identify a ghost as a Guardian Angel than we have acceptance and devoted readers, but if we label the ghost as a spirit entity, guardian spirit or as departed spirit than we have denial and condemnation from the same groups. Why? What makes one "name" acceptable and another "name" unacceptable? The answer is the perceived understanding of the "name" that has become associated with the event. Unfortunately, this perceived understanding is very restrictive and linear and resembles what many people call judgement.

Regardless of deep-seated religious beliefs, activities definitely are taking place in the paranormal realm, be it acknowledged or ignored. People imbued in traditional mainstream creeds have a difficult time accepting anything outside their established territory. Early Explorers were faced with the same dilemma in their time. The Church declared the world was flat and that sailing to the far edge of the flat earth would result in death.

Early scientific study was blocked by the Church who said the sun revolved around the earth and that the earth was the center of the universe. The Church leaders refused to look through a telescope to confirm Newton's statements about moons revolving around planets because they were so convinced that they were right and Newton was wrong that they refused to verifty it with facts.

Today, each of us must be the explorers and scientists who explore the unknown, often at the condemnation of others. The knowledge gained through our research studies of life after life may often be in conflict with established mainstream Christian religious precepts while other precepts are valid and very important for us in our sojourn after death. Our purpose is to share with you the divine nature of life after life and that as human beings, we will continue to live on after death of our mortal bodies. We are seekers of truth and knowledge and the explorers of multidimensional frontiers.

We do not judge or label the spirits of the dead as good or evil. We suggest that a spirit entity or ghost will emanate either positive or negative energy depending upon their prior earthly disposition. The ancient Greeks believed in the existence of intermediary spirits between humanity and the gods called daimons. A good daimon protected and helped people. Evil daimon led people astray with bad advice.

According to the main stream religious precepts, ghosts are considered to be demons from the depth of Hell who are cursed to roam the earth. However, this religious precept creates a dilemma when the spirit entity is a loved one who has returned as a loving, caring spirit. Perhaps this deceased loved one was a good person in life, yet has returned as a spirit to say good bye or to watch over a child or spouse that was loved very much. Is this loved one now a demon or evil? The answer is absolutely, "No!" The loved one is earthbound until the unresolved issues are settled. They will then continue with their journey to the realm reserved for them.

As a result of our research and investigations, we would generally define a ghost as follows: A ghost is a spirit entity, spirit of the physically dead, departed soul or energy pattern that has previously existed as a mortal human being, who died on the earth. This departed spirit or energy pattern has become earthbound or trapped in this plane of existence because they have become lost or confused or are unable or unwilling to continue to the next plane of existence. This alignment to the earth plane is not a curse or judgement, but a sudden shift in the reality of the spirit entity. Unable to cope with the realignment, the spirit entity attempts to find stability within our plane of existence.

Essentially, some common reasons why a departed spirit becomes earthbound and lingers in this earth plane are as follows: At the time of death, a departed spirit will see a bright light or dark tunnel before them and choose not to enter but to remain behind. These lights or tunnels are the same kind of experience that many people have reported observing at the time of their death, after their sequential return to life. Other times, the bright light or dark tunnel is not seen, either way, the reason for lingering is the same: an urgency to make sure that certain things are dealt within the proper way, an emotional urgency that keeps the departed spirit earthbound.

It was urgency in life and it is the same urgency felt by a spirit entity, once the physical body passes on. The emotions remain the same and these emotions act like a magnet, drawing the spirit entity back preventing them from moving onward. The departed spirit consciously makes a decision to remain on this earth plane because they are content to remain, it is what they know, it is what they are comfortable with as they attempt to complete unfinished business or deal with unresolved emotional issues. Their decision to remain earthbound is not a curse or condemnation.

Human emotion is a very strong energy that is just as real as magnetic energy. We call this energy "emotional urgency" which acts like an energy field that traps or anchors the spirit entity to this earth plane. The departed spirit cannot escape from this earth plane until they have accomplished the resolution of that "emotional urgency." If the spirit entities eliminate this type of behavior pattern, the departed spirit is free to remain behind or enter the bright light or walk into the dark tunnel. At that time, the departed spirit may choose to cross over to their next plane of existence.

During the mortal life, the departed spirit may have been a good person but failed to completely resolve some emotional issues within their life. Perhaps bitterness or anger filled that person during their physical existence. Now after death, they exist with that emotion until they can resolve the emotion or emotions that restricted them in life. Human emotions that are negative in nature can become a paradigm of detrimental energy that we create within us. Motivational organizations have long taught that the power of a positive mental attitude will effect changes within our subconscious mind. The positive mental attitude sets up a new pattern of energy broadcast by us.

Now consider the destructive properties associated with a negative mental attitude. During the lifetime of this person, they will feel emotionally out-of-balance, perhaps experiencing deep mood swings. This person will be generating an intense energy pattern that the death of the host cannot destroy. This intense pattern will survive the physical death transformation process and continue to coexist with the spirit entity in the Spirit Realm.

Consider for a moment the following example to better understand the notion of a negative mental attitude as it pertains to a departed spirit. In this example we will use a young woman who comes from a broken home. Her birth mother had abandoned and forced her and her brothers to live with their grandparents until their father remarried. They abused this young woman during the time with the grandparents which caused deep emotional scars to form within her psyche. Later, she directed this anger toward her own father. She held her own father responsible for this abuse and buried the altered events deep within her mind, thus blocking those memories to prevent conscious access of them.

She married a man who went through a difficult childhood that caused deep emotional disorders. Together, they share extreme emotional up's and downs in their lives. Their first child is born. They compensate for their own childhood difficulties, by giving their child all the material things they never had. This overcompensation creates new problems for the couple to work with as the child becomes older and more demanding. The mother thought she had worked out her negative feelings toward her now departed father but during her emotional swings, she becomes filled with rage toward her dad.

Now, if this woman should suddenly lose her life in an accident, she would still feel the intense anger toward her own father and the urgency to protect and be near her child. Her negative mental attitude remains with her and now she finds that she craves the negative energy of others. It is kind of like a "pity party." She is drawn to living people with the same negative emotional energy output she feels. This output of negative emotional energy helps to reinforce her own negative feelings. Her intense negative emotion doesn't suddenly vanish in death but becomes even stronger. Slowly, she learns how to manipulate this strong negative energy flow to her advantage.

Her child has become her unresolved business. She wants to watch over him. Once her child is grown, she would remain earthbound due to her intense negative feelings of anger. This woman would not be considered evil in life but in death she became earthbound. If this woman had learned to forgive and forget during her mortal life, then the anchors would not exist at death. The religious precept dealing with forgiveness in this life is very important in our ongoing progression in our life after life.

We can see from the above example why they report cases of hauntings where the ghostly entity has displayed angry responses or have displayed violent behavior toward the occupants of a home. Families experiencing emotional turmoil from stress or difficulties in communication can create intense negative energy fields.

As they are discharging this intense negative energy, the families are susceptible to having departed spirits of like nature entering their home. Many youths are at risk due to high levels of kinetic energy discharged by them as they enter the teenage years of their life. These spirit entities are drawn to this negative energy much in the same way that a drunk is drawn to bars and to others of like behavior.

Children who die suddenly as a result of disease or accidents may often be confused at the time of death and are afraid of entering the bright light or dark tunnel alone that is before them. These departed spirit children have a tendency to cling to home and family. Consider children who are homeless, upon death, they cling to buildings and areas they clung to in life. As we have found with most children, they love playing good pranks on adults.

Time does not exist in the Spirit Realm as we know it, so it does not govern the departed spirits. We don't know how long it takes to acquire talents and abilities in that realm so perhaps many pranks are a result of an accident while in the process of learning and not directed toward us.

We know from our investigations and personal experiences that death is a doorway into our next plane of existence as we continue our progression. We know that a departed spirit retains the intelligence and reasoning abilities they had in mortal life so we can reason with them as a departed spirit. Often by speaking to them as you would speak to another human being achieves results. If you treat them with respect and reverence in the same manner as you would treat a friend, they will respond in kind.

Let's talk about poltergeist activities that often relate to what we could term pranks. Poltergeist is a German word meaning, "a ghost that you can hear but not see." A poltergeist will open and close doors, move dishes around, hide or take articles of clothing or items used by the family in their everyday activities. Perhaps the most common items that disappear are keys. The keys can be in your purse one moment and ten minutes later you reach for them and they are gone!

It seems that most poltergeists enjoy playing pranks such as those mentioned above. Most of the pranks appear to be of a juvenile nature suggesting that the perpetrators are young people or teenagers who are departed spirits. A parent will know that a child will often disobey so they can get attention. Perhaps many of the poltergeist pranksters are simply wanting attention or acknowledgment. We know from experience that simply talking to them and telling them to stop that normally, for a time, the pranks will cease to occur.

No religious icons or exorcism rituals are seemingly effective. Consider that the vast majority of people who die and remain on this plane of existence are not bound to Western religious interpretations. Thus, the dogmas and beliefs that bind many in this life are not in force in our life after life, unless they believe in it.

For example, a man who was a Hindu or Buddhist does not accept any Western religious rituals, so in death those rituals will have no power over him. Instead, just by changing our attitudes and resolving our negative feelings will prompt spirit entities to depart. Our emotions will generate the energy fields that either draw or repel spirit entities.

As suggested earlier, there appears to be a learning process that occurs at the time of death when a departed spirit enters the Spirit Realm and becomes earthbound. This is an entirely new experience for the departed spirit and they have to start the learning process to become integrated in their new plane of existence. The spirit entity has the ability to move physical objects and to take form within the physical plane.

However, at first, they must learn how to develope this skill. One excellent example of this process is depicted in the movie, "Ghost." Perhaps many pranks are a result of accidents rather than by intentions as the newly departed spirit attempts to learn how to move physical objects by trial and error.

Departed spirits or energy patterns are "disorganized" or "organized" in the Spirit Realm. When a departed spirit reaches the Spirit Realm, they are "disorganized," unable to function beyond a basic level of skills. We believe the spirit entity would resemble the swirling energy vortex as seen in the photographs. This swirling energy vortex would be the basic or elementary level of organization in the Spirit Realm.

A new spirit entity would have a swirling energy vortex filled with less dense composition and appear more translucent in nature. For example, the photograph taken after a funeral clearly reveals a swirling energy vortex with translucent features and concentrated dense areas.

After going through a learning curve, the swirling energy vortex will become very dense and solid white in nature. This type of departed spirit has been around for a long time and has learned how to organize itself into its higher nature. After achieving this aspect, the departed spirit must learn how to organize itself for manifestation into the physical realm. At first, the departed spirit will learn how to manifest as a mist-like cloud or small balls of light. Later, the departed spirit will have learned how to fully manifest itself into an apparitional human shape. This would be considered the highest level of organization for the departed spirit requiring much work and energy on its part to achieve.

Now the departed spirit has the ability to fully take form into the physical realm as well as to completely disorganize itself so the living can't observe it. Remember, this swirling energy vortex is a life form with intelligence and reasoning abilities just as we have in mortal life. The same nonphysical human characteristics continue with this new life form, such as shyness or vanity. Some departed spirits may feel ashamed of not having a beautiful physical body because of their vanity while in their mortal life.

If a spirit entity does not want its picture taken, it has to simply move out of the camera lens view. By the same token, if a spirit entity wants to have its picture taken, it will allow itself to be photographed. We believe that when a spirit entity allows its photograph to be taken by us, it is in effect saying that it acknowledges that we are non-threatening and it is allowing us to see that it does exist.

This seems to open up a two-way connection between this life form and us. Often the spirit entity will protect the place it haunts or the people living or working in that place. The ghost of Sellers' Arts & Crafts emits a very calming and loving sense to employees who have become upset or distressed about personal issues.

Most of the people who have called us in to investigate their haunted homes or buildings have decided at the conclusion of our visit that they do not want their ghostly visitors to depart. Once we explain about the Spirit Realm and their ghostly visitor or visitors, the people will choose names to assign to them out of respect and reverence.

There seems to be a bonding between the visitors and the people who live there. As mentioned earlier, the ghostly inhabitants assume a protective role for the family or home. Perhaps by acknowledging the twilight visitors, we have forged a link that bonds them together until the earthbound spirits are freed to continue in their progression.

Often, talking to young spirit entities can help them along their journey and letting them know that it is okay to go into the bright light or the dark tunnel. Reminding them that they should move on and cross over from this earth plane is part of the overall plan.

Let these spirits know that what they seek, can be found on the other side of the bright light or at the end of the dark tunnel, and not to fear continuing their journey into eternity. You can provide a service to them by offering to help them continue to where they need to be.

If these children's spirits are ready, they will depart. However, most of the spirits of children, being fearful and confused, are also distrustful. You must earn their trust by treating them with respect. If you try to "force" them to leave, then they may take your attempt as hostile action on your part and the repercussions can be unpleasant to say the least.

This is one reason we suggest that you do not judge departed spirits as evil or demons, but try to understand the essence of what they are. No person, living or dead, enjoys labels, such as evil or demon. Often, these words will only inflame and create hostilities within the spirit entity.

We believe a correlation exists between the lunar cycles and the apparent earth plane activities of these multidimensional beings or ghostly entities. The correlation is based on empirical data obtained from hundred's of investigations of ghosts, haunting's and poltergeist occurrences and from our research into past events that have been recorded.

Apparently, when the lunar cycle is plus or minus five days of a full moon or a new moon, paranormal events occur in an accelerated state. Perhaps this is due to the electromagnetic or gravitational wave that is at its maximum or minimum depending on which lunar cycle we look at. In at least one living ghost town where ghostly haunting's occur regularly, the old timers suggest that low pressure weather patterns need to be present during a full moon for the ghosts to be the most active.

Dr. Gunther Wachsmuth explored the meteorological link which was published in his book, *Earth and Man*. It seems that Dr. Wachsmuth discovered two time periods each day that create meteorological conditions that we have found to be consistent with ghostly activities. According to his book, the times of 3:00 A.M. and 3:00 P.M. are both ideal because these times reflect the minimum of barometric pressure in the double daily wave, plus the minimum of air movement near the ground, and a minimum of oscillations in terrestrial magnetism, and of the minimum of the potential gradients.

While at the same time, a maximum of conductivity of the vertical electric current, and of radioactivity in the layers near the ground. These two times, 3:00 A.M. and 3:00 P.M. reflect the hours of change for variations in the earth-current. Perhaps this is why these two hours are reported most often in ghost stories.

It has been our observation that the ghost of Sellers Arts & Crafts appears to be most active during the full moon cycle and then dormant until plus or minus five days of the new moon cycle. Unfortunately, we could not document the low pressure weather pattern effect as constant low pressure patterns were moving through Oregon during the Winter months.

Our empirical investigations have revealed inactive periods with no paranormal activities during the waning or waxing of the moon. Further studies of the lunar cycle and the low pressure weather might shed additional light on the nature of these multidimensional beings we call ghosts. We have included some of the ghostly photographs in the following pages as well as in the stories associated with them.

Notice the shadow cast by this vortex energy field

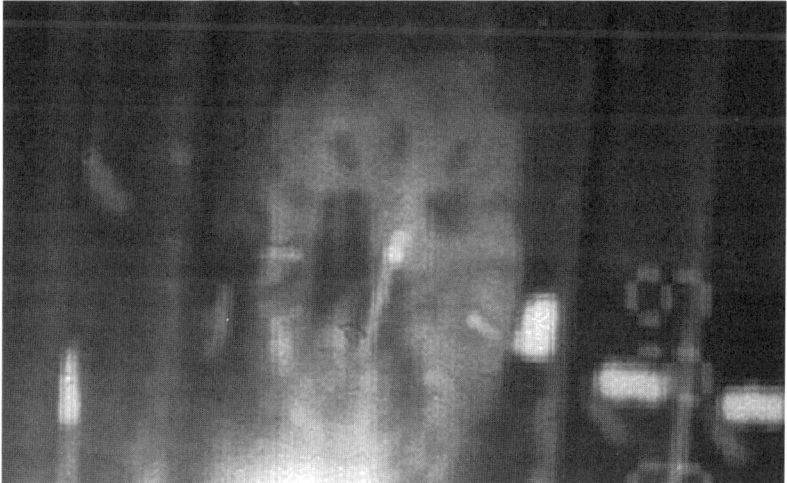

A swirling circular vortex pattern reflected in a mirror.
Credit: Virginia Burgh, Scappoose, Oregon

Eric J. Steiner Wedding Day Photograph
Credit: Eric J. Steiner, Fountain Valley, CA

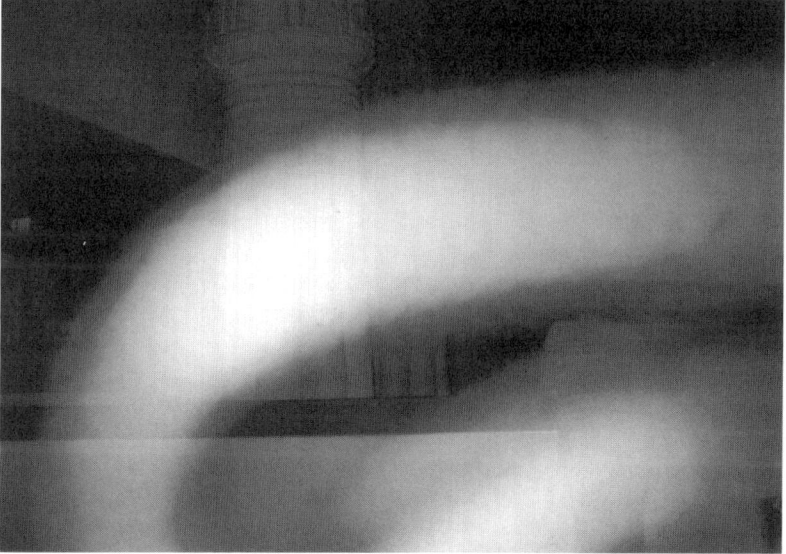

The Ghost of Luxor Hotel
Las Vegas, Nevada

This photograph was sent to us from a lady in Montreal, Quebec, Canada. The photograph was taken while her parents were visiting the Luxor Hotel in Las Vegas, Nevada. She contacted us after visiting our Web Site at http://www.aone.com/~starwest/index.html.

Notice the interesting pattern within the energy vortex cloud. Notice also that the edges are translucent and the inner composition is opaque. A tourist can be seen standing in the translucent energy field. This pattern has been repeated in other ghostly photographs sent to us.

The Haunted Reality by Sharon A. Gill & Dave R. Oester

Haunted Houses, Buildings & Places

The following ghost tales provide good examples of
ghostly entities that haunt homes, buildings and physical
locations. These spirit entities often adopt the families
living within and watches over them. Most families we
have interviewed would not want their ghostly visitors to
be expelled from their homes.

The Ghost of Sellers Arts & Crafts

The Sellers Arts & Crafts family consisting of . . .

Micky Scholl, Christie Verhoef, Doug Sellers, David Sellers & Bertha Weiss

and the

Ghostly Vortex of Sellers Arts & Crafts

Nestled along the banks of the great Columbia River, twenty minutes north of Portland, is the peaceful little bedroom community of Scappoose, Oregon. Once territory occupied by the Chinook Indians, Lewis and Clark discovered a peaceful setting, on their trek West to the Pacific Ocean. When planting gardens or leveling ground for new homes, the contractor often discovers remnants such as arrowheads, grinding stones and pottery. History abounds in this little town that in years gone by has nearly burned to the ground on three separate occasions. The strength of a community pulling together, has rebuilt and affirmed a survivorship here.

One building in particular, has a history that lives on yet today. A part of the past still roams the halls and rooms of this structure, on Columbia River Highway. It was once a place for people to gather for socializing, drinking and dancing. One room, in the rear of the building served as a nursery where mothers could leave their children, enabling them to spend the evening with their husbands. In later years, the back room became a dentist's office, where even today, the door still hangs on the second floor, nailed shut, the dentist's name imprinted on the outside. They have removed the stairway up to the door, now there is just a single reminder of that time. A single door containing a glass pane with the words "Johnson's Dental Office" painted on the glass situated high above the ground on the second floor. Today, the building holds within its walls, Sellers Arts and Crafts.

Doug Sellers, owner of the crafts store, was admittedly a skeptic at the possibility of the existence of ghosts. Until he moved into the apartment above the store, he had no reason to consider "ghost stories" anything other than the workings of overactive imaginations. However, over a short period, Doug Sellers' personal experience has taken him from being a confirmed skeptic to openly accepting the existence of ghostly visitors.

In the mornings, as Doug went downstairs to begin his day of work, he began to find various things out of place. One morning Doug walked downstairs and discovered a ribbon-display-box moved from the wall to the foot of the steps. He had to move the ribbon-display-box before he could enter the store. The strange aspect of that occurrence was that someone had taken out the ribbon-display-box of a larger cardboard display case that held many boxes of ribbon. One box was taken from the rear without disturbing the remaining boxes in front and set it neatly on the floor.

Once, Doug found someone or something had taken paint cans from behind a paint display and placed them into a box on the floor. Another time, Doug heard a crash in the store, and upon checking to see what had broken, he found a box of paint on the floor with the paint cans still sitting upright in the box. The box of paint had not fallen, it was as if the box of paint had been intentionally set on the floor. Doug returned the paint to the shelf, only to hear a crash later, again finding the paint cans, in the box, on the floor.

One night Doug was talking to a friend on the telephone and felt something cool brush against his cheek, as if someone had kissed his cheek. This night became a turning point in Doug's life, as he witnessed first hand, the existence of something unexplained in his own home. His mind no longer dismissed the possibilities of ghosts, he began to realize there was something more at work here than just his imagination. All of the unexplained occurrences taking place convinced Doug, such as the strange behavior of his cat and the sensations he was feeling. For the sake of his beloved pet, Doug needed to find some answers about what was taking place here.

All seemed normal when Doug Sellers moved into the upstairs apartment over the craft store. Something out of place or the popping and cracking of old wood as the building settled in the cool evenings would hardly have even been noticeable. However, once his cat, Skimbles, began acting strangely, Doug began to take notice of the things going on inside the building. Noises, like the sound of footsteps began to alert him to the fact that he was not alone.

While lying in bed reading, Skimbles would suddenly jump up, the hair on his body raised, hissing and fearful of something that Doug could not see. Ever more, this behavior became a nightly occurrence, and Skimbles would leave his master's side, to hide under the bed for the rest of the night. Eventually Skimbles took up residence in the back of the closet, and Doug Sellers wanted some answers about what was going on.

We were acquainted with Doug for almost a year, when the strange activity began. We received a phone call requesting that we come into the store and see if we could find out, what was going on. The strange activities were unsettling to Doug and sending his cat, Skimbles, into a state of panic. The once "macho" cat was now sleeping in the back of a closet, nervous and upset most the time.

During our research on the craft store, the storage area and the apartment, we discovered a great deal about the history of the building. We also learned a lot about the personalities of the people working in the store, the attitudes of the employees, and the overall atmosphere in the store. It was as we had suspected, an atmosphere kept business like, yet positive and upbeat most of the time. The employees are kind, sensitive women who enjoy the work they do, seven days a week. They are open-minded individuals, each of them, having accepted the fact that there is an unseen presence in their midst.

They are aware that strange things can and do happen even during business hours such as work they may do suddenly becomes undone once they turn their backs. One employee, Bertha Weiss, had just finished stacking a row of yarn onto the shelf in a neat order. She was called away to help a shopper when Bertha returned to the area of the yarn, she found what she had just neatly arranged was in a pile on the floor. Assuming they had fallen off the shelf, she again arranged them on the shelf and went on about her business. Later, while passing by the same shelf of yarn, she found the yarn in a pile on the floor. It was also on this day, she heard the back door open, but when looking up from the cash register, she saw no one there.

We arrived at the store with cameras' and our ghost hunting equipment. Our ghost hunting equipment consisted of several electronic detection meters. Our first meter for ghost hunting consisted of a gaussmeter that measures changes in the electromagnetic fields. The second electronic device is a digital temperature display meter that measures minor changes in the room temperature. The third meter is a sound-level meter which measures any subaudio sounds. Sharon has an array of cameras for capturing ghostly apparitions on Kodak ASA 400 color film.

Dave started by scanning all ground level shelves and aisles without detecting anything beyond the normal background levels of .7-milligauss or less. Dave then walked up the stairs to scan the living quarters and a warehouse found on the second floor. A few minutes later, Sharon walked up the stairs with her cameras ready for any ghostly phenomena. Suddenly, half way up the stairs, she felt a chill come over her as the hair on the back of her neck stood on end. She had the definite feeling that something or someone was following her up the stairs. When she reached the landing at the top of the stairs, she turned and snapped a photograph of the stairs.

However, Sharon saw nothing on the stairs at the time she snapped the photograph. She continued to the rear area of the second floor containing the warehouse and together we scanned shelves and aisles for unusual energy readings. Scans of the warehouse registered only normal background levels on the gaussmeter. We were disappointed at not locating any ghostly energy patterns. However, that same evening Sharon and Doug's nephew, David Sellers, heard soft music playing that apparently came from upstairs. Upon investigation, they could find no source for the ball room like music. Sharon wondered if the warehouse was the place where the mysterious music had originated from. Perhaps, a ghostly ballroom dance was in progress at the time. We returned home disappointed.

A few days later, Micky Scholl was up in the store room putting away bags of Pogs that had just arrived. She thought she heard a sound in the next aisle, and thinking that it was Christie sneaking up on her to scare her, Micky walked to the end of the aisle she was in, and just as she turned the corner, there before her was a full white, misty apparition. She screamed, the Pogs in her hands flew into the air and landed all over the floor as she quickly exited the storage area. She ran down the stairs, and seeing that Christie was with customers at the cash register, waited until she was free so she could explain what happened. Christie told me she knew something was wrong when Micky walked up to her as she was sheet white and very shaken. Christie quickly finished with the customers and Micky related her story of what happened in the store room.

Christie took Micky back upstairs, as Micky refused to go up alone to see if the ghost was still there. They found nothing out of order, except the hundreds of Pogs that were now laying all over the floor. Christie suggested that they clean up the mess, she would stay and help Micky and at the same time see if anything else would happen. While sitting on the floor and cleaning up the mess, Christie observed a spider crawling up the side of a box beside her. Now Christie can handle almost anything that comes along, but spiders are one thing that strike fear in her.

At the sight of the spider, Christie screamed, and in turn, Micky, nervous at the thought of seeing the ghost again, screamed. All the Pogs that had been picked up were again all over the floor and the two women hurriedly left the store room. If nothing else, once downstairs, they both got a good laugh out of the reaction one little spider can cause. However, Christie did tell Micky that she was now in charge of cleaning up the Pogs in the store room by herself.

As Ghost Hunters, they called us in to investigate this strange phenomenon. Again, we arrived and went in to investigate the disturbance. We chatted briefly with Christie and then went directly to the warehouse section of the second floor. Even with the overhead lights on, the isles and shelves were hidden in shadows cast by the dim lighting, creating an eerie twilight atmosphere. We scanned the shadowy area in which Micky had heard the footsteps. We were midway up the eerie isle when we discovered an anomaly residing on the top shelf. We were shocked! The anomaly registered at least five-hundred times more intense than the normal background electromagnetic field levels were displaying. The strange energy field remained in one physical location, on top of a broom box, for more than twenty-five minutes before vanishing completely. The energy anomaly was about the size and shape of a football, dropping off in intensity within twelve inches of the source, in all directions. As we were walking out of the warehouse, something or someone tossed a bag of pogs to the floor. It was as if the ghost visitor was acknowledging its presence to us.

A few days later, we picked up our photographs that included the photograph taken at the top of the stairs from the developing lab. We were both shocked and amazed! The color photograph clearly showed a swirling tornado-like energy vortex curving at the bottom that cast a shadow on the wall. Interestingly, this nonvisible swirling tornadic energy vortex had sufficient physical substance to prevent light from penetrating through the vortex, thus allowing a shadow to be cast.

Since obtaining this photograph, we have collected three more photographs showing a tornado-like energy vortex. In one photograph taken after a funeral clearly shows a horizonal swirling tornado-like energy vortex that also casts a shadow and resembles the shadow observed in our photograph. We strongly believe that our photographs, when compared with other ghostly photographs, will reveal a correlation. It is our belief that this correlation suggests that the corporeal essence of man lives on after death. We believe that this corporeal essence or intelligence can assume many patterns, such as balls of light, mist or semi-transparent apparition or a full body specter. The swirling energy vortexes often appear as a solid white or as a translucent blue.

Sellers Arts & Crafts have installed a motion detector on the flight of stairs leading to the warehouse and apartment to keep out unauthorized individuals. Sometimes, an unseen presence will trigger the alarm. A

41

corporeal presence not visible to the naked eye triggered the motion detector, as the camera has captured a shadow being cast by the swirling energy vortex. Our photographs are important because the camera records are objective and permanent without psychological or telepathic factors.

The photographic image of the swirling energy vortex is significant because it implies that these spirit entities are a component of the electromagnetic spectrum or energy patterns. Often several ghostly entities will haunt a place, much like a railway depot is a station for travelers going to various destinations. Perhaps, some ghostly entities are just visiting while others may have chosen to remain in this place.

As Ghost Hunters, we believe that when giving a ghost a name, often the pranks will subside. It is as if, the ghost is seeking recognition or acknowledgment. In addition, it also shows respect to these ghostly entities. Christie has named their ghostly visitor Billie who is welcomed as a twilight visitor in the store by the staff and customers alike. One of the first things that happened after Christie Verhoef named their ghost was that Billie stopped terrorizing the poor cat, "Skimbles," who has now calmed down and returned to sleeping on the bed, seemingly more at ease with the unseen presence.

A local television station came into the store and aired a segment on our investigation and findings as well. Billie has become a popularly mysterious part of Sellers Arts and Crafts. Now, not only do crafters enter the store for art and craft materials, curiosity is drawing those, who believe in ghostly activity into the store. They enter with anticipation of possibly catching a glimpse of Billie or hearing her actively banging things around upstairs in the storeroom.

Doug Sellers and Christie Verhoef, Doug's Mother and Store Manager, welcome the crafters as well as the curious. One word of warning though, when seeking information about Billie and her activity, Christie will openly talk of the ghost and the phenomena taking place there. She has discovered that some who come into the store presume it is okay to wander throughout the upstairs living quarters and the storage area, in hopes of sighting the entity. Christie Verhoef is extremely protective of Billie and stresses the importance of respect of privacy and private property, and woe be to the person who takes it upon his or herself to attempt investigating outside the permitted area!

Apart from all the media coverage and talk among the residents in the area about Billie, there is also a personal side to this ghost story and the people most involved with her. Scappoose is a town made up of folks who are hardworking, decent, honest and sensible. Most residents in the community are families who have been in the area for many generations. They are not hysterical publicity seekers who panic just because they cannot explain these strange happenings logically.

The employees don't seem to mind the extra work they discover occasionally, they seem to know it's just Billie making her presence known. The unexplained noises that they can hear almost any time of day, like someone is upstairs in the storage room rearranging things, dropping boxes heavily onto the floor are a common occurrence. Patrons in the store can hear all the commotion upstairs and when asking what the noise is, the employees casually explain that it's just Billie. The front and back doors open by themselves with no one in view, and even the motion sensor goes off unexpectedly day and night when no physical presence is near them. It's enough to give you an eerie feeling and yet Billie has never been considered a nuisance, she has become a big part of the Sellers family.

Apart from the many surprises that the employees find here and there, Billie gives them something that they say is difficult to explain, but it happens. Christie Verhoef explained it best, "It's like when I am feeling my lowest and need something to boost my spirits to make me feel good again. I'll feel a coolness surround me then suddenly, I feel as though I am on the highest of highs. My blues vanish and for the rest of the day and I feel a happiness that is hard to describe." More than one employee has described having the same sensation come over them.

It was a busy time, near Christmas, when Micky Scholl was walking from the front of the store back to the cash register where Christie was standing. She was feeling pretty down that day, focusing on a problem she wanted to discuss with Christie. As she reached the foot of the staircase, she felt a chilling cold around her, then as suddenly as it was there, it was gone. What remained was a joy Micky had not felt before. Her blues had vanished and as she described it, " almost felt giddy all of a sudden." The feelings lasted the rest of the day.

Billie has never been considered to be a malevolent spirit; they have accepted her with open arms. The people at Sellers Arts and Crafts feel that Billie is there for a reason, though it is one they do not know or understand. They feel she is there to protect and watch over them. They want her to remain there, they'd be happy to have her with them always. They hope one day to have a better understanding of why Billie has chosen to remain behind and hope that Billie will somehow find a way of revealing the answers to some of their questions.

Billie has already shown herself, in misty white form, to two of the employees of the store. Christie Verhoef herself, saw a distinct form, and thinking that maybe it was Skimbles, went over to see if the cat was all right. As she neared what she thought was Skimbles, it vanished before her eyes. David Sellers has also observed what he thought was their white cat running across the floor in his bedroom. When he went to see why Skimbles was running so fast he was shocked. The cat had vanished. David went downstairs and discovered that Skimbles was sleeping in the window.

As we relate these events that have taken place in and around the craft store, you may feel as we do that the presence in the building is one of caring and protecting. The employees attest to this also. Yet, we must relate to you, one story of a more negative nature when talking about Billie. This is not the tale of a negative spirit on the premises of Sellers Arts and Crafts, but one of a negative, judgmental attitude toward the idea of an earthbound spirit. As the craft store was nearing the hour of closing, Christie had set aside some extra time, after hours to let us come in and take some readings and take some pictures of various areas of activity.

The last customer was in the store and had picked out some yarn, which she brought to the cash registered to purchase. Feeling the way Christie feels about Billie, she keeps a picture of Billie on the counter. The woman put the yarn down on the counter and asked Christie what that picture was in front of her. Christie told her that was Billie, the ghost who lived there in the store. The woman looked at Christie and said very calmly, "You have a ghost here?" Christie said yes they did and at the moment the words came out of her mouth, the woman turned and walked angrily out of the store, stating that this was a place of demons.

Nothing has changed for the employees at the store, but they now find they have come to a greater awareness of their surroundings, seen and unseen. They are very comfortable with the situation at the craft store, happy for things to remain the way they are now and always pleased to share a good ghost story with anyone who is interested in hearing about Billie.

Doug Sellers related another strange event that happened to him in his office. He had had a very long and hard day. He knew he had a backlog of paperwork to catch up on at home and hoped to spend a quiet evening getting most of the work done.

He'd been in his office upstairs for some time trying to concentrate on the work before him. He'd been trying to ignore the sounds coming from the warehouse. He knew it was Billie, she was the only one who had access to the upstairs after business hours. Tonight it seemed like she was busily moving things around, footsteps were heard and the sound of boxes scooting across the wood floor.

To Doug, this was nothing out of the ordinary, but tonight he began to feel it wearing on his nerves due to the workload before him. After a time, Doug felt tormented by the sounds of activity in the warehouse. Suddenly, Skimbles came tearing into the office having been scared to death by something only the cat could see. Doug, trying with much difficulty to focus on his computer screen, was startled by the unexpected reaction of his cat.

He turned in his chair, looking out the office door toward the warehouse and shouted, "Billie, stop it now. I have a lot to do here!" His tone sharper than normal. Doug returned to the computer screen, the noise subsided so maybe now he could continue in peace. But he never expected what happened next.

The office began to get cold until the entire room was enshrouded in an unearthly bitter cold. Only the office had suddenly dropped in temperature because when he stepped from his office into his apartment, the temperature was normal. Later, Doug told us that when he yelled at Billie to stop, she felt he'd turned a cold shoulder to her so she responded in a like manner. He feels they test each other in this manner on occasion, trying to understand one another. Doug feels Billie has as much curiosity about him as he has about her.

More on Skimbles, the cat

Skimbles is continually tormented by Billie. Skimbles has become a first alert to his owner that something is present. Skimbles races down the stairs to the Craft store, stopping on the landing, turning to look back up the stairs as though something has chased after him. At times, Skimbles will watch intently, something walking across the apartment, his head moving slowly in the direction the presence is moving. He's even gotten up from his resting place to follow this invisible resident to the top of the stairs, to then stand and watch something descend the stairs.

If only Skimbles could tell us what exactly it is that he is seeing on a regular basis. He seems to have found one safe place where he gets undisturbed sleep, that is by the back door of the Craft store.

Now, Skimbles is a large white male cat, known to be very macho. He's a cat with an attitude. As a kitten he was attacked and badly hurt by a large dog which left him very defensive. Due to the serious injuries to his back and hind legs, strangers rarely get close and petting him could result in a bite.

Doug Sellers obtained Skimbles to give him a good home where he would no longer have to face those types of dangers. Over time, Skimbles has grown into a big beautiful animal with macho attitude and independent ways. He is loved and respected by his owner and family members as well.

As a result of the ever increasing nervousness, weight loss and even some hair loss, Doug Sellers has found a companion for Skimbles. The latest addition to Sellers household has been named "Herbie", of the Love Bug fame. Herbie is a bit younger, has not exhibited any signs of being bothered by Billie or any other unseen visitors to Sellers Arts & Crafts.

Guardian Angel or Guardian Spirit

In speaking with Christie Verhoef, before she revealed the details of her story, I asked her if there was anything she felt reluctant to reveal? We have found, from experience, the people we speak with about their experiences are sensitive and nervous to reveal their stories publicly or have their names used.

Most everyone begins an interview by saying, "I have never told anyone about this, people would think I'm crazy!" or "You'll probably think I'm nuts." Therefore, I wanted to afford Christie the opportunity to tell this story in a manner which made her the most comfortable. This was her response;

"The way I feel," Christie began," anything I want to tell you I would want everybody to know. I would not keep anything from anyone because anything I would have to say would be exciting and interesting because it was something I had never experienced before. I think if you try to hide things, overshadow things, then it leaves doubt in other people's minds. I would not want anyone to feel that I'm in any way, shape or form, covering up anything or try to embellish on it to make it better. I would just like to deal with the facts, for what it is, not make any changes."

One day last winter, Christie was at work, at Sellers Arts and Crafts. It had been raining very hard most all day and it was cold as well. Christies' family always teased her because of her ability to fall down, wherever she goes. Christies' Mom has even threatened to tie air bags around her, in an inner tube fashion, to act as a cushion should she fall down. She's never been seriously injured in a fall, but has sustained the normal bumps and bruises as well as a sprain on occasion.

This particular day, Christie was working with Micky Scholl. Micky is not only a coworker, but also a very good friend. Micky had also joked about Christie needing airbags. She has witnessed on many occasions, Christie falling down.

Christie had gone out to the parking lot to get her vehicle as she had some deliveries to make. She pulled her Chevy Blazer around to just outside the backdoor of the craft store, to load some boxes for delivery. The boxes had all been stacked there, in front of the glass door for loading.

Christie had pulled the Blazer as close to the building as she could to prevent the boxes from getting wet while they were loaded. She stepped out of the vehicle, not realizing there was a pothole beneath her feet, and she fell to the ground. She lay on the wet pavement, stunned, flat on her back, in the small space between her Blazer and the back wall of the building.

Micky had been standing by the backdoor, watching Christie pull the vehicle close to the building. She saw Christie step out of the Blazer and fall to the ground. She also saw Christie hit her head on the pavement and knew Christie could be seriously injured.

Try as she might, Micky could not get out the door to help her friend. On the inside of the door the boxes were

were stacked and Christie had fallen right in front of the door, blocking any chance of pushing the door outward so Micky could get to her.

Micky's concern mounted as she struggled to move the boxes enough to where she could squeeze out the opening. She yelled, "don't move Christie, don't move!" working as quickly as she could to get the door unblocked.

Christie lay on the cold, wet pavement, looking up at the dark, stormy sky and the rain that was falling on her. Micky, had successfully gotten through the doorway and now knelt beside her friend's side, asking her if she were okay. Christie told her the only thing that she thought did not hurt, was her eyebrows. Micky felt she should call 911 and get an ambulance there to help. She was concerned for her friend, and not knowing how badly she was injured, feared she would be unable to help Christie get up off the wet ground because Christie is a large woman. Christie refused, saying she would be okay, she just needed a moment.

The area around the two ladies was all open parking lot with a wide alley that ran north of the back of the store. Micky was worried, there was no one around, no one who could help them. As she knelt by Christie, she noticed two brown boots under the edge of the Blazer. She looked up, the same moment Christie looked up to see a small man standing where no one had been just a moment before.

Both women described him as a tiny little man, about 5"4" tall dressed in ragged jeans, a flannel shirt, and brown "motorcycle style" boots. He had red hair, a regular haircut, not really short and not real long, a red beard and deep blue eyes. In a soft spoken voice, he leaned over and asked Christie if she was okay? Christie told the man she was all right, she just needed a few minutes to lie there before she'd try to get up. She knew if she could get up and walk, she'd know if she was hurt anyplace. She doesn't want people fussing over her, she'd rather take her time and get up at her own pace.

Micky said, "I don't know how we're going to get you up from where you are Christie." There was very little room to maneuver her around so she could sit up and it would take a couple of strong men to lift her.

Christie recalls the man who appeared from nowhere, fondly as a very kind and gentle man. "Foolish as it may sound, in the presence of this man, I had no pain." Somehow, even through her fear of a serious back injury, she felt overwhelmed by a peace of mind she'd never experienced before. Christie explained she has Rheumatoid Arthritis so any injury from a fall of this magnitude, could be crippling to her. Her greatest concern was the severe pain in her back that she felt. However, she felt a peaceful assurance that everything would be okay.

The man told Christie when she was ready, he would lift her up. Christie responded that she didn't hardly think so. She said, "no, I am a larger lady than you think. I outweigh you probably twice and laying flat on my back, I could be of no help to you at all. No, I'll just lay here." The rain continued pouring down on them and they knew they needed to do something quickly.

The man said, "I'll tell you what you do. I'm going to grab you around your shoulders . . ." but Christie interrupted, saying, "and you're going to drop me on the ground." The man gently assured her trusting him would be okay. He told Micky to watch Christies' feet for him that he would pick her up. The odds were against the little man being able to successfully lift her but the options were much less desirable. There was still no one else anywhere around. The alley and parking lot remained totally empty.

The man slid his hands under Christies arms. "He stood me up! It was almost like I weighed nothing! Here I was flat on my back, I could not use my arms to help nor my legs to help him get me up. He told me to just lay flat and not try to lift myself, to just let him do the work," she said to me with excitement still in her voice. "I was certain I'd be laying out in the rain in that puddle of water for some time," she said. "I could not believe he just stood me up, made sure I was okay, he checked my head and asked me again if I would be okay. I was in such shock that he could even lift me!"

I hobbled into the store, it was just a matter of seconds, I turned to thank him but he was gone! I told

Micky to get his name, I wanted to send him a thank you card for all his help. Micky looked everywhere but the man had vanished. Both ladies recall he was not there when Christie fell, there was no one around, not in the parking lot, not in the alley next to the store.

Christie expressed how badly she still feels as she never got a chance to thank the man for helping her. Once he had gotten her to her feet, all she could say was "Oh my god, I can't believe you actually lifted me and stood me up." She had never seen this man before nor has she seen him since. Scappoose is a very small town where everyone knows everyone, but no one seemed to know who this stranger might have been. Had he been a local resident, chances are he would have returned at some time to check in at the store and see how Christie was doing. There was no car, no truck, no vehicle of any kind around that he could have left in so quickly.

"I'm not a trusting person. I normally would not allow just anyone to come along and pick me up after a fall. Something about this little man, gave me such peace and comfort in knowing I would be all right." Christie went on to explain, "What was strange was, I twisted my spine when I fell and had felt such pain, I figured it was severely injured. I had no spinal injury at all, not even any pain in my back from the fall itself!" Christie remembered when she fell to the ground, she had "really smacked her spine on the pavement," as well as her head. The only injury was a sprained ankle and bruising of her leg.

When Christie had looked up into the man's eyes, she recalls such a depth in the blueness, She said, "It was like looking into eternity. They were so full of tenderness and gave me such peace. It felt like he could look deep into my soul, they were electric!"

Christie described his hands as he lifted her. Normally when someone is lifting a person from a prone position and they are heavy, more pressure is required to lift that person. Chris said she never felt any pressure in the tender area under her arms. She never felt a thing. Another amazing fact was that she never had any kind of bruising under her arms from the pressure of being lifted.

Christie was amazed since she bruises extremely easily. She said he made her feel as though she was as light as a feather and that was one reason she wanted to thank him. In conclusion, Christie feels there is a protecting spirit in the old Sellers Arts and Crafts building. She has felt that since she began working there.

Christie has people coming into the store who ask about the "ghost" and if the stories are true. She, as well as other employees speak openly about the spirit they've come to know as "Billie." There are those who tell Christie that according to the Bible, ghosts are demonic or of the devil. Christie responds to them, "If this spirit is demonic, evil or bad, then are you saying that if say, this were the spirit of your Mom or Dad, Sister or Brother that this is evil? Maybe that person watches over you and gives you comfort or peace of mind during hard times, does that make them demonic?"

"It's thinking like that that is really sad, because you're cutting yourself out from an experience that none of us have an answer for. Whatever it is, whatever is allowing this to happen, for us, not always to us." Christie says she knows there are those out there who have had some bad experiences and she's very sorry for them. But the experiences that occur at the craft store have been very positive. She feels there is more than one presence, possibly two or three and they have a lot of fun with them. Now that they have a little better understanding of what they are all about, they enjoy them being there. The ghosts play pranks on them when they least expect it and do things throughout the building to let them know they are still there and want some attention!

"I think people are hurting themselves by being so closed minded when I think something good can come from this too. I've always heard that sometimes people see the ghostly appearance of a loved one and until they feel you are accepting of their passing, they find it hard to go on and remain earthbound. If you are a close family and your heart is full of pain because of their death, I think they will show you in ways they are okay."

"Whatever appeared outside that day to help me, I

feel it was whoever it is who protects us in the store. They've appeared in many ways to us in the store and help us, making our time at work easier for us. The jokes are done to remind us to loosen up a little bit.

We are all family minded people, we easily get caught up in the seriousness of business, dealing with the public on a daily basis, and stresses in daily life. We have to remember to laugh and find humor in things that happen in each one of our lives, to laugh at ourselves. We all need to be reminded of that and whomever remains here in spirit has helped us in that regard."

Christie stated not one employee has ever felt any fear even knowing there are ghosts in the building. When Micky saw the apparition up in the warehouse, it was a momentous event none of them will ever forget. When Christie saw the apparition that she had thought was Skimbles, she felt no fear but was thrilled at being allowed to see one of the ghostly residents. It all comes from having a better understanding of them and always respecting the essence of who they are.

The experience with the man outside cannot be explained away, but Christie is glad it happened and considers it to be a gift. "I feel it was a gift of understanding, understanding what is out there, understanding what we don't see. Getting back to caring, loving, thinking about others again, not just ourselves, all those feelings that got pushed aside because I was so busy in my own little world. These gifts gave me also the gifts of sight, feeling, expression and the gift of believing in something again. It was a reminder to me of all these things."

"Every person who works at Sellers Arts and Crafts has been shown something very positive as a reminder not to forget the very basic emotions of life, joy and laughter being an essential element of living. Even one-second of laughter makes it worth it. There is too much pain, sorrow and seriousness everywhere, to be able to laugh for a moment helps to break that pattern of negative emotion, and it helps." Christie firmly told us.

When Billie appeared to Micky and Christie, it gave

them something we all tend to set aside. It enabled them to be more alert and aware of their surroundings. It was also an event that enabled them to understand that this can happen at any time, in any place inside the store or outside the perimeter of the building. They've contemplated the possibility, discussed it between themselves and gave them a desire to know more and to want to see Billie again. They prepare every day for this to happen again.

Billie, by his presence and activity, has given these people a bond. They've become very close as co-workers and closer friends than they had been before. They've shared a wonderful experience that few share together and feel free to talk about, laugh about and be a part of it together on an ongoing basis.

As it is, when Billie now begins to stir up a commotion, they speak to him by name, telling him they cannot play at the moment, to go upstairs, to bed or to the warehouse. Billie listens to their words and seems to know she needs to respect their wishes, so she quiets down, until the next time.

Christie Verhoef says the employees are given something every day, there working at the store. To Doug Sellers, Christie Verhoef, Micky Scholl, Bertha Weiss, David Sellers and John Verhoef, it doesn't really matter if people believe it or not, they all know it's true. "We want to be selfish and keep Billie right there with us always." If you don't believe it, drop by and ask them about Billie. She is part of the family business at Sellers Arts and Crafts and they welcome people interested in learning what they have to share.

As Billies popularity increased, Christie found herself in a dilemma. Curiosity seekers all wanted to roam the building freely in hopes of seeing Billie. The upstairs is, of course, off limits to the public. She decided to have a motion sensor installed to alert her to anyone who might decide to explore upstairs without her knowledge.

The day the man arrived to install this device, Christie found herself wondering about certain things concerning the sensors sensitivity and function. She began asking some questions, wondering what kind of reaction she would get from the electrician. She said, "Now I have to ask a very serious question, does anything that goes by this, set it off?" He responded, "Oh yes, anybody." Christie laughed and said, I really hated to ask him this next question but, "What if it's a ghost? I have to know." He said, "Well, I guess if one walks by here, it will set it off, I'm not really sure, but you let me know if it does." He seemed to waste no time leaving the store once the unit was installed.

It wasn't two days later and all day they'd hear, ding, ding, ding, ding, all the time like Billie was just sitting there in the doorway, the sensor going off like crazy. " We'd be so busy in the store with customers and this sensor would go off. We'd run to check but no one was ever there or even close to it."

They have also put big jingle bells above both entrances to the store so they'll know when customers enter. These also frequently sound off though no one enters or leaves, at least no one they can see! When Billie comes or goes, the bells ring differently than when a physical person walks in. They've all come to know the difference. On some days when Billie seems especially wanting to play, they have to turn off the motion sensor or it alerts them to something constantly.

On a perfectly beautiful day, with no wind present at all, the back door will open, all the way outward like someone is going out. All of this indicates to all the employees that Billie does have a sense of humor and does have ways of drawing their attention to her being present.

Billie Welcomes All Outsiders

Friends of Doug Sellers, who have known him for years, dismiss his stories of Billie as pure hogwash! Not until one close friend stayed one night in Dougs' apartment did he come to believe in the unbelievable.

After having worked late with Doug one night, Doug offered his friend Tim the extra bed in his apartment to save him a long drive home. Being tired, he willingly accepted the offer.

As Tim lay in bed relaxing from a long day, just starting to doze off, he was suddenly awakened by the sound of footsteps in the hallway of the apartment. He thought it was Doug wandering around. After hearing this for some time, he got up to check but found Doug was fast asleep in his own room. He returned to his bed, a bit bewildered as he was certain he had heard someone walking around.

He'd heard the stories of Billie but was a confirmed skeptic, openly professing his disbelief to all. Tim not only heard someone walking around the apartment but he suddenly felt someone was near, watching. He pulled the blanket up over his head, which by this time he had positioned his head under the pillow.

Skimbles entered the room and jumped up on the bed. Tim welcomed the cat saying, "Yeah Skimbles, you come lay with me. Stay here and protect me." But it wasn't too long before Skimbles took off, he certainly wasn't sticking around. So Tim was left laying there alone, scared spitless. He definitely did not believe in ghosts, but he had experienced something that he could not explain away.

The next morning when Tim got up, Doug saw him and Tim related what had happened during the night. Tims' eyes were as big as saucers as he recalled every detail of the long night.

Doug told him next time to tell Billie to go back to the warehouse or somewhere else and leave him alone. Tim told Doug that his bedroom was a converted part of the warehouse, he had just wanted Billie out of there. Besides, after one experience, he swore he'd never spend another night in that apartment! All it took was one night to convince Tim, the existence of ghosts is very real. He too, is no longer a skeptic.

Another Experience

Doug Sellers had just finished putting some new merchandise out on display when Christie stopped by the store to visit. He walked Christie around the store, showing her the new items. Skimbles too was wandering casually about the aisles, following Doug and Christie as he normally does. Everything had been normal and quiet lately and today was no different, or so it seemed.

They had made their way to the art supplies, on the south wall, not far from the cash register. They were standing there casually talking, when all of a sudden, Skimbles jumped, almost falling over backwards. He acted like something had jumped out at him. He arched his back, his head moved forward then back, forward and back as he watched something very intently. Christie and Doug could see nothing except that Skimbles acted like he was scared to death of something right there in front of him.

"What in the world is the matter with Skimbles, why is he acting so strange? He acts like he's scared to death of something." Christie asked Doug. Always, when Billie was near, they could feel his presence as a physical manifestation of very cold or a very warm temperature flux. Neither Christie nor Doug had felt a sensation like that while standing there. Besides, Billie had been very quiet lately.

Doug thought maybe Skimbles had seen a mouse, but Christie said, "When is a cat afraid of a mouse?" Doug bent down and began to lift up the bottom shelves, checking for the presence of a varment of some kind. Every time Doug lifted a shelf, Skimbles would back further away. Doug tried to coax Skimbles closer but the cat would have no part of it. By the time Doug was done, the cat had done a backflip and fled the area in terror.

Christie and Doug did not understand the cat's behavior. They continued to talk and wander around the store for some time. When it came time for Christie to

The Haunted Reality by Sharon A. Gill & Dave R. Oester

leave, she suggested to Doug that he go get Skimbles, pick him up and walk toward the area that had frightened him, to see if whatever had scared him was still there. Doug found Skimbles and lifted him gently, talking to him in a soft voice, petting him and holding him close to his chest. Skimbles loves the attention from Doug and to be held like this was the absolute cat's meow. He reacted normally, snuggling closer to Doug. It seemed as if everything was back to normal once again. Doug walked over to the place the cat had reacted so fearfully before and the cat, nestled in his loving masters arms, once again became terrified. He began clawing and scratching Doug to get away from him, his hands and arms a mass of bloody scratches. The cat jumped down and ran from the store upstairs to the apartment. Whatever it was that Skimbles saw, he wanted no part of it.

Normally, Skimbles runs down to the store to escape the activity of the apartment, but never before has he run from the store, terrified, to escape something in the store. Christie explained that Skimbles is basically a cat with an attitude. He is the living equivalent of the cartoon character, Garfield. He's happiest just eating, sleeping and being lazy, not being bothered by anyone or anything at any time. He has his own agenda, don't interrupt it.

Obviously, Billie or whoever is present from the other realm, seems to love harassing the cat by keeping him on the move. Skimbles, preferring to live the lifestyle he so loves, does not appreciate being continuously disturbed. He automatically reacts with fervor upon seeing his tormentor.

Since the arrival of his new companion, Herbie, Skimbles has mellowed out a lot. That was one reason why Christie was so surprised at this latest incident. It had been quite some time since Skimbles had reacted so fearfully.

Christie wondered if this particular spirit could have been a transient spirit just passing through. His reaction was a bit more dramatic this time. It looks like only Skimbles can answer that question, and he's not talking.

58

The Last Word

On May 30, 1996, Micky Scholl was scheduled to work alone at Sellers Arts and Crafts. Business had been a bit slow lately so one person could easily run the store, or so it had been.

As it was, Micky found herself swamped with customers all day. She preferred it that way, but this particular day had turned out to be especially nerve racking. Billie had also had a full day of activity, up in the warehouse.

Micky had heard footsteps walking heavily across the floor, back and forth, from one end of the room to the other, all day long. The sounds were so distinct it was difficult to determine if it was Billie or truly an intruder. Most of Billies activity is heard when it is quiet in the store. Hearing him when the store was so full of customers was rare.

By the end of the day, Micky was tired and ready to lock up the store and go home. For the first time, Billie had really worn on her nerves so going home to relax in peace and quiet was a welcome thought. As she picked up her keys, she looked up at the ceiling, even at six o'clock in the evening, the commotion upstairs continued.

Micky considered the possibility someone had actually gotten past her to the upstairs into the warehouse. She wondered if she should go up and double check, just to be sure, before she left. She had watched so carefully all day to make certain no one went up there. Since the noise had been the same all day, she was sure it was just an extraordinarily active Billie and decided to go on home. She walked to the backdoor.

Micky opened the door and started to step out, but instead she turned, saying to the cat, "Goodnight Skimbles." Frustrated from a long day, she loudly said, "okay Billie, I'm leaving. You can have the whole place to yourself." Her tone was more sarcastic than normal, but darn it, she was tired.

Micky locked the back door and took a deep breath of the clean, fresh, cool air. She quickly walked to her car, a new one, only a few months old. She unlocked the door and got into the driver's seat. Putting the key into the ignition, she turned it. Nothing happened. The engine didn't turn over. She tried it again and then again, but nothing happened, nothing at all.

It was a new car, but maybe the battery had gone dead for some unknown reason. Her thoughts raced, trying to understand what could be wrong. There was no one else around, so she sat in her car wondering what to do.

As she sat there, she remembered her cellular phone. She had just charged the battery so she'd call her husband and have him come help her get the car started. She picked up the phone and began to push the buttons, dialing her home number. Nothing happened. The phone wasn't working either. The battery had gone dead, but that wasn't possible! The battery had been fully charged just hours before. What was going on here anyway?

Micky wondered what to do now. The only other accessible phone was back in the craft store and she really did not want to go back in there. By now she was feeling somewhat afraid because of what was happening to her. She remembered her harsh words to Billie as she left the store. It was then she realized she could try one more thing.

Micky looked back toward the craft store and loudly said, "I'm sorry Billie. I won't ever talk to you that way again." Hoping beyond hope, Micky turned back around to face the steering wheel. She put her fingers on the key and turned it in the ignition. The engine turned over and purred like a kitten. Micky put the car in gear and left the parking lot heading for home.

She had not had a problem such as this with her car before this nor since that evening. Her cellular phone had never given her a problem either until that night. Something had drained the fresh battery.

We had personally seen this very thing happen twice before, ourselves. The ABC Nightline Camera crew found all their fresh batteries were dead when they began filming in the basement of our old Seaside house. Every single one! Also the batteries in my camera suddenly went dead as I tried to photograph an old funeral carriage in the old ghost town of Bodie, in California.

Micky feels Billie didn't appreciate her comment as she left the store that night. She admits she was a bit disrespectful when she called out to her. When she apologized, Billie was willing to let her leave.

Billie is a spirit who asks little, but commands attention on occasion and demands respect all the time. That's little to ask for someone who has been around as long as she has. Woe be to the person who crosses that line with Billie because one way or another, she'll let you know, she wants an apology!

Authors Notes:

The ghost that dwells at Sellers Arts & Crafts is loving, caring and a protective entity that has adopted the people who work and live at the store. This ghost is very happy and is not wanting to move on from this earth plane. If Billie has unfinished business or unresolved issues, we are yet to discover it. Billie is most active in the days before, during and after a full moon or a new moon.

The Girl in the Nightgown

When I was fifteen, we traveled from New York to Michigan to spend Thanksgiving with my Aunt's family. My aunt and uncle had just moved to a new ranch style home in a subdivision built on farmland. There were eleven of us tripping over one another in the four-bedroom house. They gave us sleeping assignments for any available cot, sofa or bed. We managed pretty well until the second night.

They assigned me sleeping quarters in the baby's room. The room was painted a soft pink that resembles a nursery. The baby crib with hanging mobile strips was against the wall closest to the door. Next to the baby crib stood a chest of drawers on which sat a baby scale. My cot was in the opposite corner of the room against the wall.

I was just falling asleep when I heard the baby scale move. The sound was like the springs being depressed, as if something was placed on top of the scales. I told myself that I was imagining it that I had misinterpreted some sound the baby had made while sleeping. My little cousin made soft sucking sounds and murmurs in her sleep, and it was after all, a different house then the one I had been use to sleeping in.

I thought perhaps I had been dreaming and that I hadn't really heard anything. Then, I heard the sound again, clearly, unmistakably. There is no sound in the world like a creaking spring. My cot had no springs so it could not be making the noises. I began to get nervous as I stared wide-eyed into the dark, torn between a desire to hide beneath the blankets and the fear that something would creep up on me if I didn't keep watch.

Something was in the room with me. I jumped out of bed and hurried down the hall, joining the family at the other end of the house in the recreation room. All the adults were still up and I sat at the table with them, scared, not wanting to go back to that room. My aunt wanted to know what was wrong. At first, I was ashamed to say anything, just insisting that I couldn't sleep.

She didn't believe me, so finally I admitted that I was hearing things in the baby's room. I was afraid that she would laugh at me and then my mother would be disgusted with me for acting like a baby. My aunt and uncle exchanged looks, and finally said, "Well, we didn't want to say anything, but . . . we seem to have a ghost here." They went on to say that there was a cold spot in the hallway just outside the baby's room that smelled like mildew and molding leaves. The smell would come and go, and at first, they tried to blame it on the heating system creating a draft.

My aunt told me the following stories about their ghost. One night my aunt thought that her daughters had gotten out of bed and were reading books in the living room. She could hear pages in a book being turned and wondered why the girls were up. She came around the corner to tell the girls, age four and two, to get to bed and found no one in the living room. However, their four-year-old daughter had previously asked, "Where had the little girl gone?" When they asked what little girl? Their daughter said, "The little girl that plays in the living room sometimes."

Another night, my uncle and aunt were awakened from a deep sleep by the sounds of crockery crashing and shattering. They leaped from bed, thinking someone had broken into the house and charged into the kitchen. They expected to find every dish they owned shattered on the floor, but not one thing was out of place. The kitchen looked as clean and peaceful as it did when they went to bed.

My aunt looked at me and said, "Go ahead and sleep in the girls' room tonight. It's far enough away from the cold spot that I don't think you'll have any trouble."

Gratefully, I crawled into the lower bunk and listened to my two little cousins' snore. I fell asleep. Sometime during the night, I awoke with a start, having heard something heavy being dragged down the hallway, just outside my bedroom door. My mind filled in the horrifying image of a body being dragged. Terrified, I couldn't go back to sleep. I listened to the cuckoo clock in the living room sound every half hour from three in the morning until six. My heart hammered so hard I could hardly breathe. I lay stiffly, scared to death I would hear something or see something.

I knew my dad planned on getting up at six so we could get an early start on our trip back. I strained my ears listening for the sounds of his stirring. Minutes crept by, the cuckoo sounded the hour of six. I jumped out of bed and hurried out. When I reached the kitchen, my dad, who was standing in the recreation room onto which the kitchen opened, asked me, "What were you doing out here when I got up this morning?"

"I wasn't out here," I said. "I just came out here

now." I didn't want to admit how terrified I'd been all night. Now, it seemed so stupid.

"I saw you standing there by the sink," he insisted.

"Daddy, honestly, I just this minute came out here."

He hesitated a moment, then said, "Go stand at the sink and look out the window."

So I did as he asked, wondering.

Then he said, "I guess it wasn't you after all. I was sure it was. I could see your nightgown and long hair. Well, whoever was standing there was shorter." He never again said anything about it, except to insist that he had seen a girl in the kitchen. She was standing in the dark wearing a long, white nightgown.

Brazilian Ghost Tales

Both my parents are from a very small town in the heart of the Brazilian farm lands. They also know the region for its deposits of precious stones and metals. I was born and raised in Rio de Janeiro, but I used to enjoy spending my vacations with my grand folks in the little town, a twenty-one-hour bus ride. They built my grandparent's house in the late 1600's, and it used to be the masters' home of a huge slave-operated farm. Now, it is just a very old house on the outskirts of nowhere. In the front of the house is a little old church from the same period.

Maybe it was because my grandma felt guilty about all the slaves that they must have mistreated in or around the house. Because she decided, the house would serve the poor and sick. During the period when my mother was growing up, she saw lots of people die in her huge kitchen, the main room in the house. By the time I started to spend my vacations there, my grandma was already too old to take care of anyone.

After my step grandfather died, my grandma went to live with the family of one of my many aunts, just a few houses down from her own. During a summer vacation, one of my sisters' and I decided to go and spend all three months in the house by ourselves. They were renovating the little church across the road and, since my grandma was the keeper of the church, all of the religious statues from it were in the corner of the room where my sister was staying. They were a bit scary looking, because their eyes consisted of glass, and tended to shine a bit too much once the lights were out. Every night, my sister and I had to deal with bats, owls and cats roaming around, and sometimes fighting as we tried to sleep. We got use to that.

One night, I woke up hearing my sister screaming off the top of her lungs. At first, I thought that maybe one critter had landed on her or something like that. I jumped out of bed and ran into her room. When I turned on the lights, I saw that her bed had been moved to the center of the room, and that the statues were in a circle around her bed and facing it. By sunrise, my sister was in the first bus back to Rio. I decided to stay. Not because I was scared of what happened to my sister, but because my curiosity overwhelmed my fear. Besides I was having too much of a good time with my friends, especially all the attention of the girls would give me since I was the only boy from Rio in town.

During the months that followed, I had several not-too-scary experiences in or around the house. One time, a dead cat fell from the top of the church, landing right in front of me. The little guy had been badly mutilated, apparently by another cat, but I did not hear a cat fight as they tend to be very loud. I picked up the dead cat and buried it next to the church. Another day, an owl landed by the foot of my bed during the middle of the night, and I couldn't scare it away. It just stood there looking at me for several minutes, then it flew off.

Just a few nights before I was supposed to leave, I had the scariest experience of my life. A good friend of mine found out that his younger brother was dealing drugs. My friend was a very big guy, and he wanted to kill his brother. As I was walking down the street past their house, their mother came out yelling, "He is going to kill him!" (She was hysterical.) I ran into the house, and I saw my friend holding a knife to his brother. After some time, I convinced the guy to drop the knife, and I made the brother swear to his family that he would never get involved with drugs again. I took my friend away from the house in order for him to cool down. We bought a few beers, and sat on a park bench where we talked for several hours. Being a mathematics/physics/computer geek, I was never very communicative. However, that night I spoke like a priest and counselor.

While my friend and I were talking, an old stray dog came by and sat next to us. We had a bit of food, so we fed it to the dog. As we left the park, the dog started to follow us. We walked to my friend's house first since it was on my way home. For the rest of the walk back to the old house, the dog walked next to me. I enjoyed having some company on the walk back home for a change.

On the way home, I saw a goat jump over a wall and onto the street. I never heard of wild goats walking the streets, but there it was. As we approached the old church, my faithful companion started to roar and act very bizarre. Whatever it was that he was seeing scared the heck out of him. I decided to go back a couple of blocks, then walk around the longer way home to avoid the church.

As we walked out of the woods into the clearing at the back of the house, the poor old dog went crazy! It started to bark and walk back and forth, keeping his eyes on the house. He then grabbed a stone into his mouth and started chewing on it. I could see lots of blood and pieces of teeth falling out of his mouth. Finally, the dog dropped the stone and ran away. I was petrified, not sure whether to go back into the house, or to sleep on a park bench. It was a very cold night, so I went into the house.

Once inside the house, nothing seemed different, except for my level of fear. A couple of bats flew by, but that was common in that old house. I managed to calm down and went to sleep. Not much later, some very heavy footsteps awakened me. It sounded too heavy to be a person, and I could hear the old wooden floor bending and creaking.

I gathered enough courage to unlock my door and go see what it was and I saw a horse walking out of the room where my sister had her experience. I was the only person with the keys to the house and, being from a violent city, I always locked all doors before leaving home. I still have no explanation on how the horse got there. I opened the front door and the horse walked out. I couldn't go back to sleep after that.

I turned on the television and started to watch a horror movie of all things. Then it came like an explosion. All lights started to flash, the entire house started to shake. I could hear voices coming from all around, but there was nobody there, cats and bats and owls and mice running out of every corner, looking as horrified as I was. I ran into my bedroom and locked the door.

The noise stopped and I jumped into the bed and covered my head with the sheets while wandering what to do next. As I was contemplating that thought, I started to hear the sound of heavy breathing, with the sound of the wall creaking. I wasn't sure if I should take my head out from under the covers, but I did it anyway. As I looked at the wall next to me, it looked as if it were breathing!

It was inflating and deflating. I jumped out the window and twisted my foot in the process. I never told this story to anyone in town or to my family except for my sister. Whenever I asked my grandmother if she ever witnessed anything funny there in all those years she live there, she just look at me and smile, then change subjects.

The Ghostly Party

A very dear friend of mine lives in an old Victorian Mansion in Helena, Montana. We have always been aware of the other presences there as ashtrays take random leaps off tables and other things randomly move from one area to another. It was just small things at first, nothing to really attract attention. Perhaps we had forgotten where we would put the keys to the car only to have them show up in an area that we would never take keys into.

However, last summer when her entire family took a trip to Zimbabwe, they asked that I take care of her home and water her plants and feed her cat. I had the only key as only one key has ever been made to her house. My friend lives in the Carriage House and her Mother lives in the main house.

One time, I was unable to get there for three days but the cat had been left with plenty of food and water. Upon returning I entered the house only to notice in the hall that the door to the room on my right was open. Now this door has always jammed and takes nearly superhuman strength or two people to get the door open. The room behind the door was never used so there was no reason to open the door.

I looked into the room and the window was unbolted and propped open with a big metal slab. I looked to my left into the other room and that window had also been unbolted and opened. I walked further to her bedroom where the cat stayed and her room looked like a party had occurred.

The lights were on, the lamp had been moved from the corner of the room to dead center, in front of the East window and the curtains were blowing in front of the South window, although it was closed. The bedding was strewn crazily across the bed and the floor strewed with random things. Naturally, I took the cat back with me to my apartment. The cat has never been the same since. He is one of the craziest cats I have ever seen but he is still loveable.

This is not the first occurrence of anything and certainly not the last. In the main house, there is a portion in the Northwest corner that each night the electricity goes out at a certain time and nothing can turn it back on. Then a few hours later the electricity comes back on by itself.

The Ghosts of Dryden Hall

These next experiences take place in and around the old building of Eastern Washington University. My wife and I attended Eastern Washington University from 1991 to 1994 and had both lived in the dorms for a year and a half of college. We first met in college in the most haunted building on campus, Dryden Hall.

They built Dryden Hall in the 1960's as an all female dormitory. Most the residents knew that it was a haunted dormitory because of all the strange things that happened on a regular basis. Several suicides apparently had taken place in the building during the first few years of operation. They converted the dorm to co-ed in the seventies and continue to this day.

The first strange experience that I had was in the winter of 1991 on the first South Floor. I had the heat cranked up in my room to about 80 degrees and all the windows were shut. About 1:31 in the morning, I felt a very cold blast of air hit my face. It woke me out of a sound sleep. I immediately began to look for the source of the cold air blast. Being that I was laying in the middle of the room and from the direction of the air blast I confirmed to myself that the cold air came directly from above my head. There are no vents in any of the rooms so a chance of a ventilation backlash is nonexistent. It had to be a ghost.

I told my floor mate what had happened the next morning because it gets worse as the year goes by. My room mate had lived in Dryden for two years already by the time I had arrived. He stated that when he was a resident advisor he had to arrive one month before the rest of the students to help set up the hall facilities. He said that the room above his would sound like someone was opening and shutting drawers and slamming closet doors in the middle of the night.

No one was in the room because no students had arrived yet. These noises in the room above his went on for several weeks. He would go to investigate and no one would be in the room. He became scared so he quit running up to the room and would call the police or campus security. They would find the door locked with no one inside the room.

The Devil's Door of Dryden Hall may sound kind of crazy but I have seen this door and I know some of the stories behind it. The door was originally placed on a room on the 4th North floor. The door has a perfect impression of the devil's face in the grain of the wood. When the door was first installed in the building, the residents who lived in the room stated that they were scared to live in the room because of strange happenings such as personal items being moved across the room and the furniture was turned upside down on several occasions.

Finally, they removed it and moved the door to a study closet. (A study closet is a small enclosed room used for studying) We should note that every opening to the rooms and study closets are the same measurement. When they moved the devil's door, they tried the door on different rooms, but the door would not fit The door was either too big for some rooms or too small for others. The door only fit that one resident room. Yet, all the doors to each of the room were the same in measurement.

Since the first time they installed the door, the grain of the wood that resembles the devils face was at the top of the door. Over the years, the face has slid down to the middle of the door where it remains today. The Maintenance crew have painted over and sanded this face out many times but each time the face comes back. The devil's door had to be cut down in size and now hangs on a study closet on 3rd North of Dryden Hall. I studied in that closet on several occasions and nothing ever happened.

The Running Man of 4th North-floor in Dryden Hall was a fascinating ghost to say the least. At all hours of the day and night, if you were on 4th North, you may have had the opportunity to listen to the running steps that went from one end of the hall to the other. My wife lived on 4th North for one year to see if a ghost actually was making the noises, several of her friends would sit in their rooms and wait for the running footsteps. When the steps would start, they would open their doors and look to see who was running and the hall would be empty!

They could also hear the footsteps on 3rd North through the ceiling. A friend said that when he lived in Dryden they tested to see if they could hear someone running down the hall of 4th North on 3rd North. Each of his friends took turns running down the hall of 4th North with heavy boots on while the rest of them listened on 3rd North. None of them could hear each other running down the hall at all.

The Television Room of Dryden Hall was across the hall from the main office. On several occasions, the television set would come on by itself in the late evening hours. The television set would flip around the channels by itself. Many of us thought that this story was fishy. We thought perhaps the television set had a timer and someone was playing a trick on us. However, the next time the television set started to switch channels we called Security. When the security team arrived, they discovered the television set was unplugged, yet it was operating as usual.

Apparently as the story goes, on the 4th North of Dryden Hall, a woman had hung herself from the last shower stall in the women's bathroom in years past. However, to this day, that shower does not get hot water and there is nothing wrong with the water heater or the plumbing.

The ghost of 2nd South of Dryden Hall appeared in the winter of 1991 when a girl was visiting a friend who lived on 1st South. It was 2:00 in the morning and she had to use the bathrooms which for women are on 2nd South. She walked up the stairs and onto 2nd South to go to the bathroom. On her way back from the bathroom, she had to pass an open corridor that leads through two doors and into the main office area. In this corridor, a full length mirror reflects into the corner of the corridor.

As she was walking down the hall she looked into the mirror and saw a man in the reflection. When she got to the corner of the hall she looked to the corner where man should have been standing, but nothing was there. She looked into the mirror again and the man appeared to be inside the mirror. She looked into the mirror again and the figure disappeared into the wall. She never returned to visit Dryden Hall after that.

Senior Hall has its share of ghostly visitors. I had to spend a lot of time in Senior Hall which was the Criminal Justice department building. The building is very old and used to be an all woman's dorm. The criminal justice computer lab is on the third floor of Senior Hall. One night, a student was working alone on the computers when he heard two girls giggling down one of the hallways. He knew he was alone on the floor because he had checked the building before he entered the lab. He went to the source of the giggling and it stopped, but he found no students anywhere.

Another student was doing security checks late one night in Senior Hall when he walked into the main living room to witness the furniture had been moved completely around. He also heard girls giggling loudly from the third floor. Another time, a custodian was vacuuming in the living room and the plug kept popping out of the wall even though there was no one else in the building and the cord was coiled loosely on the floor. Apparently, as the story goes, the two girls were residents of Senior Hall when it was a woman's dorm. They both committed suicide on separate occasions. One girl hung herself from her room closet and the other girl slashed her wrists.

Authors Notes:

An individual who commits suicide must have had intense emotions that controlled them in life as well as in life after life. These same intense emotions that dominated them in mortality became the anchors that made them earthbound. At the time of death, the emotions were still strong and unresolved. These two ghosts are earthbound until they can release their emotions and resolve the issues that are trapping them here. No earthly ritual will release them, but only by letting go of their emotions will they be free to exit this earth plane.

Footsteps in the Night

The following account is true. It happened to me. The house I grew up in, from birth until I joined the Navy at 18, always made me uncomfortable. There didn't seem to be anything unusual about the house itself, it is even a little plain, nothing really much to talk about, though I know little of its history. However, as early as I can remember, I always felt uncomfortable being alone in any room of the house, even when in sight of somebody in another room.

When I was about five years old, I would sit in my attic bedroom which I shared with two brothers, watching television while everyone else had gone to school. While watching the television, I would swear I could see something looking like little black fingers of flames flickering behind my brother's headboard of his bed, which was just a couple feet to the right of the television set. Whenever, I would look directly at it though, I could see nothing unusual. I tried to convince myself that it was my imagination, but I usually got nervous and would go downstairs.

One day, when I was about seven years old, I headed to the attic bedroom and heard voices from the bottom of the stairs. I thought my brother must have left his AM radio on so I headed up the stairs. As my eyes came above floor level of the attic, I could see a picture on the black & white television set and still hear voices.

On my next step, and a blink of an eye, the picture and sound instantly vanished. Knowing that the picture on the television screen should have shrunk to a bright dot in the center before fading away, and knowing that the top of the television set would be warm if it were on, I decided to investigate. I felt the top of the television set but it was cold.

We have often heard floorboards creaking in the rooms at night, and were always told by my parents that it was the house settling. Eventually, they moved me to another bedroom, just downstairs from the attic bedroom. My bed was next to the door. As the days and nights passed, I began to notice a strange pattern that took place every night. It would start with a creak in the attic floor, then another on the attic steps near the top, and again near the bottom.

Then, the attic door would make a slight creaking sound, as if lightly pushed upon, then on the ultra-squeaky board near the head of my bed, just a slight little squeak. Then, my door would make a creaking sound, then a squeak out in the hallway, and lastly on the steps headed toward the living room.

This would occur every night, just after midnight, and then would occur in reverse order after two o'clock in the morning. The sounds did not go by in rapid succession, they moved quite slowly, perhaps even a bit slower than an old person would be walking. Until I got moved to another bedroom at age sixteen, I never got a decent night sleep, waiting for this apparent thing to pass through the rooms.

These noises did not only occur at night when almost everyone was asleep, but they did not always follow the same pattern. One night, I was laying awake and heard a couple squeaks coming from the floorboards in the attic. The sounds were light and far apart, not at all like the heavy and close sounds of one of my brothers getting out of bed and walking across the floor. Suddenly, I heard a sound which sounded like a small AA battery fall to the floor, roll across the bare wood part, and down three steps. Then total silence.

The two older brothers' beds are at the extreme other end of that room and could not have knocked something over in their sleep, far across the room near the steps, perhaps twenty feet. The next day when both brothers were in the living room, I asked them if they had knocked over anything during the night, anything that could have rolled down the steps, and had they found anything laying on the steps in the morning?

My Mom heard me ask the questions and said that she had heard it also, and thought they had bumped into something while headed to the bathroom. My brothers said that they had not bumped into anything and that they didn't see anything on the steps.

Sometimes, I would be sitting in the living room by myself, reading a book and hear a floorboard squeak in the same room. I would try to ignore it, though when you've witnessed some strange things happen, you become suspicious of every sound you hear. Sometimes we would be sitting in the living room and hear a couple of dishes in the kitchen cabinet clink together, or hear the sound of something falling over in the next room. Yet, when we looked around that room for anything that might have fallen, everything was in its proper place.

One Christmas Eve, around 7:30 in the evening, we were having our annual family gathering and the living room was quite crowded. I decided to sit on the floor next to my Mom who sat in her recliner. It was quite noisy as two conversations were taking place at once, each with several participants. However, I was not in either of the conversations, I was just sitting and listening.

Suddenly, I heard a noise off to my left, in the dining room which was dark because the lights were off. It was just a little noise that got my attention for a moment. My attention returned to the conversations, and I was feeling a little strange. Then, I noticed movement off to my left and looked to see that the hanging planter was swaying gently as if caught in a draft or lightly bumped. I thought that to be odd, but I returned my attention to the conversations.

Suddenly, I felt this cool draft on my back and my neck, and felt my hair being lightly brushed. This sent a chill down my spine, and I looked to my right and saw the other hanging planter suddenly begin to lightly sway. I had enough, I wasn't going to experience anything else that night unless someone else did too. I got up and crossed the room and sat between my two older brothers who were also sitting on the floor.

One evening, my sister and I sat on the couch in the living room, she was reading the newspaper and I was reading a paperback. We both noticed movement off to our right and looked over to see a closet door open fully by itself, silently. This was most unusual because the door was usually stuck closed. It also dragged on the carpeting because the door wasn't trimmed when they installed the carpet.

The carpeting prevented the door from opening more than three quarters way open. There was indeed something in the house. I got up and inspected the door and closet and found nothing unusual. Great force was necessary for me to get the door closed, because of the carpeting, and the hinges squealed loudly. It took a couple bumps with my shoulder to get the door closed into its frame again. On top of this, the screw on the door handle was missing, meaning that when you try to turn the knob to unlatch the door, you had to push the knob downward somewhat while turning. If you turned the knob too far, then the knob would slip back and the door would be re-latch with a loud snap. Furthermore, the latch assembly and the door hinges needed oiling and squeaked loudly when turning the knob or opening the door. Yet, when the door opened by itself, it opened completely silently.

Something interesting to note about this closet, it is only about six to nine inches deep, and apparently was the front door at one time. My Mom said that the front door was found in that position before the newer front porch was added, and that they had filled it in and they installed a new doorway to match the porch. Though they filled in the outside to look like the rest of the house, the inside doorway was left there as a small closet. This is the same closet whose door opened all by itself.

On another occasion when I was about fourteen, I sat with my Mom as I waited to depart for school. It was just another typical weekday morning, all my brothers and sisters were at work or at school, and my dad was asleep upstairs. We could hear his loud snoring from the living room. Suddenly, we saw something to our left, we both turned to look, and saw a Styrofoam picnic cooler, that had been in the kitchen, flying through the air. We saw it enter the dining room from the kitchen, as it flew a strangely downward curving path, not natural looking. It hooked downward from about four feet from the floor, and suddenly forward, lodging itself under a dining room chair. We gaped at each other for a second before I hopped up and checked the kitchen, but nobody was there. I even checked all possible avenues of escape, but the back door was locked and the bathroom was empty. Nobody else was home.

One night, when I was about fifteen years old, I was laying in bed, dreading the beginning of the series of creaks and cracks that made their way from the attic through my room, and down toward the living room every night. Suddenly, it started with the usual creak on the attic bedroom floorboards, then another closer to the top of the steps. Then, the slight cracking sound as if someone was lightly stepping onto one of the steps. Then, as usual, another sound near the bottom of the attic steps. I waited, expecting to hear the sound of the attic door which was only about three feet from my bed, to make its usual cracking sound as if someone were pressing firmly against it.

Then, something happened which I didn't expect, and which began to make me nervous. That something was silence. The pattern was suddenly broken, the sounds made their nightly succession down from the attic, but stopped at the bottom of the attic steps this time.

After what seemed like several long minutes of silence, suddenly a scratching sound against that door broke the silence. It sounded like fingernails scratching at the door. I was totally petrified, nothing like this ever happened before, and I really wanted to wake up my brother who was sleeping soundly in the other bed, but I figured he would think I was nuts, so I just listened. As the scratching continued, I tried to think of ways that might scare it off. I tried clearing my throat a few times figuring that if I didn't scare it away, at least it might awaken my brother, who might also witness the scratching sounds. Neither worked. The scratching continued, and my brother continued to sleep deeply.

My heart was pounding so hard that I thought I might have a heart attack, my chest ached and my stomach felt queasy, and I was sweating profusely. Still, the slow scratching continued at the door just a couple feet from my head. I went over to the door, looked all around the outside for anything that might be causing it and found nothing. I grabbed the handle of the door and slowly pulled the door open. As soon as I started pulling open the door, the scratching stopped.

I looked all around the inside of the door, assisted by the streetlight outside shining into the doorway. I could find nothing unusual. My heart rate started to return to normal and I started to relax, confident that my suffering was over for the night, but after a couple of minutes the scratching sounds started again. That was enough for me. I got out of bed and went to the basement where my Dad was working on his Radio Shack TRS-80 computer. I didn't tell him what had happened, I just hung out with him down in the basement until he went to bed.

Strangely, after that night, I have never heard the succession of floor board squeaks coming down from the attic or going back up. I never saw or heard anything strange again.

The Haunted Lighthouse

I would like to share with you an experience that I had several years ago while working on a lighthouse on Lake Superior. Standard Rock Lighthouse is on a shoal about thirty miles from the nearest point of land. They constructed it on a hollow cylinder of concrete reinforced with a belt of steel which rises about thirty feet out of the water.

They have not occupied the Lighthouse since about 1961 when a fatal accident occurred to the lighthouse keeper and his crew. Somehow, the kerosene tanks that fueled the fog signal exploded. A fire followed so intensely that it consumed part of the stone structure. The only way some of the crew survived was to hang over the side of the structure suspended by lines. It was several days before they rescued the crew, and then only because a vessel passing at night had reported the light extinguished.

In the spring of 1993, they tasked our unit with making repairs to Standard Rock Lighthouse prior to the Coast Guard turning it over to the National Park Service. After loading suitable materials on board we steamed from Duluth, Minnesota en route to the lighthouse. The weather was fine during our trip to the lighthouse, but as soon as we arrived, the weather deteriorated. Eventually, it began to blow so hard that we had to drop the anchor and ride the storm out. After two days the weather calmed sufficiently for us to launch a small boat to take the work party over.

We made it to the lighthouse, off-loaded our supplies, and went to work by about two o'clock in the afternoon. Then by five o'clock, the weather was turning badly again and the ship wanted to bring us back. However, we wanted to stay the night so we could finish the job, and hope that we could get back to the ship the next day.

The jobs ahead were big but simple, fix what needed to be fixed, clean and paint. Each of us had a task to do. I was on the main level, several of the crew were on the top level and the rest of the crew was scattered about. When I finished my job, I went down to the keeper's kitchen where my friend, Jeff was working, to give him a hand.

As we worked the talk turned to the fire that had occurred at the lighthouse and the fate of the three keepers. One level below us was the bottom of the light. When we first came aboard the light house, we all walked through it to check it out. This area reminded me of catacombs, one main chamber with tunnels leading in different directions. It was cold, dark and damp and not a very comfortable place to be.

Around seven o'clock Jeff and I decided to take a break. I walked over to the door leading to the lower level, opened it and called down jokingly, "Hey George, we're going up for a bite to eat, want anything?" Immediately they could hear sounds in the level below, scraping and knocking, but the most chilling was the sound of footsteps coming up the stairs. Jeff and I looked at each other, his eyes were as large as a Volkswagen head lights, I bet mine were just as big. We both raced up the stairs to the main level.

We ate our dinner, calmed down and decided that we had imagined the whole thing. Jeff related the story to the rest of the crew and everyone had a good laugh. Jeff took another job on a different level and we all went back to work. At about 11:16 that evening, a couple of the guys suggested going down to the basement at midnight to see if anything would happen. I really didn't want to go but not wanting to be branded a coward, I agreed to anyway.

At midnight, five of us made our way into the basement. We called out, shutting the lights on and off and waited. We didn't hear or see anything, but I sure could feel something. The hair was standing up on the back of my neck. I swear that I could feel something moving around us. When nothing appeared to happen, we went back upstairs to the keeper's quarters.

As soon as we were all out of the basement the sounds started again. The five of us stared at each other, until the footsteps started coming up the stairs again. At this point, there was total chaos as we all tried to get up the stairs at the same time. As luck would have it, I was the last in line, as I was going up the stairs, I glanced back and saw just for an instant, a shadow with no definite shape emerging from the basement door.

Nobody said much, we just went back to work. When we finished, it was about three in the morning. We moved up to the upper level of the light and tried to get some sleep. It wasn't easy because for the rest of the night we heard everything from banging on the walls to distant moans.

When the sun finally came up we went back downstairs and found that some of our gear had been scattered. A garbage can had been turned on its side and looked like someone, or something had jumped up and down on it.

Spook on my Screen

My Computer is a year and a half old. It is a Macintosh Performa 467, with a 68030 processor and 4 megabytes of Ram. I have ample room on my hard drive, approximately 160 megabytes. I purchased this micro machine from one of those large discount warehouses. This computer has become my personal electronic surfboard to the Internet.

This home computer ran great, except for a few mishaps with system software conflicts and my beginner's curiosity. Nevertheless, last summer, the monitor began to act funny. I generally thought it was a hardware defect, so I called Apple Computer for an exchange. I told the belligerent technicians that I had seen black lines and running screens, which made it nearly impossible for me to do my word processing and other functions. I sent my monitor for an exchange.

When my new monitor arrived, I thought my problems were gone. It was the same model as the old faulty monitor. Then after two months, the lines and running screens began to appear again, but this time there was a sickly green glow to the whole screen. Each time I sat in front of my monitor, I began to feel nauseous and dizzy. This time I sent it to a local repair shop. I left it at the shop for almost a week.

The repairman phoned me at work to tell me that the monitor was causing them problems. It would flash on, even though it was not connected to a CPU nor an outlet. The technician told me that it was due to extra energy that was collected in the cathode ray tube, and that my home may have higher than normal electrical surges with the wiring.

Then he began to lecture me about computer maintenance. He said that I should always turn off the screen if I am going to leave it for a long period of time. He went on to say that pictures would burn into the screen and leave a permanent etch on it, a footprint of what was on the screen. I felt like a child, during the talk. He advised me to purchase a screen saver.

Then, before the technician hung up, he told me how I had created that ghastly picture of a zombie-like face that was etched on the screen. I had no idea what he was speaking about. I only used my computer for word processing and playing Tetris. He said that the image seemed to be realistic, a gruesome head stared outward with bony hands that grasped the corners as if it were trying hard to get out. I was amazed at what the technician said.

I told the technician that I had no picture files on my computer, nor had I used the paint program to generate this picture. I told him whatever it was, I had not done it and that I should not be at fault for that burnt in image. Laughing sarcastically, he told the other employees in the background that it wasn't of my doing. Then a silence. He came back on the line and told me that the image had suddenly disappeared. He told me he was going to send the monitor back to the manufacturer and request a refurbished, but different model and then he hung up. So far, my new monitor works well but I am waiting, just in case.

Movie Theater Ghost

I used to work in a General Cinema in Redondo Beach, California. There were three theaters located in three separate buildings. The longest theater was the one I worked in. This theater was also directly adjacent to a large old cemetery. When I first started there, I heard the other workers joke about, "the ghost" in the theater. I didn't think much about it, thinking the proximity of the cemetery would lend itself to ghost stories, legitimate or not. After a few weeks, they gave me a tad more responsibility. I would open or close the theater with one of the assistant managers.

The theater had an upstairs projector like any other theater. There was a small employee locker room since we wore uniforms. We had to pass through the projector room to get to the locker room. The projectors are automated, so there was never anyone up there. Next to the projector room was a tiny room where we popped all our popcorn. For starters, the projector room always freaked me a little.

It was very dark and shadowy, and unless you happened to be coming on or going off a shift, the exact time as someone else, you were always up there alone. I thought I saw things move in the shadows out of the corner of my eye as I walked through the projector room. I could have imagined that, I guess, but what was definitely not imagined was the really Cold Spot.

This happened on the wall that divided the popcorn room and the projector room. Popping corn always generated tons of heat and was thus the least favorite duty of the theater workers since there was no ventilation in the room. It got stiflingly hot in there. The wall between the two rooms always heated as well, except for the Cold Spot. This spot was at eye level, roughly the shape of a head and shoulders, like a bust of someone. No matter how long you had been popping popcorn or how hot it got in the popcorn room, the wall always had a cold spot.

What's worse, the spot moved. Not while anyone was actually feeling it, but it would be at different places along the wall, and it would move sometimes within minutes of someone locating its position. It was weird. Once another woman reported seeing "eyes" in that corner of the projector room. She never went upstairs again, just stashed her personal stuff in the manager's office and changed in the restroom. One of the assistant managers also refused to go up there, at least by himself.

My own experiences, other than the cold spot and the generally creepy feeling up in the projector room, were mainly limited to the concession stand. It doesn't sound like a very spooky place, does it? As I started opening and closing, often back-to-back, I began to notice weird things happened overnight. Cabinets I know I had locked with keys and a small padlock were unlocked and opened in the morning. This unlocking of the cabinets after being locked occurred for over a year.

Supplies were moved around and knocked over in the supply room directly behind the concession counter. Several times, I felt a cold chill and a breeze, like someone had just run past and I was feeling the wind in their wake. Twice, another worker behind the concession stand reported feeling the same thing, the same time I had.

The assistant manager was closing the theater with one other worker, a woman. They were getting ready to leave and the other woman had gone back up to the employees' room to get her things. There is an in-house phone in the projector room, and she called down to the office to tell the assistant manager that there was someone in the theater. She said there was a weird woman standing down by the curtain. The assistant manager went to check it out. This wasn't all that unusual, sometimes transients tried to stay in the theater after closing, and since the alarm hadn't been set it was possible that someone had managed to sneak in the exit doors and was down there messing around.

The assistant manager went into the theater. What she saw was a pale, grayish-looking woman in a plain, long skirt and a blouse. She had long hair pulled back at the nape of her neck. The assistant manager distinctly remembers seeing the skirt moving and strands of hair moving behind her head, as if there was a breeze blowing, and there wasn't a breeze inside the theater! As the assistant manager walked down the aisle toward her, she told the woman the theater was closed.

As she got closer, she could see the woman's mouth moving, as if she were talking, but the assistant manager couldn't hear her saying anything. The woman wasn't looking at her but out into the theater. As she got closer, the strange woman suddenly looked straight at her as if noticing her for the first time, and suddenly vanished. No movement, no disturbance behind the curtain, nothing. She was simply there one moment and gone the next.

The assistant manger was extremely shaken. She ran out of the theater back into the lobby. She nearly had a heart attack when she thought she heard footsteps coming after her. She did hear footsteps but they were those of the other worker running down the stairs from the projector room. She had seen the whole thing. She had been watching from the window in the projector room until the strange woman vanished, then she freaked out and ran out of the projector room and down to the lobby.

My Sister's Ghost

My sister and her husband stayed with some college friends who were renting a large house built in the late 1800's while attending college in Montana. The first night after my sister and her husband arrived, she awakened and thought she saw a shadow in the shape of a man in the doorway. When she noticed that it couldn't be a shadow, she woke her husband and told him to look over at the door.

As soon as he looked at the shadow, this dark shape in the form of a man ducked down and crawled underneath their bed. This scared them, they looked under the bed but could find nothing out of the ordinary. They decided to spend the remainder of the night in the living room on the couch.

The next morning when they were all eating breakfast, the two room mates said they had experienced a similar account. One of them said that when he had gotten up in the middle of the night to use the bathroom, he was walking down the hallway when he thought he saw the other room mate walking toward him. When the room mate did not respond to a question, he began backing up to the wall. Then the shape walked right up to him and then right through him!

The other room mate said he didn't believe him. He must be imagining things. The next night, suddenly the other room mate was awakened. He noticed that the bed felt wrong. There was too much weight on the other side of this queen size bed. When he looked over to the side, he noticed that there was a person laying beside him, but the person was all black as if a shadow. When he spoke, the person suddenly disappeared.

Now, the two room mates were both thoroughly scared and went to the landlord to get their money back. The landlord asked what was wrong and when they told her what had happened they were surprised when she just laughed and laughed. She told them this was "Frank." He generally did similar stunts to welcome people when they first arrived. He wouldn't do the pranks twice. Besides he was often a big help to the tenants.

For instance, once when the previous tenants were out for a week, someone decided that breaking into the home would be easy. When the police finally arrived, the would-be burglar was pounding on the door from the inside, begging to be let out. Apparently, "Frank had surprised the burglar," who kept locking the door over and over.

Then according to the burglar's description, moved the kitchen chairs around to keep him from going anywhere. The two room mates decided they had enough so they moved to another house a few miles away. My sister and her husband decided that having a ghost might not be all that bad so they rented the house from the landlord.

They had made me aware of this ghost on my first visit, I decided it would be a fun experiment to take a video camera with me. I set it up to record when I pushed a button, so that I would push this button when I first woke up. Well, the next morning I woke up and thought that nothing had happened, perhaps Frank hadn't come to visit me. Since I was just passing through, I collected and packed everything up.

When I finally reached my destination at Mt. Rushmore, I took out my video camera and started recording. Unfortunately, my battery was dead. All my batteries were dead. Figuring I had been stupid enough to forget to recharge them, I took the normal photographs and then headed back to my sister's place. I was not there for the night this time but I plugged the video camera in to record my sister's house for my other siblings and parents. What I found was really surprising. The video tape was already at the end of the reel. Strange, the tape had been bought just the day before. Well, I rewound it and played it on the television. The first hour was just me sleeping. At this point we figured I had just fallen asleep on the switch, then at 12:03 in the morning the camera did something strange, it moved! As if someone was actually moving it.

There weren't any footsteps or the sounds of breathing from the camera operator. The camera moved around a little erratically at first then moved toward me, where it zoomed on my face. Well, at this point, I thought it must be my sister or her husband. Still, my hair started moving in ways as if someone was running an invisible hand through it. But you couldn't see anything in my hair. Then the camera moved back to where it had been originally and filmed me, sleeping some more.

Since I sleep very deeply "Frank" probably could not rouse me when he was running his hands through my hair. He probably was planning to scare me the same way he did everyone else. I have not been to my sister's house since but she has said that they have noticed little things having gotten done. For instance "Frank" actually does the laundry if they put clothes in the washer.

It starts all by itself. "Frank" has even been credited with doing little favors like rolling up car windows on visiting friends cars, when it started raining or the cat gets fed sometimes even when no one has been there for a day. Anyway, "Frank" has turned out to be a very friendly ghost except for the first night encounters which the landlord calls "Frank's test."

The Haunted Reality by Sharon A. Gill & Dave R. Oester

New Hampshire Poltergeist

I am an avid hiker and camper, and I love the outdoors. In the summer of 1992, I had a bizarre experience at a fishing and hunting resort in the town of Pittsburgh, New Hampshire, which is about fourteen miles from the Canadian Border, at the very end of U.S. Route 3. There is not much to do out there in the summer time but fish and hike, and that's what my husband and I had come to do at this little resort.

The second night we were there, we decided to take a hike up Route 3 around midnight. Oftentimes, we can see the best wildlife in the middle of the night, when things are quietest and there are no people around. So we took our flashlights and went a couple of miles up the road. We saw a few moose, but that's about it. Not being tired, we decided to go back to the cabin and get the car, and travel to the Canadian Border, really slowly. At that time of night in the Northern New Hampshire wilderness, you can do that. There are literally no other cars, because there is no sign of human life again until Chartierville, the first town over the border in Canada.

We got into the car and started up the road, going slowly, looking for nocturnal wildlife. Located on the right-hand side of the road there was a white cross stuck into the shoulder of the road. It looked so weird and out of place that I said to my husband, "Can we pull over and look at that? What is it?" He pulled the car over and I shined the flashlight on the marker, but I couldn't read the inscription without getting out of the car.

I was just thinking about doing that when I began to feel really uncomfortable and kind of upset. I got chills and goose bumps, my eyes started to water, and I just got panicky and turned to my husband and said, "Can we get out of here?" He looked uncomfortable too, nodded yes, and we peeled out of there and went back to the cabin.

On the way back to the cabin we saw some more moose, a coyote, and other night creatures, but it was

88

enough to take our minds off of the spooky stuff for a while. We got back to our cabin and I took a shower and went to bed. While my husband was in the shower, I started hearing this funky clanging noise but if you've ever stayed in a cabin with a rather rustic hot water heater, you probably know that they make all kinds of noises and is nothing to get upset about. Anyway, the clanging didn't phase me at all and when my husband got out of the shower, he said, "What the heck was all that banging?" and I replied that it was probably the hot water heater.

We climbed into bed and were drifting off to sleep when we heard what sounded like the front door to the cabin close and the sound of heavy work boots on the board flooring of the cabin. Our eyes flew open practically at the same time and since I was closest to the night table, I switched on the lamp. The noise stopped. We really didn't know what to make of it, and at that point we were too freaked out to open the bedroom door, so we just switched off the light again. Within five minutes, the footsteps started again, in what seemed like a diagonal line from the front door to our bedroom door. This time, my husband reached over me and switched on the light. I was sitting bolt upright in bed, my eyes were watering, and boy was I uncomfortable.

I knew I wasn't hearing things because obviously my husband heard them too. He was pretty upset. He wanted to pack the car but I was reluctant to even move, I felt rooted to the spot. Finally, I got out of the bed and threw open the bedroom door. Naturally, there was nothing there, the room looked exactly the same as when we'd gone to bed.

I still felt like I was being watched or something. However, I shrugged and closed the bedroom door and climbed back into bed. Again, we shut off the light, and again, the noises started, but this time we watched in horror in the semi-darkness as the bedroom door latch clattered.

We turned on the light and this time it stayed on. Eventually, I fell asleep while my husband stayed awake all night. On the way home in the morning we discussed

the possibilities of what we had heard and I remembered
the cross marker, and suggested that we go back and look
at it again, but my husband said no way and wanted to get
home.

About a year later, I went back to the same area with
my husband. While my husband was taking his shower, I
took the car and drove back to the spot where the white
cross stood. I read the inscription on the marker. The
marker said that an anonymous man was buried on this
spot, found frozen to death sometime in the 1930's.
Apparently, he was a drifting logger and was thought to be
Canadian.

The Panama Furniture Ghost

I used to live in Panama City, Republic of Panama,
a city with an ancient and very violent history where
ghosts and believers in ghosts were as common as
tourists. The Spanish Gold Trail had its southern
terminus in the city and the northern terminus was on the
Caribbean Coast at Puerto Bello, the site of the eerie and
mysterious Church of the Black Christ.

I visited Panama City in the summer of '93 and
stayed in the suburban Ciudad Radial, where relatives and
neighbors were very quick to warn me away from the
corner under a tree in a yard where they had frequently
seen the dangerous Lady in Black. I tried to spot the Lady
in Black but did not have the good luck to ever see her,
though I did take a picture of her "spot."

The Lady in Black would appear around two o'clock
or three o'clock in the morning. People in the
neighborhood claimed that her voice would carry through
their windows entreating them to come outside.

Panama is sweltering hot and they use louvered
tropical windows that are kept open at night. Since in
Panama the Lady in Black is a death-omen, no one was too
inclined to answer her call. However, apparently one of my

rash cousins worked his courage up and did go out into the yard, only to encounter a dreadful red-eyed spectra draped in black, from which he quickly retreated.

Now, back to my story about the furniture. That was an earlier time when I lived in the Bella Vista district of Panama, a relatively new area of fewer haunts. The high-ghost areas of Panama City are in ancient Panama Viejo and the SantaAna district.

Nothing compares to the Colon side where, among other villainies, 300,000 to 400,000 slaves died in the effort to build the French Canal. It was here Pizarro plotted the eradication of entire races, and it is there where they see the horrifying forest night-demons with pointed heads standing by some account's twelve to fifteen feet tall.

My small apartment had a hard tile floor with an open balcony on the third floor overlooking the city. They furnished the room with a small bed, an easy chair and a primitive wooden table and two wooden chairs, both pulled up to the table. One late night I was sitting alone in one of the two chairs reading the newspaper when the other chair very slowly pushed away from the table, making a loud scraping noise on the tile floor.

I watched bewildered as it slowly made its way across the room. Because of the way the legs were chattering, it seemed to be carrying a heavy weight like someone weighing 300 pounds sitting in it as if someone else reluctantly dragged the chair. I thought my chair might break. I watched wide-eyed as it slowly made its way across the twelve-foot room.

Then it stopped. I approached the chair, touched it, and it was clearly empty. I checked for any and every possible explanation, but there was no way to explain the movement of that chair. All that remained were some scrape marks on the tile.

The White House with Red Trim

In 1974, Oakridge, Oregon was a bustling little logging community with two saw mills, two Forest Service officers, and a ski lodge about twenty miles up the road. There were simply more people than available housing. For those who moved there, this resulted in a sort of musical house swap. It was easier if you were single as there were a lot of cramped shanties around town and the turnover there was high. For new couples, however, they took whatever accommodation they could until something better opened up. Starting at the bottom, the low end joints were very tough, but if you hung in long enough, the pickings got better. You paid your dues and moved up the ladder.

I got there in the winter of 1973, taking a job with the Forest Service as a forestry technician. It was now early fall 1974 and I was about to get married. I had been in town long enough to have made connections. I put the word out that I needed to move into something bigger and better, something more fitting for a wife. Getting married and at the same time expressing a desire to remain in town gave me an additional degree of prestige and social clout. The system went right to work for me and within a few weeks I got word back that a place was about to come open. A small white house with red trim right along Highway 58, not more than a mile and a half from work. It looked like a good deal.

My future bride and I went to check the place out. We discovered that an old man lived there. He was in the later stages of Black Lung, a disease caused by working many years in coal mines. We chatted for a while. He was a polite man and the situation was a sad one. He said they gave him only a couple weeks more and he would be gone. He then asked if we could wait that long. That struck us as a bizarre request and made us feel as if we were a couple of buzzards circling overhead. We wished him well and left. As the man predicted, two weeks later the house became vacant.

We signed the papers as the new renters and the landlord gave us the keys to the house. The house was a cozy little one bedroom house with an unattached, windowless, cinder block garage to the west. I looked forward to being able to park my car out of the rain for a change. The yard was over grown and mixed among the weeds were many decaying concrete pillars and walkways. Remnants of somebody's long forgotten dream. The sound of the log trucks and the soothing sizzle of their tires against the rain drenched highway was never far away. Cleaning the yard would have to wait until spring as winter was fast approaching.

When we first went into the house, we found there was a peculiar odor throughout. It was a heavy smell, the one that accompanies when death is not far off. We attributed it to the deteriorating condition of the last resident. We cleaned and scrubbed and painted the insides. The smell was persistent. We had no choice as somebody was waiting for my old place. This house represented a quantum leap up the housing chain. We had pulled strings, there was no turning back.

Miraculously, the smell went away when we moved our bed in. We took that as a good sign. A week later we got married and settled down to being newly weds. My new wife took over the house, making the drafty little cottage more a home. Me, I took charge of the garage and the adjoining shop and that's when I first felt something strange. In the ceiling above the workbench was an uncovered crawl hole leading into an attic space. Curiosity pulled for me to look up there. I dragged my ladder over and went to crawl up inside to where I could investigate.

As my head crossed the threshold of the darkness, I felt a cold firm presence envelope my upper body. There came a sudden pressure as if it were pushing me back down the ladder. It was a creepy feeling and I obliged immediately. I stood on the floor looking up at the hole, thinking what a strange thing that was. I started again, but as I got higher I felt the presence still there above in the darkness.

It didn't need to push the second time. I had experienced a similar feeling one other time and that was enough. I moved the ladder and went inside the house where I told my wife about it. We kidded a little saying perhaps it was the ghost of the old man. Then we realized that the old man probably died in the house and the joking stopped and I never went up there again.

Over the next few months, I discovered an eerie pattern setting up in the garage. Keep in mind there were no windows in this cinder block building, no way of knowing day from night unless one opened the door and looked out. I discovered that no matter what I was working on or doing in the garage area, there came a time when I would get a cool chill. It came like that of somebody standing inches from my back, watching. It would send shivers down my spine and I would spin around to find nobody there. Each time this happened, I got a feeling that it was time to stop my projects and leave. Each time it was precisely as the last beads of sun were dropping over the ridge line.

I declined one night to ignore the uncomfortable presence. Belligerently, I continued working after the sun went down. I wanted this project done and I didn't want to work outside in the drizzle. As it was the middle of winter, the sun went down shortly after I got home from work, leaving me no time to get things done. I felt him telling me to leave as usual, but I told the ghost, "Piss Off!"

A short time later I felt something bounce off my shoulder. I turned around, but there was nothing. I looked down at the floor to find the biggest, most succulent spider I had ever seen in the northern United States. So big, you could hear it sliding across the floor as it walked. It had dropped from the hole above me.

I stomped on it but it was as if the creature consisted of rubber. It still moved for I had barely injured it. The thought of it rolling under my shoe again or squirting like a grape disgusted me. I grabbed a shovel, scooped him up, and took him to the highway. There I tossed him out into the busy traffic, figuring a log truck would get him. I went back inside to continue working, but found myself staring up into the dark hole, fearing another such creature would drop. Snakes and other reptiles have little effect on me, but spiders, that was, and still is, my weakness. I finally gave up and conceded that the garage was his, the ghost that is.

My wife thought I was acting nuts, and said so repeatedly after that when I would bring it up, but I noticed that she would send me out there if we needed something from the building. She did admit that she too got creepy feelings from time to time.

Spring finally came and I started working hard to get the yard cleaned. I hauled a lot of crumbling concrete shapes off. I mowed the weeds back into something resembling a lawn and repainted the outside of the house. We were trying to make this place a home in spite of some small and not so small drawbacks we found.

For laughs, I would send friends into the shop after sundown and watch them react. We actually started to have fun at it and I thought I had developed a kind of working relationship with the ghost. However, that came to a close the night I woke up to find him standing at the foot of our bed.

I awoke to a cold chill like the ones I had felt in the shop when I first tried looking into the attic. As the sleep slid from my eyes, I began to see a shadow standing at the window. IT then grew more clear. It was that of a man dressed in a long coat wearing a hat like from a late forties, early fifty's movie. Fedora, I believe they call the hat. At first, I thought it was somebody outside the window, perhaps a peeking-tom. I sat up and stared more closely. I felt a sudden sweep of anger, then I realized that th shadow was inside our room, silently standing perhap foot from the bottom of the bed.

"Get out of here!" I yelled, but it stood motionlessly looking at us.

My wife stirred and then started to wake. She asked as she wiped her eyes.

I tried to speak again and it was as if my · not work. I could breathe, but not speak. I b my wife in the side and pointing, trying to br so she would see this thing with me. However, as she came around, the dark silhouette broke apart and vanished before my eyes. She told me I was dreaming and rolled back over. The rest of the night I laid there listening to every creak and pop of the house.

The same thing happened a second time about a month later. I awoke to the silhouette at the foot of our bed. As before, I found that my voice would not work and I had to resort to poking my wife in the ribs. Again, the apparitions vanished before my eyes prior to her actually seeing what I was referring to. That was it. I had all I could take from the house. The house was too small for the two of us, let alone this third being. It was a small drafty shack, nothing more. The tinsel hung sideways on the Christmas tree from the wind blowing through the living room walls. Rain caused a stain on the ceiling near the front door. Camp trailers had a bigger bathroom.

A retired trucker lived in the trailer park across the way. He had the power on his CB radio cranked up so much it bled over into our stereo and television. He kept a constant string of chatter going well into the night. Every trucker buddy of his with a fancy horn had to show it off, didn't manner when.

They half painted the windows shut and there were a hundred kids and a thousand cats using our newly cleared backyard as a war ground. I put word back into the system that we were looking for a move up. It took about a month this time, but we hit the jackpot and found ourselves slipping to the head of the line, snagging the top place. A house with an attached garage and carport on a dead end street. No kids, no CB antenna's, only one cat and no ghosts.

I moved my things out of the shop first. It felt good. I remember staring up at the hole, thinking that I should try to look up inside again. Then, I decided not to push my luck and closed the door, never to go back in again. The bed was the last item we took out of the house. A peculiar thing happened when we moved it. The smell came back at at very moment the bed went out the door.

The new couple was waiting anxiously in the living

room ready to get started moving in. They noticed the smell too. We told them that the smell was there when we moved in and that it went away. It turned out that they needed a bed. We sold them our old one and moved it back into the house. Surprise, surprise, the smell went away.

We all laughed about it, though my wife and I for different reasons. We didn't bother telling them about the other things that we had experienced in the house. We didn't know them well enough. We didn't want them thinking we were screwy and we didn't want to spoil the place for them if we weren't. We'd leave that to the ghost.

Authors Notes:

This story illustrates several common elements associated with haunted houses. The first is the sudden chill that descends upon the person in the presence of a ghostly spirit. The second common element is the feeling of being watched, of feeling the presence of something that is not natural to this domain. Third, an apparition appeared as a solid form silhouette then dissolved and vanished right before your eyes. Fourth, the smell or odor that seems to come and go without rhyme or reason.

Spooks in the House

A number of years ago, as a poor student, I was renting the top two floors of a house with seven other school chums. We thought ourselves lucky to get the house for such low rent, and all utilities paid. With seven of us, we each paid about $75.00 a month.

The house had its fair share of windows facing east and west, so it should be a brightly lit house in the daytime, but somehow, the house was always dark and dim. We could never figure this out. Often at night, we'd hear bumps and creaks, we always put it down as the old hundred years plus Victorian style house settling down

It was a Friday night, just about Spring time, exams were done with, Winter was almost over. We were all really overjoyed and happy. We felt that we did well on our exams. That evening, six of us went to the movies, then had dinner. After the dinner, we headed home. The celebration continued when we got home. We were drinking soda pop while some of the guys were drinking beer. We were all laughing and joking in the kitchen, when we heard the door open, and footsteps coming up the stairs.

We thought, Jenny and Sue were home, they had opted to go to a fellowship rather than join us at our celebration. We called out to the two sisters to join us, when we received no answer, Tom poked his head outside the kitchen, the dim hallway was empty. We figured, incredible as it sounds, the two sisters probably had not heard us, so Tom went upstairs to the girls' room. A few minutes later, he came back downstairs looking very puzzled. The girls weren't home, yet, we heard someone open the front door and come up those stairs. We shrugged it off as the house settling down or a streetcar coming by shaking the house.

A week later, as I was sleeping, I woke up quite suddenly. Unsure what had awakened me, I switched on the light. Looking around, peeked outside the door, nothing. I went to the kitchen to get myself a glass of water. While walking to the kitchen, I met Frank who had just as suddenly awakened. We made some cups of soup and talked for about half an hour and then headed back to our respective rooms. Frank shared a room with Alex.

As I couldn't sleep, I sat in bed reading when suddenly, I heard a loud, high-pitched cackle. I froze, my eyes quickly scanning my small bedroom. Nothing. When I heard movement in the next room, I ran to the door, swung it open, just as Frank and Alex were about to crash into my room. The guy's looked rather angry, they thought I'd given that laugh. I swore that it wasn't me when Dave and Rich joined us, while John, Sue and Jenny came running down the stairs from their rooms. We'd all heard that cackle. Alex and Frank, the oldest of us, calmed us down and gave a very logical explanation about what happened.

We figured that the tenants renting the basement and first floor of the house were partying and the sound carried through the vents to our rooms. Sounds reasonable, Right? The next day, we called on our neighbors, but no one came to their door. Puzzled, we went to the house next door, our landlord lives there. Our landlady told us in a rather cold voice that the other tenants had gone home for the summer vacation, we were the only ones in the house.

Things went fine for a couple weeks. Then one night, while we were having dinner, a sudden cold blast of air came from nowhere and the lights got dim. We stared at each other, we all looked very nervous. The already dim hallway was black as night. Suddenly, a low, very evil sounding laugh started, its volume got higher and higher then the evil cackle joined the laugher. Just as suddenly, Rich gave a loud yell. The lights went back to the way they were before. There was no one but us in the kitchen. After that point, the conversation around the dinner table was, "why did Rich yell out?" and "How soon do we move out?" Rich swore that he felt someone grab his throat, squeezing it. Eventually, we decided to stay on, the rent was very cheap, and we couldn't afford anything higher. Besides, we were such good friends who didn't really want to part company. Most of us were from the same town.

The next day, we had to call an ambulance for Rich had suddenly developed a dangerously high fever overnight. At the Hospital, they diagnosed Rich with throat cancer. A very strange thing as he didn't smoke and there was no history of cancer in his family. They did not explain the fever, the doctors did not know what caused it as it went away soon after he was admitted. They hospitalized Rich for about two weeks. Sometime after the first three days, Rich decided that he didn't want us visiting with him anymore. He arranged for his things to be packed and moved to a storage facility until he could be discharged from the hospital.

A few days after Rich had moved out, Alex and I were on Dinner duty. When we heard the front door open and slam shut, we figured the others were home. We hollered out at them that dinner wasn't ready yet. Our announcement was greeted with silence. Immediately, Alex and I froze and stared at each other, our eyes mirroring the horror we felt. We heard footsteps coming up the stairs. We peeked out at the hallway, nothing there.

No one was coming up those stairs but the footsteps reached the top of the stairs, the carpet depressed as the footsteps came closer and closer. Alex yelled at the "Nothing," "Stop! Go away, leave us alone!", the footsteps just continued. We both felt a sense of foreboding danger, as though whatever it was that was approaching us was evil. The footsteps got to the middle of the hallway when Alex, said in a hoarse whisper, "Get out of here kid!". He grabbed me very hard by my arm and shoved me away from the kitchen door then ran toward the large kitchen window, grabbed a chair, smashed the window and practically half dragged and half threw me out the window.

We were on the second floor, but we were past caring, all we knew was we had to get away from that thing. The jump gave us some bruised limbs and a couple sprains. We looked up at the window, a shadow was at the window, then the whole kitchen slowly grew darker and darker until the window looked like a black gaping hole in the house. Suddenly, the lights came back on in the kitchen again. In spite of the fact that all we had on were T-shirts and Jeans, Alex would NOT let me go back into the house, it was late Spring, and the temperature was still very cold.

Alex made us wait on the porch until the others came home. An hour or so later, when the other guys got home, Alex made me wait outside as they trooped into the house, got me a jacket, packed our things, called a cab and we all headed for a motel on the lake shore. We rented a room and stayed there for about a week until we found other accommodations.

The next day we went back to the house to talk to the landlord and pay for the window. The landlord was not thrilled with us. His wife started cursing and swearing at us. We'd told them, take the last month's rent and here's extra for the window, she called the cops on us! Luckily for us, the cops were quite understanding and polite. The landlady insisted that we did more damage than the window. We entered the house to look. What a change! The whole place smelled dank and the walls, the paint looked like someone run something sharp over them. It really gave us the creeps. The landlord took one look at the walls, turned pale and refused to come into the house.

One of the police officers told us that many years ago, a man and his wife had lived in the house we rented. One night, the police got a call, the couple in a drunken fit had killed their children and the husband's mother. Then the husband killed the wife as they were fighting about where to stuff the bodies to hide them. After killing his wife, the man became depressed and hung himself. Apparently, the police frequently got calls from people who had lived in that house about intruders that weren't there. The police officer had grown up a few blocks away and knew the story very well. He said he had never known the house to be occupied by any family for more than a year at a time, or less. We were in the house for about two months.

A True Story

What you are about to read is absolutely true. We have exaggerated nothing, and we changed none of the names. It involves an experience my girlfriend and I had over a six-month period between 1988 and 1989. My name is Bill and I met my girlfriend, Stacey in Brentwood, Long Island in September 1987. Almost a year later, we decided to get married. We found an apartment which was really a basement converted into a student apartment.

Strange things started happening the very first night we moved into the apartment. Stacey was cooking dinner while I was in the shower. I was in the middle of shampooing my hair, when I heard a female voice say just above a whisper, "Billy." I peeked behind the shower curtain, thinking Stacey was talking to me. No one was there. I then called out to her loudly, asking what she wanted. She called back saying that she didn't say anything, and that it probably was me hearing things, with shampoo in my ears.

I shrugged, went back to my shower deeds, and was finishing rinsing my hair, ready to put conditioner in, when again, I heard it, but a bit louder. It seemed to come from the hallway right outside the bathroom. Stacey came running in, shaking, saying that this time she heard it too. Needless to say, I didn't condition my hair that night.

After dinner, I convinced us both that it was probably the landlady Liz, upstairs talking to someone else, and that her voice was carried through a vent or something. Then around eleven o'clock that evening, I picked up a book to read in bed while Stacey stayed up playing a game on my computer in the living room. Around one o'clock in the morning, I noticed that the lights were gradually dimming in the bedroom. Finally, it got so dark that I couldn't read, and in less than a minute, the light was completely off. I got up and looked at the switch. It was one of those round knob switches you have to turn to make brighter or dimmer. I turned it up, and all was fine. I told Stacey what had happened, and she said that maybe it was an electrical problem.

That night after she was sleeping, I was still reading, and fell asleep with the book on my chest. I awoke to find her still asleep but the light off again. I never turned it off, and asked her when she woke up the next morning and she replied no she hadn't turned off the light.

Subsequently, every night at around one o'clock in the morning, our bedroom light would turn itself off, gradually dimming until off. We would joke about it, and show the little trick to friends, pointing out that no other room does it. One day, taking my friend Ken's advice, I turned the switch all the way on, and put a pencil mark on it, all the way to the right.

We got a flashlight ready, and waited for the one

o'clock hour to come. Then, the lights dimmed and went out, and Ken turned on the flashlight, shining it at the switch. Sure enough, the little pencil marks that I had made at the five o'clock position was now at seven o'clock position.

The Whirlwind

The following story comes from England and describes the ghost of a little girl that haunted their home.

When I was in college, both my housemate and I were into the paranormal. We rented a 1930's style home that was semi-detached. What was interesting about the house was not the outside appearance, but the ghost inside. At the top of the stairs, outside the bathroom door, there was a cold spot. Neither my housemate, Alison nor I could bear to be on our own in the house, and both of us had, on occasion, sat outside on the doorstep until the other came home.

After we had been there four or five months, the cold spot would start to move around the house like a tiny whirlwind, skipping from one room to another. We were not the only ones to feel it. Many of our friends refused to use the bathroom in our house because of it, and many friends had followed it around the house in curiosity. It just frightened the willies out of me. Having a bath was a very traumatic experience. Oh yes, and the light-bulbs at the top of the stairs used to blow on a regular basis, every week or so. Then you would be in the dark with this cold pillar following you into the bathroom.

A friend of mine had a mother who made her living as a psychic named, Sandra. Anyway, we asked Sandra to come and see what was what. She was a lovely lady, very friendly and chatty. She did some regressions on members of the group which seemed to work on everyone except me, and I was a little skeptical by this point.

"What do you think of the house?" Alison asked her

without telling her of the whirlwind.

"Very transient." She said. "However, there is something on the landing, isn't there?"

My mouth dropped open, maybe there was something in this after all.

"It's a little girl and she is very frightened, isn't she, Ann?" Sandra looked straight at me.

After that evening, we took to talking to the whirlwind, verbalizing our fear to her, and making her realize that she was frightening us. Although it never stopped, and we were always apprehensive about being in the house alone, it became better after that day.

Authors Notes:

It is interesting that they describe the ghost in this story as a whirlwind, a cold pillar and as a cold spot that moved around the house. Consider the photograph taken at Sellers Arts & Crafts store because it also resembles a whirlwind and was a cold pillar that followed Sharon up the stairs.

This swirling energy vortex cast a shadow on the wall. This is interesting since it represents that the whirlwind had density and can reflect light. This means that one can feel this sensation since it has density which has mass.

The Substation

Shortly after graduating from high school I found myself moving to a community on the southern end of the Willamette Valley called, Cottage Grove, where I lived for three years. I consider it one of those places that just seemed right to me. Within a year of moving to the town I had more friends than I knew what to do with. I had melded myself into the social fabric of the younger community enough that many thought that I had been raised there and actually graduated with them from their high school. It is a nice feeling and a nice town and I still love it and will always look back on those years fondly.

It was a wild period. A time of some of my greatest happiness, but I also will reflect on it as where I encountered one of the most frightening experiences of my life. It happened not long after I had moved from the place. I took a job in Oakridge, some fifty miles away. Oakridge didn't offer much in the social category for a young man in his early twenties. So every time I found myself with more than fifteen hours of free time and ten dollars in my pocket, I jumped in my 1964 Karmen Ghia and sped off for Cottage Grove.

It happened that I met a girl there on one of my trips. Like the town, she possessed all the qualities I was looking for and everything felt right and natural. She eventually became my wife, but before that happened, we were simply two young people deeply in love, living fifty miles apart and looking for things to do, places to park and spark.

One Friday night in the heat of summer, I drove down out of the mountains to Cottage Grove. I was staying with a young married couple I had grown to know rather well. We were sipping on beer that evening and talking about places to drive to where two people could be alone. In the conversation they mentioned a place not to go because it was haunted. It was the first time I had ever heard the stories. I knew of the place and had driven by it a hundred times and never once gave it a second thought. A power substation out in the middle of nowhere, south of town on the way to Cottage Grove Lake.

The next day I went into town to do my usual socializing. I happened to mention the spot to a group of my friends who then preceded to tell me all sorts of stories about "the substation." Some of the stories were very outlandish and some of them somewhat believable. The stories varied from a young demented ax-murderer stalking the area, to some ghost of a kid who drowned in a nearby creek, to werewolves and such.

I took into account who told each story and weighed my own opinions as to validity. There tended to be a common element, however, to each story. Every person who said they had actually tried to park there after dark, claimed they had the hell scared out of them and would never try it again and they said these things with profound conviction!

At the time, I didn't take much stock in such matters, yet I was looking for something different to do and this sounded like something fun to investigate. My girlfriend seemed willing to help so we went back to the young couple's home where I was staying for the weekend. We told them about our plan to go out to the substation and park that evening after dark. They did not think that was a good idea but they knew we intended to check it out with or without their approval. They suggested that I not take my Volkswagen and offered me their Monte Carlo instead. A car with a few extra thousand pounds of Detroit steel armor and an engine that could place some distance should the need arise. After thinking about it for a while, I accepted the offer.

That evening after the sun had set and it grew about as dark as it was going to get, we drove out to the spot. As I turned in, our headlights raked the substation which looked like some kind of eerie erector set encased in a tall cyclone fence. On the north side of the wire was a bladed out area where someone had pushed the trees back for parking. The substation had been there for a few years so the brush was starting to encroach. Still, there was plenty of clearing around so theoretically a person could see somebody, or something, coming.

As luck would have it, there was no moon. Once the headlights were off, it became pitch-black beneath the canopy of the woods. I switched off the engine and locked the doors, then settled back. It was a hot August night so I left the driver's window down a crack. We sat there for about two minutes, nothing happened. No strange feelings, sounds, or sights.

We began to notice that the car was bigger and a whole lot more comfortable than the Karmen Ghia ever thought of being. Since nothing else was happening, it seemed a waste of time and gas to sit there staring into the darkness. Besides, the smell of my girlfriend's perfume was driving me crazy and it was a Saturday night. We laughed the whole idea off and started to engage in some smooching and such.

Very shortly after we turned our attention from outside the car there came a sudden chill that swept inside of the car. I would best describe the sensation as bitter cold. It came as the combined thrill of every ax-murder, werewolf, and monster horror story we had ever heard all rolled into one. It was an icky sick feeling that surrounded us everywhere and nowhere, leaving us gasping for air as if drowning. The romantic mood vanished like a splash of ice water and my girlfriend and I literally flew apart and simultaneously made sure the windows were up tight.

Whatever it was, it was real, so help me, God! From out of the blackness we felt as if something that was extremely evil and dangerous was rushing toward the car. The doors on the Monte Carlo were thick steel and lots of it. Nevertheless, the glass was just glass and it was right there all around us only inches away. I fumbled for the ignition key. I fully expected to have something like an ax-blade come flying through the window at us. I expected to see burning red eyes or teeth smeared on the glass that licked and bit at the windshield or clawing at the handle. Our hearts pounded and my girlfriend began to whimper and scream. It came upon us with such speed and force that we had nothing else to do but panic.

I managed to start the car and hit the headlights. I saw nothing unusual in the beams to the front. I found myself wishing that I had the foresight to have turned the car around before we shut it down. I slammed the car into reverse and spun the wheel. Dust and rocks boiled around the front, cloaking us in a dingy brown cloud. I yanked the shifter into drive low-range and the car shot out of the dust and I turned the wheel for the road out of there. The headlights again flashed across the substation, illuminating the strange angles and shapes. Still, I saw nothing unusual, but I could feel this presence and so could my partner and it was as close as reaching from the back seat.

With my back and neck tingling, I mashed down on

the gas and could hear the sound of gravel churning under my tires. The car eased forward slowly and I realized that I might be digging the wheels down to where we could get stuck. I eased up on the throttle and the car leaped forward. We hit the road squealing the tires, turning toward town. We kept going until we found ourselves surrounded by the lights of downtown Cottage Grove. We both were deeply shaken. We took the car back to our friends and I thanked them profusely for letting us borrow it. We told them our story and got back an uncaring "we told you so" lecture. Neither of us actually saw anything out there, but we felt it and we won't ever go back there after dark again, not even today.

To this day we still have trouble talking about it in a darkened parked car. One thing is for certain, I am now a believer of things which go bump in the night. Not everything necessarily has to have an explanation or be seen merely to exist. Even now, years later, I refuse to park in dark places or else my mind leaps to that dark night at the substation. In fact, as I write these words I find myself looking over my shoulder as I feel faint ripples of panic still echoing off the walls of my soul.

Authors Notes:
This story illustrates an important concept in understanding the players found in the Spirit Realm. The substation was a source of electromagnetic radiation that acted as a magnet attracting the presence of a negative energy pattern like bees are attracted to water.

The negative energy pattern attached itself to the substation and began feeding on the energy radiated by the substation. The negative energy pattern may or may not be the spirit of a deceased person. It may be an "unconscious pattern of negative energy" that had drifted in the cosmic sea and became stuck in the radiation net of the substation.

We can liken this "unconscious pattern of negative energy" to jellyfish that float about in the ocean. The tidal movements dictate the direction and speed of their movement, not intelligence. Some jellyfish are harmless while others have deadly stings. If a jellyfish drifts up on the beach and someone accidentally steps on it and is stung, we do not say that the jellyfish is an evil demon. In the same manner, we should not judge intense negative energy as evil or demonic for we are then labeling and judging them according to a singular belief system.

The Haunted Connor Hotel

The history of Jerome, Arizona is a story of tough men, hard rock, hard work, hard liquor and hard play. Jerome is a town propped on a thirty-degree mountainside two thousand feet above the Verde Valley floor in central Arizona. The town main streets are switchbacks in a narrow highway that snakes over Mingus Mountain with twenty mile per hour curves.

The town of Jerome sits on Cleopatra Hill, directly over the Jerome Fault and atop eighty-five miles of underground mining tunnels. The town of Jerome has a fifteen hundred vertical foot elevation differences between dwellings at the Gulch, which is the bottom of Cleopatra Hill, and the upper-level homes.

Prehistoric Indians, the Sinagua, were first attracted to the mountain by the colorful stone that they mined almost a thousand years ago. They ground the colorful blue azurite into powder for jewelry and as pigments for coloring pottery and as body paint. When the Spanish gold hunters, Antonio de Espejo in 1583, and Farfan de los Godos in 1598 arrived to claim the land in the name of the Spanish crown, the Indians led them to the mines. The Spanish gold hunters were disappointed in finding no gold, just colored stones, so they departed shaking their heads at the Indians for mining colorful stones.

History does not say if any white man visited the area until 1865 when the American settlers from Prescott arrived in Verde Valley. They established a cavalry post in Verde Valley to protect the settlers from Indians. Legends have it that Al Sieber, Indian scout and guide, staked a claim on the copper mountain, but failed to work the claim. The town had its beginnings when a group of prospectors staked ten claims and a millsite in 1876.

The beginning of the town was typical of most mining towns. As miners flocked to the area, tents and wooden shacks started to dot the thirty-degree hillside. This community of tents and shacks finally grew to an incorporate city of 15,000 people in 1920. When the mines played out, the population finally decreased to 120 people and a ghost town. Later the artist community discovered the town and started moving into the abandoned buildings and established studios for their artwork. Today, the town has a population of 470, mostly merchants and artists who are very proud of their town.

We drove around the tight twenty-mile per hour curves that slowly climbed the Cleopatra Hill. Old cement foundations with crumbling walls and abandoned wooden frame houses complete with fallen porches dotted the steeply sloped hillsides as we arrived in town. As visitors, we were very interested in why the local residents called their town,"The Ghost City." The rumors of haunted buildings intrigued us and we wanted to explore the shadowy side of Jerome. As Ghost Hunters, we were loaded with our camera's, video equipment and ghost hunting paraphenalia.

After rounding several bends and steep curves, we glimpsed a sign that read "Ghost Inn" attached to a Bed & Breakfast. Later we would realize that the town was full of such good natured signs as Haunted Hamburger, Spook Convention, Spook Crossing, Spirit Room and the Ghost City Goodies bulletin board that greeted visitors. We parked our rig next to the Sliding Jail that originally was found much higher on the hillside.

After dozens of quakes, both from natural occurring and from the underground mining explosions, the jail ended up sliding downhill to its present site. The weather was great, a storm was moving into the area and dark angry clouds filled the horizon. The wind was blustery as a gust lifted our hats from our heads and sent them sailing in the wind. What a spooky day to be in Jerome, the Ghost City.

After walking around town snapping photographs of the "ghost" signs, we decided it was time to get to work by asking questions about ghostly haunts. We stopped in at the Jerome Grill and had some iced teas and asked about haunted spots in town. We chatted with the waitress about ghosts and things which "go bump in the night." She laughed and said the upstairs was haunted. Almost everyone who worked in the Grill has heard strange sounds coming from upstairs. She then asked if we would like to investigate the upstairs.

We were led up a set of steep green carpeted stairs to the second floor which turned out to be a Bed and Breakfast Inn that is housed in this 1899 green stone building. At the top of the stairs was the waiting or receiving room where we set up our equipment. The small room was nicely furnished with two couches and a fireplace. We walked through some French glass doors and found a long dark carpeted hallway. The individual rooms had a bed, sink and television set and perhaps a chair or two. We explored each of the rooms with the EMF meter looking for energy anomalies and taking photographs of the interior.

The upstairs maid was busy making up one of the rooms that a guest had recently vacated. We talked to her about ghosts and she laughed and said that she hadn't seen any. She sounded like she thought we were nuts for asking. We investigated each room until we finally reached the last room at the far end of the hallway. Managment had given each room an individual name such as Victorian Room, Dance and Romance or the Spooks, Ghosts and Goblins Room.

Managment must have named this room because of prior poltergeist sounds heard by the restaurant staff found directly below this room. We scanned the room and detected a small energy anomaly registering 1.8-milligauss that moved around the room. The energy anomaly was about the size of a football and was very fast moving. One moment it would be in front of me and the next moment it had floated to a different location in the room. Since the meter reading was low, we suspect this was a recent visitor who was not yet able to generate a stronger energy field.

When we finished, the waitress told us her friend, Tisa Conlin, at the Mandolin was very interested in chatting with us about ghosts. The waitress gave us directions and we walked up the hill a block to find the Mandolin located next to the Spirit Room tavern. The Mandolin was a small shop specializing in medieval decor located on the first floor of the old Connor Hotel. The second floor of the Connor's building, the actual hotel, takes up the entire block. The old stone Connor Hotel has had a colorful history, in that it has burned to the ground many times leaving only the stone walls standing.

Today, the owners of the building are restoring the Connor Hotel to its original condition. However, the day we were there, the lone workman was busy in one of the old hotel rooms. Stepladders were in the hallway, scraps of wood yanked from walls lay on canvas and the dreary hallway seemed eerie. Much has to be done on the second floor to update the wiring and plumbing so as to meet the city code specifications. Someday, the owners plan for the hotel to open for business once again. The first floor consists of small business shops and the Spirit Room tavern where locals' gather for a cool beer, listen to Country Western music and relax for a spell.

The history of the Connor Hotel is very important. David Connor of Massachusetts moved to the mining community of Jerome and purchased a corner lot from the man who had laid out the town. Connor decided to build a saloon out of stone which he called the Stone Saloon. The town folks thought Connor was a nut for building his saloon out of stone instead of wood and canvas as did the other merchants. None of the local merchants knew how long the town would survive as a mining town because as soon as the payload played out, the town would become a ghost town over night.

Connor was different, he had a dream and he constructed his buildings to stand the test of time. The Connor corner burned down six times, always rebuilt each time with ingenuity and insurance money. The town folks have credited his stone building with saving the town from burning down several times.

This massive landmark is on the corner of Jerome Avenue and Main Avenue. Connor built the first floor out of native stone and two other floors built out of bricks made in Jerome. The first floor housed a restaurant, stores, bar room, card room and a billiard/pool parlor. The second story floor had twenty-three rooms for boarders and transients. The hotel bus met the narrow gauge railway train bringing boarders to stay at the hotel for $1.00 per night.

The 1897 fire, occurring on December 24, brought a gloomy Christmas to Jerome. According to the Jerome Mining News, the only structure to escape the flames was Dave Connor's building. Apparently the fire started to the east of this building when a fight broke out in Japanese Charley, a lodging house that was actually a sporting house, with girls occupying the second floor.

An eye-witness account by Oscar Wager, as quoted in a 1959 issue of Arizona Days and Ways, is as follows: "Apparently some sort of free-for-all was going on and we stopped and looked through a window . . . While we looked on, a woman picked up a kerosene lamp and threw it at a man. It missed the mark, but broke against the wall and almost instantly the interior of the flimsy building was a mass of flames. The flames spread so rapidly through the business section that there was almost no time to save the goods. The saloon keepers hollered 'Come and get it! All the whiskey you want for carrying it away!' A good many irresponsible people desisted from fire fighting, sacked the saloons of all they could carry, and guzzled whiskey while the major portion of Jerome's business district burned to the ground."

The hotel was gutted in 1898 and 1899 with only the walls left standing. Connor cleared the site and rebuilt the hotel out of bricks. We were unable to learn if any boarders or transients were killed in the many fires that gutted the hotel over the years.

The Winter 1991 edition of the Jerome Chronicle, the Quarterly of the Jerome Historical Society, contained the following article titled, "CONNOR HOTEL AND ITS PROPRIETOR." The article is reprinted from the Jerome Reporter dated December 28, 1899. The article reads as follows: "Phoenix-like, Hotel Connor has again risen from the ashes. It has only been eight months since the large brick structure known as Hotel Connor was destroyed by fire, yet today there is no signs visible of the Jerome destroyer. A complete two-story brick has replaced the old, new and costly furniture is in every room.

The second floor of the building has 20 rooms and a parlor. The first story contains the hotel bar, office, Boyd's drug store, Goldberg Bros. clothing store, and a restaurant. As a whole it will be seem that the property is a money earner and its favorable location will make it more so in the future.

Dave Connor, the proprietor, is one of the most unassuming men in town, and is not spoiled by the good returns that seem to attend all his investments. He is about 35 years old, a native of Ireland and Democracy is his religion. The Connor block was known for its fine restaurant (the Connor Cafe) and the many stores servicing the mining community."

The old Connor Hotel in Jerome, Arizona could be deemed the hotel where time stands still. Though in the process of restoration, a new face will never remove the atmosphere that remains from the days when the copper mines were active and the population soared to an amazing fifteen thousand people.

The feeling that takes over when entering the hotel is like stepping into a time warp, where modern technology and conveniences have not yet invaded the premises. It is wonderful as in ones imagination, a person can picture the gaiety and activities which took place there so many years ago. Imagine having an elaborate room in the hotel, settling down for a quiet evening of rest after a hard day of travel, only to find talking and laughter filtering up through the floor boards from the tavern below. The tavern is still active, now it is called, The Spirit Room. A person could get caught up in the swishing of ladies long skirts, boisterous laughter, clanking of glasses as well as glass breaking.

The carpeted stairs are solid beneath your feet as you walk up the indoor stairway to the vacant hallway and large rooms on the second floor. Nearing the top of the stairs, the atmosphere begins to feel heavy, bordering on oppressive. You can feel the strength of the building itself. It is old, but solid with high ceilings and light fixtures from another era. New to the ceilings are skylights, though they permit little more light to penetrate into the darkened hallway.

Maybe the dark green carpet and darkly painted walls and doorways contribute to the heavy atmosphere in this hotel. Something about the place creates an invisible weight strong enough to make even the boldest of people have second thoughts about exploring here. It is the perfect setting for ghostly activity.

According to Ms. Tisa Conlin, daughter of the owner of the old building, room #1 has been reported as the area of haunting. She herself has felt the true source of the paranormal activity emanates from room #5. She has spent many nights alone in the hotel, bedding down in room #1, sleeping undisturbed. She has not attempted to stay all night in room #5, however, many daring people have been turned away in fear and repulsion from that room. As we walked the hallway, though thickly carpeted, like the stairs, the wooden floor beneath us, creaked and groaned, adding an eeriness to the silence.

Ms. Conlin, not being fearful of paranormal activity, says she has experienced little that was abnormal in the hotel. Her focus has been on the business, a unique little gift shop called, The Mandolin, on the first floor. She feels she is not sensitive to the ghostly activity taking place on the second floor, or as she explained it, she is "numb to it." Yet she has an awareness of something present due to one experience that remains vividly in her mind.

The only bathroom available to Ms. Conlin during

working hours is a remodeled, updated bathroom on the second floor. When business slowed in the gift shop one afternoon, Ms. Conlin ran upstairs to use the facilities. As she sat on the toilet, she heard someone call her name. It unnerved her as she was alone and feeling quite vulnerable. She thought a workman or someone had come upstairs without her knowledge. She called out, "Who's there?" No one answered so she dismissed it, attributing it to imagination.

A few moments later, she once again distinctly heard an eerie voice call out her name. It was soft and distant but she could have sworn it was a man's voice she heard. She was so startled hearing her name called the second time she learned very quickly that it is extremely difficult to pull up and fasten jeans while running down stairs!

Ms. Conlin firmly believes that visitors from the past are roaming the hallways and rooms in the old Connor Hotel. She knows she is not as sensitive to their presence as many who have visited. Other people have felt the presence of something of a negative nature. Her children visit regularly and express no sensation of ghostly inhabitants, in fact they are very comfortable being there. They have displayed absolutely no fear while in the building.

The workmen restoring the upstairs hallway and rooms express a disbelief in the Hotel being haunted. Yet there have been more accidents and injuries to them than normal. One workman had an angry looking gash on his upper arm from one such accident. He did admit that the restoration work at the Connor Hotel was the most difficult he'd ever encountered on any job. Too many things go wrong up there.

As we returned to investigate and photograph the Hotel, the second time, we encountered a few oddities ourselves. It was 4:45 in the afternoon when we set up our equipment and the only sounds we heard were traffic on the streets below. The hallway was dim from lack of natural light, we did not wish to use artificial lighting. We wanted the hallway in its natural state for that time of day.

As we wandered the hall, taking photographs and getting a sense of times past, we both began to hear a faint and distant beeping sound. It was almost inaudible so we dismissed it, thinking it was something outside. The beep was intermittent, five minutes or so between the sound. As we continued to randomly shoot pictures, the beeping increased in volume and became more frequent.

We discovered a smoke detector on the ceiling in room #4 as the source of the beep. At the time, room #5 was locked, as were most other rooms that evening. Room #4 had increasingly drawn our attention that evening as a source of activity. Along the north wall of the room, which divided rooms' #4 and #5, our EMF Meter spiked, showing momentary electro magnetic intensity. This drew us to investigate further. The more we photographed the area around room four, the faster the electric smoke detector beeped, until the beeps were occurring within seconds of each other.

We finished our investigation, collected our equipment and started down the stairs to meet with Ms. Conlin once again. As we began our descent, we realized we no longer heard the beeping of the smoke detector. The hallway and rooms were deserted and silent once again. While taking photographs, the batteries in one of my cameras had gone dead, very suddenly. We have had this happen to us in the past in allegedly haunted places so it came as no real surprise. Ghostly entities have a tendency to drain the energy from even brand new batteries. Having learned this, we've made it a policy to always carry extra batteries, should this occur.

As it turned out, our efforts were well rewarded as we captured the energy vortex of one invisible resident on the stairway. Whomever it was, passing before the camera lens, allowing us to capture him on film, remains nameless. Ms Conlin as well as ourselves, remain hopeful that one day, a name will be revealed for this ghostly entity.

Another interesting story that Tisa Conlin told us, was about a large glass case in the Mandolin. When she bought the old display case, she was told, up front, that she would never sell anything that she had displayed inside the glass case. She was told it was hexed! The case, being a very large, very old piece of furniture was so attractive to her, she bought it anyway. So far, nothing inside the glass case has sold.

The customers of the Spirit Room tavern talk about the footsteps and thumps that they have heard over the years coming from above them in the Connor Hotel. They smile and say that the ghosts are having a party upstairs. The haunting footsteps and thumps are so common that it has become a way of life for the patrons of the tavern.

The Connor Hotel

The busy street in front of the Connor Hotel where tourists are busy buying gifts from the many small shops. The Spirit Room is one of the watering holes on hot days for locals as well as visitors.

The Ghost of Connor Hotel
Jerome, Arizona

The dark and eerie stairs leading to the second floor of the Connor Hotel. It felt almost like someone was following us up the stairs. The strange white vortex was not visible to us, but was captured on film. It is interesting that its configuration is similar to the vortex captured on film at Sellers Arts & Crafts.

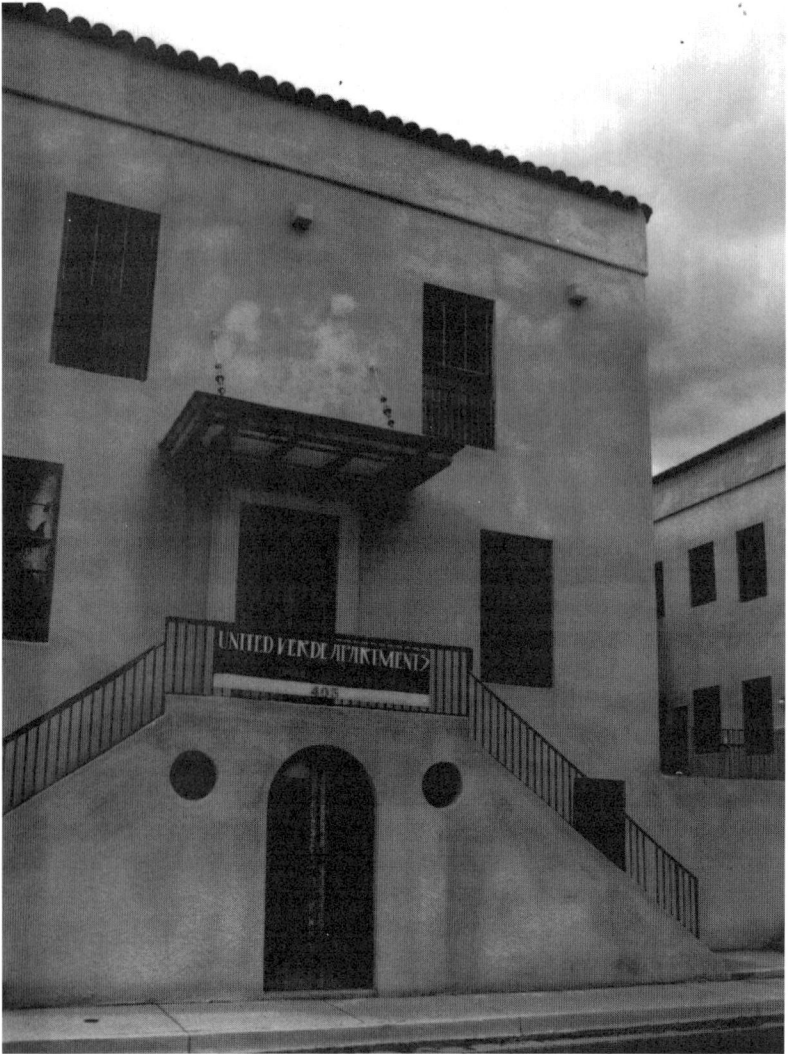

Is that a Ghost in the window?

While passing by this old building in Jerome, we took a photograph and discovered an interesting figure in the window. Could this be a ghost? We did not see anything strange at the time the picture was taken.

Why should it be strange in a town noted for its ghosts? Most old timers have tales of ghosts and most of the merchants say that the old hospital is perhaps the most haunted building in town because of all the miners who died in that building.

The town folks treat the ghosts and hauntings as if it were a perfectly normal part of their town. They are proud to be a Ghost City and appear to coexist with the spirits of the dead miners who walk the town, unaffected and unafraid. This was the first time that we found a town whose citizens accept ghostly entities as a normal state of affairs.

Perhaps the ghostly residents from the past are thankful to business people for bringing life again to the town. We suspect that the ghostly miners enjoy seeing the tourists visiting their town and taking a moment to acknowledge the many miners who have died here.

You can imagine that Halloween is a favorite time for the residents of Jerome as they arrange special events around their ghosts and spooks. It is no wonder that Halloween is the biggest event in Jerome and more elaborately celebrated than Christmas.

The town folks are not afraid to talk about the spooks who haunt the old abandoned buildings especially during the full moon. Some suggest the best time is when a low pressure weather pattern is moving through the area. Jerome is perhaps the most haunted town in America and the Conner Hotel is the most hauntingly active!

For more information about Jerome, please contact:

Jerome Historical Society
P.O. Box 156
Jerome, AZ 86331
520-634-1066

Unresolved and Unfinished Business

The following ghost tales relate to unresolved issues or unfinished business that becomes an anchor making the spirits earthbound. Unfortunately, the ghostly entities are earthbound until they can finish their business or are able to let go of unresolved issues so they can continue in their progression beyond this earth plane.

The Ghost of Captain Jack

Along the state line between Oregon and California lies the beautiful Klamath Basin. Among many of the natural features of this basin is the Klamath Basin Wildlife Refuge. This Refuge is home to one of the largest concentrations of Bald Eagles during the late Winter months. Photographers come from around the world to film the Bald Eeagles that perch atop the cottonwoods at dusk. Snow capped, Mt. Shasta provides a photogenic back drop for these majestic eagles.

South of the Lower Klamath Lake lies Petroglyph Point which stands out as a lone sentinel amid the bleak and barren landscape of Northern California's Lava Bed National Monument. This desolate and windswept landmark is a few miles south of Tulelake, California and about twenty-five miles south of Klamath Falls, Oregon.

The original inhabitants of the Klamath Basin region dwelled around Tule Lake that lapped against the low cliff side of Petroglyph Point. The flat cliffs that lined this outcropping were ideal for the carving of rock art. Muddy volcanic layers of tuff created the smooth cliff sides some 270,000 years ago. Magma from deep within the earth welled up through cracks, or faults, in the earth's crust, erupting when it contacted the shallow waters of Lake Modoc, later known as Tule Lake.

The Modoc Indians who occupied the area later referred to these early people as the "Ancients," but did not know of their language or meaning of their mysterious symbols carved on the cliff walls. Considered sacred by the Modocs, this place was used as a site for "power or vision quests" by Modocs seeking to come into a closer spiritual relationship with the animals and the earth around them. They have dated some rock art to more than 5,700 years ago and may have originated with the earliest inhabitants of the region who came into the basin more than 11,500 years ago. There are more than 5,000 symbols carved on the cliff side also nearby boulders and in cave shelters. This site is one of the largest concentrations of rock art in North America.

This area is dotted with old volcanic cones and expuded black lava that are rough and jagged laying naked upon the land. The lava beds are like a no-man's land, dotted with lava caves and natural walls offering concealment and tactical advantage for defense. This desolate lava bed became the retreat for some proud people driven from their homes by the white man's hunger for their land. Many of the local residents also consider the lava beds to be haunted. One of the most interesting ghost stories of this region is the tale about the ghost of the Modoc Indian named Captain Jack.

The story begins with the "People of the South Lake" or Modocs and their leader Kientpoos or Captain Jack. They had been forced to move from their beloved lakeshore homes to the Klamath Reservation, north of Klamath Falls by the U.S. First Cavalry. Captain Jack was a peaceful man but to avoid bloodshed with the Whites, he had agreed to the move only after the government made specific promises to the Modoc Indians if they would move to the Klamath Reservation. However, once moved to the Reservation, the government did not see fit to live up to their promises to the Modoc People. The Modocs felt the government had lied and cheated them. Greedy white settlers were anxious to sell this prime Indian land to new homesteaders arriving in the valley spreading lies that drove the Modoc people from their traditional land.

Captain Jack, provoked by the many broken promises made by the government, decided to return to their traditional home on Lost River on the Oregon-California border. It wasn't as if Captain Jack and his people hadn't tried to live in peace with their related brothers, the Klamaths. Almost immediately after arriving on the Reservation, the Modocs were resented and badgered by the Klamaths and made to feel like outcasts. The government did not understand the differences between the two tribes because all they saw was the skin color.

Captain Jack could not tolerate this shameful abuse to his people and unable to obtain relief, he moved his people back to their traditional lands on the Lost River. Captain Jack knew that he would be unable to keep his people clear of trouble with the white settlers. There was too much fear and resentment by the white settlers against the Modocs. Captain Jack asked for a Reservation on the Lost River but the white settlers pressured the military to not grant this request. They wanted this prime land for their homesteads instead.

The government answered Captain Jack's plea for help on November 29, 1872 by sending in an armed detachment of the First Cavalry. The armed detachment looking for blood and retribution entered the Modoc's camp and ordered Captain Jack and his men to disarm and return to the Klamath Reservation. As the Modoc's were complying, they exchanged angry words, then shots rang out and when the smoke cleared, one soldier was dead and seven were wounded. The Modoc's were headed for the lava beds.

Over the next five months sixty Modoc braves held off an Army twenty times their strength. This was no small task since the First Cavalry was using four Coehorn Mortars and two mountain Howitzers. Captain Jack did not want this war but some of his men felt it was better to force the whites from the valley than to stay and be killed. Finally after much fighting the Modocs retreated from the Stronghold. They were half-starved, encumbered by the women, children and old people, and divided by conflict over leadership, as the Modoc's were finally captured in small bands. Captain Jack surrendered to save the women and children who were starving. The cultural identity of an entire people was lost!

They arrested and took Captain Jack to Ft. Klamath where they hanged him on October 23, 1873 at 10:30 in the morning. Apparently they beheaded him before his burial and his head was sent to the White Fathers in Washington, D.C., as a trophy. According to the Modoc beliefs, a warrior had to be buried with all of his body parts if he wanted to enter the Sacred Hunting Grounds after this life. When they removed Captain Jack's head, it was the same as cursing him to remain in this world, forever barring him from his afterlife rewards. Captain Jack is angry at what the white man has done to him and his people. They say that on February nineteenth of each year, the ghost of Captain Jack walks along the trails of his Stronghold in the lava beds. Many have reported images of gloom and doom enshroud them as they walked along the lava bed trail following in the footsteps of Captain Jack.

According to some local residents in the area, they can hear the sounds of gunfire and angry screaming as they walk the dirt trails around Captain Jack's Stronghold! It is certainly eerie to walk along the lava bed trails in absolute stillness with only the wind for company. Walking this trail toward sunset can be nerve racking. Narrow pathways wind through steep lava walls to Captain Jack's Cave and the many fortified positions built by the Modoc band of warriors. They spilled the blood of innocent men on both sides on these jagged and bleak lava beds inducing a sacred bond between the dead and the ground they died upon.

Captain Jack's Stronghold may be the prison for the cursed and doomed Captain Jack. He wanders amid the rocky outcropping of the lava beds searching for his severed head. Sadly they doomed him to wander until his severed head is finally returned and laid to rest in his dirt grave. Then and only then will his spirit be free to depart this mortal battlefield and enter his spiritual peace and rest.

Authors Notes:

This ghost tale is a perfect example of a spirit entity who has unfinished business that is so compelling that he becomes earthbound. Captain Jacks beliefs during his mortal life were very strong concerning the importance of being buried whole so he could cross over to the other side. We do not understand why February 19 was the date that Captain Jack chose to return to the Stronghold.

The Wedding Visitor

Joyce Gill hadn't spoken to her father for four long years. In 1985 she relocated from Florida to New York, the parting was bittersweet, many painful issues were left unresolved between Joyce and her father. In 1989, Joyce telephoned her father and during the course of the telephone call, some of the issues were approached. Tears were shed, feelings were shared and forgiveness resulted.

On December 27, 1989, Joyce Gill telephoned her father at work, to let him know she was going to be married. She was elated and wanted only to share her joy. The voice on the other end of the telephone was strange to her, someone she did not know. She asked to speak to her father, giving his name. The strangers voice was terse, saying, "he's dead, I'm in charge now." Joyce Gill hung up the telephone in total shock.

It was three days before the biggest day in a young woman's life and the shadow of her father's death, hung heavy all around her. Joyce made every effect to enjoy her day, to begin a new life, yet her father was the forefront of her thoughts for three days. He was with her, throughout the days and nights, in her mind, memories whirling through her every thought.

On December 30, 1989, Joyce Gill was married to Scott Burdick at the Wesleyan Church in Syracuse, New York at 11:00 in the morning. She was excited and happy as any new bride, yet grieving at the loss of her father. After the ceremony, the reception was held and photo's were taken of the bride and groom and the wedding party. A member of the Burdick family was snapping photo's randomly in the Church sanctuary.

Joyce Burdick Wedding Day Ghost

Upon receiving the prints from the photo lab, one photograph included a bright circular pattern of light across the print. This anomaly was also on the negative and was not a chemical stain from developing the negative or color print. Something strange had been captured on film, something that was swirling and very white and resembled a circular energy vortex.

The photograph clearly reveals some kind of strange circular pattern of solid white. She still wonders if the ghostly apparition captured on film was the departed spirit of her late father attending her wedding.

Authors Notes:

Upon receiving this story and photograph, we compared this unusual addition to other ghostly photographs we have in our possession of similar anomalies we've identified as energy vortexes. We have found Joyce's photograph to be consistent in its patterns to existing energy vortexes.

Joyce Burdick has asked if we feel it could have been the departed spirit of her late father. We suspect it may well have been the essence of her late father, his love for her and his need to know that she was doing well could well have enabled him to be present at the wedding.

The Ghost Biker

The following was told to me when I was a boy scout in Basingstoke, Hampshire, England. The Scoutmaster who told the story swore it was true. I found the tale quite scary, though I was eleven at the time and we were sitting around a campfire on a dark blustery October night. It just goes to show that atmospherics really help to make a story.

The storyteller, Mike, used to have a friend named Dave, who owned a British racing green Norton motorbike. The bike was very distinctive; There aren't many Norton's left nowadays or British motorbikes for that matter. Anyway, this guy was frequently seen riding out of town on the A30 highway on his motorbike and Mike would often pass him on his way home from work.

The motorcycle guy then went on a touring holiday on the Continent. Before he left, he met with Mike in the pub and described the route he was going to take. He was going to take the cross-channel ferry to France, ride down into Bordeaux and into Spain and then double back into the German Eiffel and Switzerland. The bloke was really enthusiastic about the whole trip;

Ever since he was little he had wanted to see mainland Europe and now was going there and combining the trip with an opportunity to ride his beloved Norton. They parted company and the guy promised to send Mike a postcard from each country he visited and they would meet up when he got back. Mike went back to work wishing he was going with him.

After a while, Mike started to receive the postcards his friend had promised him showing beautiful views of southern France, the Alps and other areas of great natural beauty. Then the postcards stopped as soon as the guy had entered Germany. Mike thought nothing of it; perhaps he had been too busy touring to write postcards.

Anyway, the day arrived when the two of them were due to rendezvous at their regular pub in Tadley, a small village to the north of Basingstoke. Mike drove out to the pub and en route his friend overtook him on his motorbike. The guy turned round and waved at him and signaled that he would meet him later. Mike acknowledged him and continued on to Tadley.

When Mike arrived he went up to the bar and ordered two pints of bitter. One for himself and another for his friend.

The barman said, "Expecting someone?"

Mike said that he was waiting for his friend who just was on a touring holiday of Europe.

The barman said, "Do you mean Dave?"

"Yes," said Mike, "I just saw him coming up the road five minutes ago on his motorbike." At this, the barman turned very pale.

"Are you sure it was Dave?" He asked. Mike said that he was sure since Dave owned the only Norton he knew of and anyway, he recognized the license plate on the bike.

The barman leaned forward and said in deep serious tone, "I don't know how to tell you this. However, Dave had a crash near Euskirchen, Germany, two weeks ago. He had a head-on collision with an articulated lorry. He died instantly."

Authors Notes:

This story is an example of unfinished business that prevented Dave from letting go of the anchor that holds him to this physical plane. He had to fulfill his promise and return to the pub.

The Circle K Ghost

This is a true story that happened in Tucson, Arizona to my friend Wendee who used to do clerking at various convenience stores in Tucson so she could work her way through college. She worked at the 7-11's, Quick Mark and finally the Circle K's from 1990 to 1992.

Wendee's first gig was at a little Circle K which is a highly visible convenience store chain, especially here in the Southwest. This little Circle K was in a quiet neighborhood on the south side of town. She worked the graveyard shift that lasted from 10 o'clock in the evening until six o'clock in the morning.

At first things were busy. A road construction crew was building an off ramp to one of the main freeways in town at night and so Wendee experienced brisk business from the husky and burly folks. The road work was done about a month later and business reduced significantly.

In order to pass the time, Wendee brought in a small

clock radio to listen to late night talk shows. Occasionally, during mopping detail, Wendee would tune the radio to top 40 radio and turn it up again. She noticed over time that the radio's volume would go down slowly until it was inaudible. Wendee would then simply walk over to the radio and turn it up again. Again, over a period of an hour, the volume would go down. As the days went by, Wendee began to notice that the radio would completely shut off when she tuned to the Top 40 stations. Despite the fact that the radio was brand new, she took in a boom box from home and the very same phenomena occurred.

However, Wendee would hear signals and noise coming from the stereo even though it was shut off and sometimes even when they unplugged it. She eventually took the stereo home where it worked well. Spooked, but far from calling in parapsychologists, Wendee decided not to listen to the Top 40 or any radio at all and the occurrences stopped.

A few months into her employment at Circle K, Wendee began to get the feeling that she was being watched. She had just stopped dating a very possessive man at the time and she confided in me that she felt that he might be stalking her. There were times she felt that she was being watched from across the street.

One night, she looked out the window and saw a small man who appeared to be hunched over sitting on a bus stop bench across the street. The man appeared to be looking in her direction. Later, she figured that the man had been sitting there for about three hours. A few hours before dawn, a police officer came in for his nightly dose of coffee and snacks.

Wendee asked him if he could go speak to the man who was sitting across the street because she felt uncomfortable with his peculiar behavior. The police officer looked at her oddly and asked, "What man?" Wendee pointed at the man on the bench and said, "That Man!" The police officer insisted he did not see anyone sitting on the bench across the street. Wendee swears that the man disappeared moments after the police officer departed.

The man would reappear from time to time and Wendee would attempt to take a picture of him or go outside to try to confront him. By this time, she was convinced that something ghostly was going on. After a time, Wendee did not see the man ever again. Yet strange occurrences continued.

At first it was a few strange noises, some bumps and clicks, then things were falling off shelves and the video game getting unplugged. Soon Wendee felt like a babysitter for a bored ghost. She eventually got use to it and called the ghost, 'George' after her dead brother whom she believed the ghost was.

One night the milk guy came in with a shipment. Wendee went back to the rear of the store to open up the refrigeration storage area. Wendee was bored so she decided to chat with the guy and help him unload. Expecting him to come through the rear, Wendee was startled when he came through the front. He looked at her a little curiously and asked her, "What is the deal with your boss?"

Not having the foggiest idea what he was talking about, Wendee responded, "What boss?" The milk guy explained that there was a strange looking man in a Circle K shirt with a sour look on his face. The guy then went on to describe the man as having a hunchback and glasses. Wendee said the man across the street wore glasses and was a hunchback.

After that night, Wendee decided that her days were numbered at Circle K and she gave her two weeks notice, partly because of the ghost and mostly because she got a job at a 7-11 during regular day hours. The day before she left, she found herself very tuckered out and tired around four o'clock in the morning. She did not look forward to the fact that she would start her new job that very day at eight o'clock in the morning, just four hours from now.

Around 4:30 a.m., a group of young ruffians came into the store and bought a variety of cokes, candies, and nachos. They stood around the magazine section and chomped away at their goodies. Wendee watched them carefully but soon found herself falling asleep.

A few moments passed and she fell asleep. Maybe five minutes passed when she was awakened by the noise of a paper boat of nachos hitting the floor. The boys were nowhere in sight and there's a big cheesy mess on the floor. Wendee looks up at one of those circular mirrors to see if the boys was up to some kind of scheme and she notices a dark figure for an instant. Wendee goes out to the aisles to investigate but finds no one.

About a year later, Wendee ran into her old boss at a bus stop. They chatted for a while and the boss mentioned that the store was shut down about three months after a big AM/PM convenience store opened up and forced the Circle K out of business. He also mentioned that they could never keep anyone to do the graveyard shift and that Wendee worked that shift the longest at four months.

He also mentioned that she broke the record set by the guy who worked it before her, a small nearsighted hunchbacked man named Jerry who had been shot and killed in an attempted robbery a month before Wendee started work there.

Authors Notes:

An example of a departed spirit who chooses to remain earthbound, perhaps remaining in this earth plane to look for his killers. The emotions of knowing you are going to be shot and killed apparently angered Jerry so much that he couldn't let go of the emotions and continue to that plane he should be on after death of his physical body.

The Confederate Soldier Ghost

Slowly, the fog rose out of the hollows, drifting, swirling upward toward the old cemetery. It flowed like a slow tide, absorbing all things within its shifting haze until the things faded from view. The swirling fog like mist acted as if it had a life of its own. Independent movement within the fog appeared from time to time. Shapes and figures were slowly forming within the fog, becoming more real then illusion. Late February often brought the dark angry storms that threatened to flood rivers and streams.

The sky had darkened with angry black clouds that promised to drop more rain later in the night. Rock Mills, Alabama was a still town about fifteen to twenty miles from the Georgia state line. The country road from Rock Mills to the state line was typically hilly and the rural roads apparently were made by a herd of old milk cows slowly taking the long way home.

Unfortunately, the paved road twisted back and forth for the entire length until the state line. Then the rural road curved and twisted up one side of the hill and then down the other side. This was to be repeated again and again. The trees grew right up to the edge of the road, further blocking any moonlight which would have fallen if it hadn't been a stormy night. Drivers had to be careful along this country road at night as deer feeding along the side of the road were noted for jumping out into the approaching headlights of cars. This could be fatal for both the deer and the driver.

Julie Roberts had stayed in town late to take in a movie that began at seven o'clock that evening. It wasn't often that she stayed after work but tonight was different. Today was her birthday and she was celebrating it with dinner and a movie. After all, she was thirty-one-years old today. Besides, it helped her take her mind off of her life. She had been feeling in the pits lately and needed something to look forward to doing.

The dinner had been great and the movie just added

the extra touch. Her husband would be returning home from his business trip next week. He was upset to be out of town on her birthday, but his company needed him to debug some problems in their client's business in Atlanta. She knew that travel was part of her husband's job as a computer troubleshooter.

Her mind was still on the movies as she rounded one of the many twisting bends on her way home. She reached down and pushed in the cassette tape of her favorite music group into the cassette player, adjusted the volume and bass and stared ahead at the black road. The long black road twisted and turned, the white dotted line passing slowly on her left. The drive back home gave her opportunity to reflect on her life.

In the back of her mind, she was watching for red eyes of any deer that might be grazing along the roadway. She knew the damage that could be done if she accidentally hit a deer. Julie noticed the swirling fog in the hollows between the hills. The fog swirled in the gentle breeze that filled the valley this time of night. In the summer, the breeze was cooling after a hot day, but in the winter months, the breeze would move the fog around creating dense patches of fog on the roadway.

Two old cemeteries, one on each side of a steep hill dotted the landscape. Sadly, the first cemetery was unkept, old tombstones had fallen over, other tombstones had been pushed over by careless teenagers. Weeds had grown up covering many of the old markers, some reaching back to the Civil War days. Patches of fog had absorbed portions of the cemetery, fading out the lone statues and standing headstones.

The second cemetery was no better, farther from town, it was unkept and had fallen into disarray. Thick vines covered many of the old Civil War tombstones and markers. Rusted pipes linked together like tinker toys marked the boundary of old plots, now hidden with tall weeds and thistles.

The rural road twisted up a hill, then dipped down to a hollow. Then back up to another hill that is between the two old cemeteries. The hollow had filled with the swirling twisting fog, fading in and out as a shape started to take shape. This shape was more transparent then solid at first, slowly more definite edges took form, until at last, the figure was contoured against the drifting fog.

A large gray hat turned up on one side rested on the head of the figure. A gray blouse buttoned high on the neck and gray trousers with a black strip running the length of each leg became visible. Around the waist hung a silver saber. Black riding boots that rose high on the legs were mounted in stirrups. The figure was sitting on a great white horse with raised head and fuming nostrils. Quickly, the figure withdrew the long silver saber from its leather sheath, holding it up next to his head and waited.

Julie Roberts had passed the first old cemetery and had climbed the first hill, slowly descending into the hollow. She was not far from home. Just pass the second old cemetery was the dirt road leading to her house. The fog had settled over the highway in patches so she was forced to slow as she entered the hollow.

She was reaching down to turn the cassette tape over when suddenly she thought she saw movement on the road ahead. Julie stared straight ahead in her headlight beams, at a figure mounted on a horse, enshrouded with a hazy fog. She became alarmed as the figure was in the center of the road.

Julie panicked for a moment as she slammed on the brakes but too late. Her car had plowed directly into the figure of a man in gray uniform sitting atop a white horse that was reared up, blowing steam like smoke out of its fuming nostrils.

As her car slammed into the figure, she realized that the horseman was dressed in a Confederate Soldier Civil War uniform. Julie remembered seeing the horseman raise his saber at her as she passed right through the figure. The car came to a dead stop on the road, she jumped out and looked back along the road, but nothing was there.

No horse, no horseman, no nothing. She was shaken and had to lean against the car for support. Her lungs had forgotten to take in air as she realized she had been holding her breath. Julie started breathing again as she glanced around for some answer to what had happened. Seeing nothing, she got back into her car and drove home.

Over the next few weeks Julie Roberts researched the old cemeteries. She spoke to Miss Millie, one of the oldest residents of Rock Mills. Julie learned that in the spot between the two old cemeteries is a lone grave, with a headstone reading 'Unknown Soldier of the Glorious Cause'.

Julie learned that a wounded young soldier had come through, sometime after Sherman's march to the sea, and had lost consciousness in the yard of Miss Millie's father. He died without regaining consciousness, and a search of his personal effects left no clue to his identity. Miss Millie said that they had seen the ghost on the white horse a few times over the years, as it prepared for battle.

Authors Notes:

This young man who served the Confederate States was so emotionally involved with the events surrounding Sherman's bloody march to the sea that upon his death he still had to protect the land from the invading armies.

This strong emotion anchored him to this earth plane and will continue to anchor him unless this young man can let go of his pain and emotions. This appears to be a common occurance among soldiers of the Civil War. They were very devoted to their cause.

A Friend Returns From the Dead

Ten years ago I saw my first ghost. It was a very pleasant experience, not frightening at all. I was a sophomore at UC Santa Cruz, living on campus, when a good friend named Doug died suddenly. He had suffered from Marfan's Syndrome and had a pacemaker, but his death was unexpected.

He was tall and lanky and always seemed to be in a good mood. He had days that were painful for him to even move around.

I felt bad, guilty because a few days before he died, I had broken a date to see Doug. I had been involved in a small mishap with my hand. My hand had been in the car jam when the car door got slammed shut. I did not break any bones, but it was sure sore. I was feeling sorry for myself and wanted to be alone as I nursed my hand back to health.

I had a hard time dealing with the guilt I felt. I mourned hard for a week for Doug then started to feel like the grief and guilt was ebbing. That night, I couldn't sleep, which has happened maybe four times in my life. I lay in bed for a couple hours while sleep eluded me. Suddenly, I sensed a presence in the room. This presence that was sitting on my bed, illuminated by the half-light through the blinds, was Doug!

I recognized his lanky form, with long bangs falling over his face and his unusually long physique. He was holding a stuffed toy squirrel in his left hand and sort of hopping it along the bed as if he were playing. I sensed that he was trying to tell me that he felt playful as a squirrel, free from a body that had always caused him pain.

As I turned to look at him full-on, he vanished. I was skeptical at first, figured maybe I'd just seen what I wanted to see, yet the experience did make me feel much better, as if something had been resolved, as if I were forgiven for breaking the date.

In the days that followed I felt better about myself. I wanted to share the visit from Doug with his father. During my visit with him, I mentioned the experience and he surprised me with the information that Doug had collected stuffed animals and his favorite was a squirrel, which I didn't know.

Somehow, it all came together for me at that moment. The squirrel was a fitting symbol to leave behind for those that knew him. Even today, when I am walking in the woods and see a squirrel, I think of my friend Doug.

Authors Notes:

Few of us understand the bond of friendship that can develop in his life. The bond of friendship forged with Doug apparently continued in his life after life. Doug returned to give assurance to his friend that he was okay and not to worry about him. How many of us have friends where true bonds of friendship exist such as the bond that Doug had?

The Crying Girl in the Cemetery

As a Funeral Director in Pittsburgh, Pennsylvania, I am constantly inundated with the reminders of death and the effects death has on people. Many people ask me how I got interested in the field. My back yard borders an old cemetery. There were burials in that cemetery, but they got less and less frequent. I would always watch, and became interested in how we care for our dead. This also gave me my interest in ghosts.

I would sit in the back yard on summer and fall nights, just watching and waiting to catch that one glimpse of something out of the ordinary. I personally have not seen any kind of apparition, but I'm told from some of the old-timers in my neighborhood that they've seen "weird goings-on" in that graveyard. I have, however, heard a great many odd sounds emanating from the mists there!

One night, in 1984, I was reading on the enclosed patio behind the house, when I heard a soft cooing, like that of a small child. This sound was interspersed with sparse laughter, and words that I couldn't make out. It was dark, and there wasn't a moon to see by, and it had begun to fog over, as it does the time of year of late May or early June. I thought that someone was walking on the road on the other side of the cemetery, and I paid it no mind. I went back to my reading, but was again disturbed by the persistent cooing. I heard no adults and looked at my watch, trying to reconcile a small child out alone at 10:30 at night.

I got up and went to the light switch and flicked it on, immediately casting a bright flood light on the back yard, far into the distance, where I could see the rusting back gate of the cemetery entangled in the vines and weeds of a now rarely used footpath. Turning on the light was like turning off the child. There was no sound but the crickets and the breeze.

I resisted the age old flaw of calling out into the darkness, remembering all the poor saps in the scary films that did this only to find more than an answer awaited them. I actually thought of that, because this whole incident was beginning to unnerve me. I wasn't going to let a child frighten me, I told myself. So I did the next stupid thing that all poor saps in horror films do. I got a flashlight and went out to investigate what was going on. I walked out about fifty feet, and heard nothing.

I didn't need the flashlight yet, as the light from the flood lamp was still bright enough to illuminate my way. The grass in my yard is well trimmed up to the rockery, where my mother (before she passed on) would place rocks in ways that mimicked a flower garden. I started walking the narrow path made between the rockery's two halves, and still heard nothing.

I got up to the gate, the light from the house now struggling to pass through the thicket at the yard's end, and I pointed the flashlight out to the gaping darkness. I saw fog and a field-mouse near the foundation of the wall where the gate delineated the two properties, and some vigil candles in the distance.

I stood there for a minute or two, trying to use my ears like radar, trying to get a fix on a sound, any sound, and aim the light in that direction, but heard nothing. Even the crickets had stopped, and the field mouse darted out of sight and hearing range immediately upon being discovered.

I began to think about how silly and cliché this all began to seem just as the realization of damp night air rocked me back to my senses. I turned out the flashlight and walked back to the house, part of me relieved that I found nothing, and part of me sure that I heard something. I decided it must have been just passers-by and left it at that.

As I walked through the patio, I switched the light off, and in that exact instant it was like switching the sound on. The crying started again, and I stopped in my tracks, you know that feeling you get when you think someone has the advantage on you and is watching you. I began to think the obvious: Someone is playing a very bad joke on me. I reached for the light and flicked it on, and the sound stopped. Now the poor sap in the horror film crept out and I yelled out with a booming baritone something to the effect of, "Very funny, folks. Just get off my property, now before I call the cops."

The darkness was silent. I almost dreaded hitting that light switch again. I even thought of going to bed and leaving the lights on all night. However, I thought of the lecture I'd get in the morning on how electricity doesn't grow on trees. When I start paying the electric bill, then I can leave the lights on all night, ran through my head.

I pulled the light switch down, very slowly, as if to think that the quieter I made the switch, whoever was out there wouldn't pick up on the fact that I was trying to trick them. It didn't occur to me that the light going out was probably just as big a tip off to the pranksters. As I expected, the sudden dark cued the minute voice, but it seemed louder, now. I began to get really frightened. Whoever was doing this was good at practical jokes, but I wasn't going to let them get the better of me.

I grabbed the flashlight, ran out the screen door and rushed toward the thicket and gate, anger now replacing fear. I purposely made as much noise as possible, giving the jerks one last chance to vamoose before I discovered them and ruined their fun. I reached the gate, the waif-like sounds still carrying across the night air, and zoned in on the sound. It seemed to be coming from the left of me. I opted to jump the wall rather than fight with the rusted gate. As soon as my feet touched the hallowed ground the silence returned.

Nevertheless, I had already pinpointed the source and switched the flashlight on to navigate through the veritable sea of markers, sure I was going to beat them at their game. I reached the spot I thought was the sound's source, keeping my peripheral vision honed for some surprise from the flanks. I was scared beyond belief, wondering what I had gotten myself into, and would I be able to handle a possible group of angry or drunk people!

I stopped suddenly and looked around attempting to get my bearings; There was McSorley's mausoleum on the left, the large black obelisk marking the O'Tool family plot right next to it, and the flags of the veterans' graves to the right. Everything where it should be. The moment would have been serene if I wasn't so frightened. It was, however, anticlimactic. No girl crying, no pranksters, no drunks, no gangs, nothing.

I looked around, thinking they still might be in the surrounding thicket, and I started shining the light in all directions, the fear and the pounding in my head still not completely gone. I searched a part of the thicket to my left, where I saw some graves I had never noticed before, or had forgotten years ago, and it looked like I wasn't the only one who forgot them.

They were in terrible condition. Four headstones, and part of one that was obviously destroyed by lack of attention. I shined the light on them to see if I recognized the stones, at least the names on the stones, only to find I was completely unfamiliar with them.

Two of the stones belonged to the Herlihy family, a mother, father and two sons. The parents both died within one year of each other in the late 1930's, while the sons both died in World War II. The third stone belonged to a Caroline Miller, who died in 1968. The fourth stone, when I shone the light on it, froze my blood. You guessed it, it belonged to a little girl of five years old-- A Louisa McHale, who died on May 26, 1917. The very day this all occurred!

Authors Note:

Some people might think it strange for a funeral director to feel this way, but our experiences had revealed that most individuals when faced with a similar circumstance react in much the same manner. All the little girl wanted was acknowledgment or recognition. Isn't this what most of us want to feel good about ourselves? We work hard in our day jobs, hoping for recognition and acknowledgment that we are performing our task well.

The dead who are earthbound need to feel acknowledged and recognized. Our emotions do not die at death. As we come to understand life after life, we realize that spirits who dwell on the spirit plane or dimension have the same needs as they did while they were living on the earth as mortal beings. We will replace the physical body with an energy body, but our emotions, our intelligence, our loves still remain the essence of whom we are.

The Mail Man

Marge Taylor had lived all her sixty-eight years in Knoxville, Tennessee. Her great-grandfather had home-steaded the farm back in the early 1800's when he had immigrated from Londondary, Ireland with his family and brothers. Her great-grandfather had fought Indians and her great granduncle, Caleb Taylor, had been killed in one of the many raids on the farm.

The hollow she lived in was remote by today's standard. Only six other families were living here. The hollow was actually a long narrow valley between two mountains. Her farm was the furthest from the main highway. The old barn had fallen down years ago after a freak storm had blown through the valley destroying her barn and her neighbors.

Marge lay in bed listening to the wind chimes that hung on the front porch. The chimes softly echoing in the breeze. Her window was open to help cool the bedroom from the late Indian Summer heat. The days would be hot and the nights would cool off fast with fog forming in the hollows during the night. She had just put down her novel and was deep in thought, enjoying the serenity of the moment.

They had taken her grandchildren to the train station in Knoxville and put them aboard the Amtrack bound for their home in Lexington, Kentucky. Her daughter and her husband had settled in Lexington after getting married. He worked for the State as an Auditor and she worked for an Insurance company as an Underwriter. Their two children would often spend two weeks during the summer with their grandmother. She loved them very much and knew that in a few years she would be getting too old to have them visit.

Marge was worn out from her grandchildren's visit. They were full of energy and kept her on the go the entire time they were here. Now, in the calmness of late evening she was grateful for the silence. She enjoyed laying in bed listening to the wind chimes and feeling the light breeze blow through the window. Tonight, she was tired and exhausted so she retired earlier than most nights.

Suddenly, she awoke to the sounds of clop, clop, clop. In the twilight between being awake and asleep, she thought she heard the sounds of shoed horses pulling a wagon with steel rim wheels. She had not heard those sounds since she was a kid. Her grand father used to repair their wagon wheels. He would heat the metal strip and bend the two-inch metal strip around the wooden wheel. The metal shod wagon wheel made a distinctive sound as it rolled along the road.

Marge opened her eyes and glanced at the clock. Three o'clock in the morning. She lay in bed thinking she must have had a dream, when the sounds of clop, clop, clop could clearly be heard once again. She sat straight up in bed, swung her feet over the bed and into the slippers on the floor. She got up and walked to the window and glanced down to the road in front of the house.

A misty fog was drifting across the road as an image appeared to take form and substance in the swirling fog. Slowly, the image materialized into an old fashion mail carriage pulled by six black horses. A figured sat atop the carriage wearing a top hat and cape. Marge rubbed her eyes in disbelief, staring through the window for a second time. The ghostly apparition stopped in front of her mail box.

The driver jumped off and inserted something into her mail box. The horses were fuming, anxious to be away from this stop. The driver climbed into the carriage and with reins held in his hands, he slapped the reins hard on the horses backs, immediately the team of horses trotted into the drifting fog and vanished.

Alarmed, Marge hurried down the old wooden stairs to the living room and out the front door. She rushed to her silver mailbox and opened the hinged door. Inside the mailbox lay a single letter with a canceled stamp. She retrieved the envelope and headed back toward the house. Once inside, she went over to her favorite sitting chair, sat and turned on the small lamp on the end table next to her. She held the off-white envelope in her hands, gently turning it.

She noticed that the letter was addressed to one of the members of a family living in the next hollow, a Mr. Tim Johnson. She wondered why they delivered the letter to her, especially since her regular mailman, Mr. Hayes, didn't normally arrive at her home till around four o'clock in the afternoon. She was on the end of the rural route and the last stop for the mailman. She wondered why they had delivered it in the middle of the night, and why an old fashion mail carriage pulled by horses? Marge tossed the letter onto the end table, turned off the lamp and went to bed.

Marge did not go to town the next day nor the next to drop off the letter to the post office. She had been feeling ill and had stayed home in bed. The third day after she received the letter, she drove to town to do her grocery shopping at WinnDixie. While shopping, she bought a newspaper. After the grocery store, she drove by the post office and dropped off the letter.

When she returned home, she put away her groceries and went into the living room, to her comfortable chair to read the newspaper. She always scanned through the obituary page to see who had passed on. Suddenly, the name Tim Johnson jumped up from the page. It was the same Tim Johnson that the letter had been addressed to that she dropped off earlier in the day. The date of death was the same day she had received the letter from the mysterious mail carriage driver.

The next morning she went out to her mail box to put in some letters containing payments that needed to be mailed. When she opened her mail box, there was another letter in it addressed to Samuel Cliffton. She left the letter in her mail box, raised the red flag and went back into the house. A few days later when she went to town on some errands. Upon buying a newspaper she discovered Samuel Cliffton had died of natural causes on the same date she had received the letter addressed to him. Over the next few weeks, she received mail addressed to people that within a few days would die either from natural causes or from accidents. She tried to intervene when she received a letter but upon calling the name addressed on the letter, she would be dismissed as a crank caller.

Then one morning as she found a letter addressed to her. She was distressed. She had planned on flying to Cleveland to see her twin sister that afternoon. She knew that if she flew out of the airport, something would happen in route and she would be killed. She was in good health so she knew she wouldn't die of health related problems.

She fretted all morning over whether she should fly to Cleveland or stay home. Finally, in desperation, she called her sister and told her she would be staying home. Her sister thought she was silly to fear flying as there just weren't that many accidents' now-a-days. Her sister told her it was safer to fly then to drive. However, Marge would have none of it. She stayed home, locked her doors and waited out the day. She knew that within a few days flying to Cleveland would be safe.

After a week, the twin sister tried to call and encourage her to fly up to see her. After calling for two days without finding anyone home, she became concerned and called the Sheriffs Department. They dispatched a deputy to check on Marge. The deputy sheriff arrived and found

146

no one home yet the car was in the driveway. He found a window that was not locked so he entered the house.

"Hello Marge, this is deputy Quinny, are you here?" He did not receive any reply to his shouts. He climbed the stairs and checked each room. The last room was Marge's bedroom. The deputy knocked and went into the room when he received no response from knocking.

Marge was laying dead on the floor, her eyes and mouth wide open in terror. Still clutched in her hands was an off-white envelope addressed to her. A muddy boot print was found next to the body. The sheriff's department investigated the death, but all they could gather from their research on the boot print was that the boot was standard issue used by the post office in the 1880's.

Returning for the Rosary

In 1988, I lived in Dublin, Ireland, in a boarding house on De Burgh Road, a tiny little lane next to Phoenix Park, across the Liffey from the Guiness Brewery. There were two other boarders, an older gentleman from the south and another man abut my age (I was 21), and the landlady. One night I had retired to my room and had just laid down on my bed and turned the light off. I rolled over, away from the bedroom door, which wasn't locked, to face the window.

Suddenly, the temperature in the room dropped about ten degrees. It hadn't been cold, but it was now. I thought I'd left the window open, and was surprised to find when I raised my arm to close it that it was already closed. I was thinking that was odd, when I felt all the hair on the back of my neck stand up. That had never happened to me before and was really strange. I remember thinking, "So this is what it is like to have the hair on the back of your neck stand up!"

I still hadn't connected the two events, the drop in temperature and the hair standing up on end, until I rolled over and was about to turn on the small lamp at the side of my bed. At that moment I felt someone sit on the edge of the bed. The mattress sank and it felt like someone heavy had just sat down beside me. I didn't even think this was odd, the older man who lived with us frequently went out to the pubs in the evenings and came home intoxicated. His room was right next to mine at the top of the stairs and it was entirely conceivable that he had mistaken my door for his. He could have come in, since I had left the door unlocked.

When he started to lie down, I decided it was time to say something since it was only a twin bed. This time I did turn the light on, and when I did, I almost fainted, there was nobody in the room with me. The heavy feeling that someone was laying down vanished, as did the cold and the hair standing on the back of my neck. I stood up and looked around, unable to believe there was nobody there, because I knew there had been.

The most surprising thing was when I went to check and see if the older man was back from the pubs and found out my door was locked. These rooms had the old turnkey style locks that must be locked from inside the room. The key was in the door where it always was, but because I'd heard stories of people not being able to get out of their rooms during a fire because they locked the door, I always left my door unlocked.

I told the landlady in the morning what had happened over breakfast. She went pale and was speechless for a few moments. When the neighbor, who was having breakfast with us and I, finally got her to talk again, she told us an interesting story. The previous inhabitant of that room had been an old man, a profoundly religious one, and a devout follower of Padre Pio (Catholic). His wife had left him many years before and he was slowly drinking himself into a stupor.

He had moved out several months before, leaving a picture of Padre Pio still on the wall in the bedroom and his treasured Rosary behind. She said she had heard that he had died a few weeks after moving out, having successfully drunk himself to death.

She felt terrible that she still had his Rosary, and had been trying to find one of his relatives to return it to. She told me she had heard creaking on the stairs and had felt cold drafts, but had dismissed them as normal occurrences in an old house. Now, she is convinced that this guy was returning for his Rosary.

Authors Notes:
An interesting fact is that we often place extreme value on our possessions. Even something as simple as Rosary beads can be extremely important. The beads represented a belief system that transcended death and the sufferings experienced in this dimension. Once his Rosary beads were recovered, the energy pattern that was the essence of the man could now move forward and continue to the higher realm.

Shadows in the Mist

The mist slowly rose out of the moor, a gentle pungent breath released at the end of the day. Heavy rain clouds reflected the orange glow from the Manchester city street lights some forty miles away. This amber luminescence was the only light on Stanford moor at night, and the only way you could tell a fog was rising.

The ground mists had a life of their own, slowly filling the hollows and old peat quarries dotted across the moor. It flowed like a slow tide feeling its way along the stream beds filling out the gullies and gradually rising.

The scent of bog weed and sedge grass mixed with wild herbs and moss making an aromatic blend diffused with an intoxicating oxygen content. Just standing on the moor at night made you want to inhale deeply. Not that many people came to the moor after dark.

The occasional car would pull off the main road leading to Halifax and drive a small way up one of the many quarry lanes, a romantic destination for couples. Very few actually left the security of their cars, and those that did, did not linger for long. Imagining some sinister apparition watching in the gloom was all too easy.

Stanford's moor breathed out again and the mist grew thicker, thin tendrils reaching into the chill night air. Areas of the fog coalesced forming shapes, some of which held together for a time, moving of their own accord then fading to nothingness.

Explaining the twists and turns of the fog is easy as the moor is a hot bed of organic activity producing warm and cold currents as a natural part of its daily cycle. Watching the mist move through gave the impression that these movements were far from random, any more than a dance might be.

Here and there contours in the mist formed, becoming almost defined. The ground mist gave way to these twisting forms and the dance of seen and unseen gained a purpose. It was plain that the dance was over and the phantoms now had an objective. Several shapes in the mist moved in a single direction against the general flow of the fog around them. A fragile wake formed as the still undefined shapes moved forward.

The silhouettes in the mist had a direction. Now they faded and changed as they went in the mist, impossible to say whether there were the same number or not. They passed through each other then sank into the ground only to rise again at a different location but slowly they were moving as one group in the same direction toward the main road.

Near the banking that sloped down to the road, the shapes came to a standstill. They were better defined now, the still swirling moisture at their core was denser taking shape, filling out. Seven dark shadows forming an increasingly distinct line over looking the road. The air was completely still and a freezing chill accompanied the ominous silence. The shapes were waiting.

John Riley was driving, tapping his fingers to the rhythm of the heavy metal beat as he steered the battered Ford Transit van through the dark. Next to John was Tony

Carter who was trying unsuccessfully to find a music cassette that he would prefer to listen to. Beside him was Richard Marsden, his small finger deeply imbedded in his left ear. He was twisting it round and round then slapping the side of his head.

"I'm deaf." He bellowed at the other two.

"We'll all be deaf if you keep shouting like that." Tony turned to face him as best he could. They were cramped for space on the front seat of the van, but it was better than one of them having to ride in the back, especially with all the gardening tools John kept in there.

"Are your ears still ringing?" Tony was pinching his nose and blowing, trying to make them pop.

"What?"

Rick said, "I can't hear a thing, my ears are still ringing."

Tony laughed, "Are your ears ringing John?"

"Ringing? It's a wonder they're not bleeding. They were loud, and Rick just had to get us up front next to the speakers."

"I'm telling you, it's the last Motorhead concert I'm going to."

"Yeah, that is what I said last time." Rick held up his T-shirt.

"You know how much this cost? Twenty quid, twenty quid. Bloody rip off."

Tony tried to see the image on the T-shirt but the only light came from the headlights on the road ahead. Rick squinted at it holding it up as a car passed them going in the opposite direction but unable to make out the image.

They were heading back home to Mytholmroyd, a small town in West Yorkshire, having attended probably the last concert the three of them would see together again. Not that they would admit it, not even to themselves, but heavy metal concerts had started to lose their appeal once they had turned thirty.

This was a fond farewell without needing to state the fact. Motorhead had been playing at the Apollo in Manchester and they had grabbed the opportunity of 'a night out with the lads', even traveling in John's old van rather than taking any of the three sensible cars at their disposal. They were traveling back by the shortest route available, over Stanford moor. They could easily have taken the M62 which would probably have been quicker, but John had wanted to call at a pub on the way back, just for a quick pint.

When they left the public house it was nearly half past eleven and they still had about forty miles to travel. They all knew they would have some explaining to do once they got home. The street lights ended long before they turned onto the road which led over Stanford moor and once on the road they did not see or pass another vehicle. The road wound its way steadily higher and higher, becoming more remote, finally leaving even the farms behind.

Tony switched the cassette player off and to his surprise neither of his companions complained. 'Must be getting old', he thought? All three had fallen quiet as they had started to climb the hill toward the moor, with only the occasional comment being passed around.

"Tell you what, my bladder says its busting." Rick looked over at John and said, "Do you fancy pulling over John?"

"Gee Rick, can't it wait?"

Rick frowned back. His bladder was full of ale. Why he hadn't gone at the pub, he didn't know.

"Come on John, I got to go."

"Yeah, I could do with shaking the snake too." Tony grinned.

"Of course, if you just wind the window down, I could unravel it from where I sit." John laughed.

"Okay, just wait till the road levels out a bit, the handbrake is a bit dodgy."

They continued up the slow incline. Suddenly Rick rammed his face against the window and grabbed Tony's arm.

"Did you see that?" His shout startled both Tony and John.

John slammed on the brake and skidded the van to a halt with the front end turned slightly toward the edge of the road.

"Did you see it?" Rick still had his face up against the glass, then he spun around looking over his shoulder through the back window.

"See what?" John said angrily. He was breathing heavily and gripping the steering wheel hard.

"I saw something or someone." Rick said as he wondered who or what would be up here at this time of night. Rick asked Tony if he saw anything. Tony didn't speak at first. The other two looked at him as he stared intently at the rear view mirror.

"I think I saw something white, by the side of the road." His voice was steady and he had not taken his eyes from the mirror. "Something white, like a little girl."

Rick pulled on the door handle, letting the door swing open. The strong scent of the moors hit them followed quickly by the chill. As he stepped down from the van Rick noticed for the first time that a ground fog had appeared, it swirled round his knees and was thick enough to prevent him from clearly seeing his feet, though in this half light it was hard enough seeing anything but what was in the beam of the headlights. Tony climbed out after him and stood looking at the mist and then started off back down the road.

Tony had only walked about fifty yards down the road but when he looked back to the van, the swirling fog hid it; with only the red glow of the rear lights showing through like a couple of shining eyes on an indistinct face. He slowed his pace then came to a standstill. Tony felt sure he had walked back far enough to be at or to have passed the point where he and Rick had seen the white shape. He squinted his eyes trying to see further down the road. The fog was definitely getting thicker and he shook his head and smiled to himself.

"Must have been a sheep, or a trick of the light?" Tony said as he turned to head back but was stopped in a half turn. At the top of the grassy banking to his right was what appeared to be a small figure clothed in white. Before his eyes focused on it, the figure moved back dissolving into the darkness. Tony headed straight to the point on the banking, scrambling and slipping as he went.

When he reached the top of the bank he gulped for breath, he had been holding it without realizing it. He quickly scanned the area. The moor was pocked with hollows and mounds and covered with coarse tufts of grass making walking difficult. There was no figure to be seen. He stood for a while catching his breath, though his heart was still pounding.

The hair on the back of his neck suddenly stood on end and his stomach tightened. He was being watched! He was certain of it as he quickly scanned the fog left and right forcing his eyes to see more then he could. When that failed, he turned his head to one side listening as hard as possible. The mist rolled toward him parting around him depositing fine droplets on his clothing. Then directly in front of him through the thinning mist and startlingly clear, was the shape of a small girl.

She was aged about nine or possibly ten. Her hair was shoulder length and lank, soaked to the shape of her face, saying what color was impossible. The short pale dress was saturated, clinging to her slight frame making her seem pathetically thin. Tony took the details in an instant but her eyes held his attention. The girl's face was ash white and framed her deep-set dark eyes. The opened face stare could easily be fear but her eyes pierced him defiantly.

Tony took a step forward, keeping his eyes fixed on hers. She took a step back. Tony said, "Wait." His voice was tight and his mouth had gone dry. He licked his lips. "Please wait, don't be frightened." Her look was not fear. Her look was knowing.

It was a trap, he found it hard to swallow, he couldn't move. The mist was closing in again and the girl was fading. She turned and started to move off, back into the mist. Tony wondered how he could have hesitated as this little girl was probably lost. Perhaps her parent's car had crashed and she was out looking for help and had become frightened. How could he be afraid of a tiny child?

"No, don't go, wait for me." Tony said as his courage returned, stepping off toward her. He stumbled forward tripping on the grass and sliding on the peat. He could see the tiny shape of the girl but couldn't gain ground on her. His foot missed the next step and he went down splaying spectacularly on the sodden ground, the impact forcing a grunt of air from him.

His mind was racing, what must the girl be thinking, some total stranger chasing after her in the dark. He stood up and looked around. There was a loose circle of children around him. They were at an equal distance from him and they all watched with the same dark eyes in pale expressionless faces. The mist enveloped them all.

Rick could not be sure if he had heard Tony call. The fog had a way of dampening any sound. Even his footsteps on the tarmac were dull. The fog was definitely getting thicker. He should be able to see Tony by now, surely he had not gone any further. He stood looking around him. The cold was biting into his face and a steady dampening moisture was soaking his jacket.

Something in the corner of his eyes attracted his attention. The peat and tufts of grass at the road edge had been disturbed, a clump of grass had been torn from its position. Rick moved closer, scanning the area as best he could in the half light. There was a foot print, it had to be Tony's.

Rick struggled up the banking slipping in the footsteps his friend had taken. There it was again, he felt sure now he had heard Tony cry out some way off onto the moor. What the heck was he playing at. If this were a joke, he wasn't going to be happy about it.

He was tempted to shout back but somehow the oppressive silence kept him quiet, he did not want Tony thinking he had been worried or felt tricked. He stumbled in the guessed direction, he was confident he could turn back if he needed to, after all, he was not going far.

The fog closed in around him. Its swirling motion disorientated him and he had to stop for a breath. He yelled out for Tony but received no response. Rick turned and headed back toward the road. His pace gained speed as he went, he was wiping the moisture from his face, staggering over the grass hillocks and sliding in the slimy peat.

His heart was pounding and his muscles were already starting to ache so he slowed to a more steady walk, gulping in lungs full of air. The sweat ran down his face, mixing with the moisture from the fog and when he licked his lips, it was bitter on his tongue. He kept walking going careful now, his head down and back stooping.

Rick should have been back by the road my now as his pace slowed even more. He could not see more than a yard in any direction. He stopped, no matter what direction he looked, it was the same blanket of churning moisture. He could feel the panic rising in him, he must be near the road, he had to be.

He stood motionless and closed his eyes, perhaps he could hear something. He let his arms relax by his sides and tilted his head to the right breathing lightly. The fog moved around him as a darker area in the charcoal gray solidified and moved closer. Rick was sure if he listened hard enough he would hear the van engine or something. The shadow was close now, solidifying, moving in. Rick has his eyes tightly shut. Eventually a car would drive by then he could find the road.

The figure was by him, within arms reach. If worse came to the worse, Rick could stand there shouting till either John or Tony found him. A tiny freezing hand slipped into his and gripped his fingers. Rick screamed and spun round, pulling his hand free, his eyes wide with shock and fear. He staggered back a couple faltering steps then fell. There was no one there.

He lay prone, staring wide eyed. The hand slipped back into his, its icy grip squeezing his index finger. Rick rolled away then leapt to his feet, spinning to face where he had lain, again nothing. The adrenaline was pumping through his body making him light headed and dizzy, he stood gasping, his mouth open. This time the hand gripped like cold steel, his fingers crushed in the vise hold.

He pulled against the clutching hand but his strength was gone, only fear remained. Rick was helpless, he looked down at the pale faced child and saw the emotionless depth of his eyes. He wanted to run or to scream or to attack, anything to break free of this chilling grip. Instead, he allowed himself to be raised to his feet and led by the hand deeper into the waiting darkness.

John Riley peered into the rear view mirror again, then the side mirror and finally turned in his seat to look out of the back window. He tried to make out the time on his wrist watch twisting his hand in an attempt to catch the low light. How long had they been gone, he wondered? He just knew that Tony and Rick were out there in the darkness, waiting for him to get out of the van so they could leap out and frighten him. This was the type of childish prank they would play on him. What he ought to do was start up the van, then they would come running.

His hand touched the key in the ignition, stroking its shape. Something prevented him from turning the key. Perhaps, they had not been gone that long, he looked into the mirrors once more. The fog was definitely getting worse, he could not see the grassy banking to the left of his van now. John was trying hard not to think of the many tales he had heard of creatures in the fog, of mad men escaping from asylums. He breathed out heavily, dispelling his morbid thoughts.

Outside of the van the figures had gathered as darker outlines in a boiling gray mass. The shapes varied in size, some no bigger than a four year old child, the others could be teenagers. Their expressionless faces were the same, an ashen hue with penetrating eyes of deepest pitch. They were all drenched from head to toe, the material of their clothes defining the pitiful slightness of their frames. Then without a word spoken or gesture made, the figures moved as one toward the van.

John sat bolt upright, had he seen something; it was hard to tell with the mist moving the way it did. Surely, a shadowy figure had passed through the reflection in his mirror. It was probably Rick or Tony. As he changed his focus from the mirror to the windscreen, he gasped jolting backwards, directly in front of him were dark silhouettes.

There they were, it was Rick and Tony, about time too. Then a third shape moved forward and then a fourth.

157

As he concentrated, he realized that the figures were too slight to be his friends.

John quickly pushed the lock on his door then jerked across to do the same on the passengers' door, he jarred his shoulder as the seat belt stopped him short. His fingers missed the fastener and as he fumbled, his eyes flicked to the windscreen, the shapes were closer, moving round to the doors, moving to the unlocked passengers' door. Why hadn't he locked them earlier?

His concentration came back to the seat belt fastener. Blood coursed through his veins deafening him and his breath came in short gasps. John's fingers missed and skidded across the metal fastener in his haste to be free. The metal tongue flicked out and he was released. He leapt across the seat his hand coming down hard on the lock. Too late, the door swung open. John's momentum carried him forward splaying him across the passenger seat.

The dark shape rushed forward gripping Johns shoulders, raising him.

"John, John it's Tony. I thought you had a heart attack." Tony smiled, a thin and forced gesture, that quickly gave way to a far more worried expression.

"John, I think you'd better get out." Tony said as he released his friend and stepped back.

John sat up, when he saw Tony move away from the door, he rushed to follow him, dragging himself across the seat.

"Where's Rick?" John asked as his voice was shaky and his hand shook as he climbed out of the van.

"I'm here." Rick said as he stood next to Tony watching the other shapes close by.

"Who are they?" John asked in no more than a whisper.

"I'm not sure who they are, but I think I know what they want."

John tried to see the expression on Tony's face, but he had turned away moving toward the back of the van. John's eyes flicked to the shadows in the mist. He could not see how many stood there silently watching.

"Come on." Tony's voice startled him.

"We've got a job to do."

Tony handed both Rick and John spades from out of the back of the van and took the only shovel for himself. Then with barely a word he set off up the grass banking using the shovel to steady him as he went. He did not look back. Rick shot a glance to John, then quickly followed, heaving himself up, darting looks at the disturbing figures close by. John only hesitated for a moment, when he saw Tony move on without stopping, his heart began pounding. He avoided looking at the shapes.

Back on the moor, the tiny figure at his side was leading Tony by the hand. They were weaving a path through the squelching moor. Rick and John hurried forward wanting to keep close but afraid of Tony's pallid companion. Tony and his thin guide came to a halt and his friends forced themselves parallel. They stood not speaking, the child stepped reluctantly away from Tony, releasing his hand.

Rick said, "What now?" The tremor in Rick's voice stilted his speech. Translucent companions joined the child. They slowly fanned out turning to face the trio. Tony could feel the moisture from the child's hand dripping from his fingers but he left them wet. Rick had started to shake, his head, jerking slightly as he shivered, and John was rigid, his eyes were unblinking.

Slowly the figures in front of them knelt down, one after the other, then sat back lowering themselves down. Gradually they lay back stretching out on the moor, the ground mist swallowing the more distant ones. Then they faded from view. The fog wiping them away like chalk on a slate. The last to vanish was the little boy who had led them there, he gestured serenely as he laid down his hand showing the small mound now revealed in the places the figures had settled.

The mounds were randomly spaced but of roughly the same size, long narrow protrusions. Tony started to dig, after a moment John joined him, then finally Rick. None of them spoke as they carefully displaced the peat probing with the spades as they went. After several minutes, the earth gave way falling loosely aside as they scraped with the shovel blade.

A small skeletal hand caught the light, a shred of cloth attached. The fog flowed into the shallow grave covering the child's remains. The police uncovered a total of fifteen children's bodies, eventually fourteen of the bodies were identified. The one remaining unnamed child was a small boy, age nine or possibly ten.

Authors Notes:

This tale suggests that the location of grave sites are especially important to departed spirits. In this case, the fifteen spirits allowed their presence to be known so their earthly remains could be discovered. We do not know why this is important to those who depart this life, unless the deaths are the undiscovered tragedies of some violent act. Then, it seems essential the spirits of victims, indicate where their remains are located to give closure to their families.

The Lost Sheep

What follows is an account of real events that occurred to a couple that lived at the farm next to me on the Yorkshire moors.

Fog illuminated by a hand-held-torch (flashlight) and seen through the rain on a pitch black night can be very deceptive. It takes on a life of its own, images imagined and real meld. Shapes seen out of the corner of the eye vanish in the time it takes to switch focus. Sometimes pathways open up enticing you in one particular direction, then close behind you, cutting you off. Experienced in a familiar environment, in a town or park, it can be misleading or disorientating. On rain drenched moors pocked with abandoned peat quarries, it's lethal.

Some parts of West Yorkshire are quite remote but very picturesque. Heptonstall is a village which sits at the top of the Calder Valley. Its boom time was during the Industrial revolution. The valley is full of derelict mills some of which have been renovated or rebuilt in the past few years. Though in most cases only the towering mill chimneys remain. During the late sixties and seventies, any remaining cotton mills were closed down and unemployment rose.

Many locals had moved away seeking employment, and as a consequence, the house prices stayed low. During the eighties, however, the local council developed the towns and villages giving birth to a prosperous tourist industry. This attracted those people seeking an escape from the cities and offered them the chance of buying large properties at decent prices. The indigenous population referred to them as 'offcomers'.

One such couple were the Robinsons. They sold their semidetached in Ealing West London and bought a small holding on the edge of Wadsworth moor in West Yorkshire. They were both in their mid thirties and had managed to make enough money from the sale of their London house to buy a run down farmhouse and twenty acres of pasture land. The farm had been left empty for nearly a decade though all the locals, myself included, referred to it as 'the Denny's farm', the name of the previous occupants.

Harry Denny, the patriarch of the family, had died and his two sons had moved out of the area, one to manage a large farm in Buckingham and the other son to the promise of work in Manchester. Irene, the mother, held onto the farm as long as she could, but the place gradually deteriorated and it was not long before she moved out to a Nursing home. A couple of years later she sold the farm and land to the Robinsons.

They didn't move into the farm straight away. For over a year, they would seen on an occasional weekend attending to the property. Then, in the spring of eighty-four, the activity increased and they employed local craftsmen to set about repairing the farm proper. In the

Summer of that year, they moved in. The biggest shock to the locals was, that after only a week a cattle wagon turned up with thirty ewes and a ram. Isaac, the wizened old farmer with a pronounced limp and conical hat who had lived all his life in the farm next to the Robinsons was the most surprised.

He took great interest in the couple and dedicated a large portion of his time to pointing out the mistakes they were making and the best way of rectifying them. The one thing Isaac was right about was the type of sheep they had elected to buy. David Robinson incorrectly stated sheep were sheep, whereas, Isaac and all the other locals knew each breed of sheep had its own particular traits.

David had bought Swaledales. Now, Swaledales are the Steve McQueens of the sheep family. To them, the great escape is a walk in the park. If Swaledale had a motto, it would be 'the grass is greener on the other side of the fence and no bugger on Gods earth is going to stop me tasting it'. Escapism is in their genes.

David and Melissa Robinson settled into the job of farming. The sheep escaped regularly, the locals returned the sheep regularly, and Isaac became the mentor the Robinson never expected. David and Melissa became regular attendants at the Red Lion in Heptonstall that is to say they were there regularly any night except Friday nights. Friday night was the only night Isaac went to the Red Lion where his endless information on farming techniques was more than they could face.

The problem of the sheep escaping came to a head a few months later. Winter comes quickly on the Yorkshire moors. Bouts of thick fog accompany the early nights which are breathed out by the vast expanse of Wadsworth moors, acts like an enormous sponge that soaks up the rain and slowly releases it. Large areas of that moor become treacherous in the winter as the saturation reaches a peak. Venturing onto the moor is best avoided during the day and never to be attempted at night.

In early December, the Robinsons were returning from a late night drinking bout at the Red Lion. As they approached their farm, they stopped their Landrover.

Through the torrential rain they could hear the bleating of sheep. In a very short time, they had learned many things, mostly about fencing and walling in sheep, but also about the sounds sheep make. On this particular evening the bleating they could hear was the sound of sheep in trouble, the incessant cry of sheep in distress.

David rushed inside the farmhouse, grabbed some waterproof (raincoat) and a torch (flashlight) and headed off into the fog and rain, in the direction of the sheep. Melissa was only a few steps behind and kept calling at David to slow. They moved through the top pasture, then came to a standstill (gate) at the gap in the fence that led to the moors. The fog was at it thickest there and the torch light could only penetrate a few yards into the swirling gloom. The bleating was much nearer though the dense blanket of fog flattened its resonance.

The couple trudged slowly onto the moor and rapidly the fence that bordered their land faded to a faint contour, then nothing. They headed off toward the calls of the sheep, Melissa suddenly screeched as she slipped and sank up to her thigh in the brown putrid water. She quickly pulled herself out with David's help, though the suction was a poignant warning of the danger they had placed themselves in.

Their progress was slow as they went forward. More than once, they considered going back for extra help or at least to get some rope. The desperate cries of the sheep held them, drawing them onward. Eventually, the first sheep came into sight. A wave of relief swept over the couple when they realized that most of the sheep were huddled in a tightly knotted group for comfort and warmth.

Once they came up close to the group, they replaced their relief with a stomach tightening realization that at least a dozen of the flock were up to their necks in moor land bog. David stood looking at them helplessly for a while, unable to speak or think straight. Already, two or three of the larger ewes were showing strong signs of exhaustion and had given up struggling, their heads resting on the tufts of coarse grass which poked up

163

through the mire.

They stood watching some of the ewes struggling to clear themselves but their winter pelts were sodden through and the weight held them down. The ewe nearest gained strength from them being there and turned toward them pawing at anything to gain ground. Slowly, she made progress toward them and David carefully moved into the sodden pool. He was surprised to find the bog was not that deep and seemed solid enough for him to wade toward the struggling sheep. As he drew close, he sank deeper without any warning and found himself flaying around trying to step back.

Melissa stood on the bank shining the torch light toward him, calling him to come back. Somehow he managed to gain a firm footing and when he stood upright managed after a couple of attempts to snag hold of one of the struggling sheep's horns. Then with as much strength as he could muster, he bodily hauled the sheep toward him. It was slow going but he managed, eventually to free it from the sucking mud and out onto the coarse grass beside Melissa.

When David turned to step back into the bog, Melissa grabbed hold of him preventing him from going any further. He stopped panting for breath, a look of helplessness across his face. There was a frenzied splashing as one of the previously motionless ewes put her last strength into an attempt to break free. Her neck strained and her head thrashed about as she desperately searched for footing, then suddenly she was gone.

The surface broke only once as she gulped in a lung of air, then nothing. No movement, no bubbles. David waded in without thinking and stood up to his waist in the bog looking across to where the sheep had gone under. A second sheep started the same actions, thrashing about perhaps panicked by the loss of its fellow. David and Melissa watched desperately, unable to do anything but listen to the bleating of the sheep rising to a new high.

Beyond the pool on the opposite side of the couple, a faint light suddenly blinked into sight through the gloom, then out again. Then a shadow in the distance solidified, then was lost as the fog enveloped it. Eventually, they could see the figure of a man dimly opposite. He seemed to be carrying an old paraffin lamp with a rope slung over one shoulder and a short broad plank under his arm. The shape of his odd conical hat and his limping movement, they knew without doubt who it was.

Isaac shouted across to them but the fog flattened his voice and the sheep drowned out any of his words. With signs and gestures he made it clear that the ground was firmer on his side and with the help of the plank he could slide himself out to the entrenched sheep. This he did. He threw the length of rope over to David, then dropped onto his stomach and moved out across the plank to the first of the remaining sheep. Luckily, the sheep became oddly calm as he approached them and he seemed to have no trouble tying the rope around the horns.

David and Melissa then pulled for all their worth until finally the sheep was clear. Using this technique, they struggled for several hours throwing the rope to Isaac and him securing it on the next sheep, then pulling back his plank before sliding out the next one. Melissa and David were exhausted by the end of the ordeal, though they marveled at the strength Isaac, a man more than twice their age had displayed.

David signaled at Isaac through the fog to go around the mire and join them back at the farmhouse. Isaac clearly signed back that he would join them for a drink at the pub the following night. They had no doubt who would be paying. The Robinsons got their sheep back safely to the low pasture making sure they were secure, then went to bed tired, but relieved that they had lost only two sheep.

The following evening, the Robinsons went to the pub early. They hoped to see Isaac and thank him for saving ten of their sheep and for stopping David from risking his life further. They were surprised he wasn't already at the pub. They bought their drinks and waited, and waited and waited. After a couple of hours of turning to face the door every time somebody new entered, the landlord (barman) asked whom they were waiting for.

They explained the events of the previous night. That Isaac had come to the rescue and that they owed him at least a night of free drinks. The landlord went pale and at first seemed quite angry until he studied their faces and saw that they were telling the truth.

He was obviously quite shaken and poured himself a large glass of whisky. He explained it could not possibly have been Isaac as he had been found dead on his farm two days previously by the home help. David and Melissa Robinson were stunned into silence, they ordered a pint of Isaac's favorite beer and left it undrunk on the bar in tribute to the old man who had done so much to help a couple of off-comers. To this day, on any Friday night that the Robinsons go to the Red Lion, there is always a pint of undrunk beer waiting for its owner to claim.

Authors Notes:
The neighbor loved his sheep and somehow knew that David and Melissa were having problems with their own flock on that stormy night. He came and saved the lives of the sheep as the good sherpherd he was. He knew that David and Melissa lacked the knowledge to know what to do in the circumstances and felt a need to come back and aid them in saving their sheep.

The following set of ghost stories relates to ghostly entities that conduct themselves as guardian spirits. Often times these stories are related either as guardian spirits or as guardian angels depending upon the belief system of the individual.

The Apple Scent

I was twenty-four years old in 1978, at the time and it was a very bad time in my life. They confined me to a hospital bed, IV's were hooked-up and dripping vital fluids into my veins, trying their hardest to sustain a life that didn't want to be saved. I had gotten into the wrong crowd and ended up getting messed up with drugs.

I could hear the doctors talking to my Mother about my condition, about the amount of drugs I had put into my body to do the damage that was done. I could feel my Mother's tears on my face, her strong, warm, caring hands holding mine, her aching voice asking me over and over why, why had I decided life was not what I had wanted.

Now what I am about to tell you is true. First some background so you can understand what happened next. As a child growing up in Scappoose, Oregon, my Swiss Grandpa was one of the most important people in the world to me. I spent many weekends and summers with him and my Grandma in St. Helens, Oregon, while my Dad was at work. The summers only a child can have, free from worry and pain, full of love and attention.

My Grandpa always wore bib-overalls with his pipe sticking out from one of the pockets, work boots and a brown felt type hat. He was what they called in those days, a tinker. He would work out in his workshop tinkering with various things. Their house always smelled of good food cooking and Grandpa's pipe tobacco. Every night after dinner, Grandpa would take an apple then peel and slice it for everyone to eat.

He would smell of apples from the juices of the apples he sliced and the Prince Albert pipe tobacco he smoked. My favorite place was to sit on his lap at the end of the day as he sat enjoying his pipe full of Prince Albert tobacco while Grandma fixed supper. He loved to watch Gunsmoke and Wrestling on television. Unfortunately, Grandma died and then Grandpa died six months later when I was twelve years old in 1966. I had a sensation of loneliness come over me that I never forgot.

I slept for a while and when I awoke, my Mother was gone and the only company in the room was the constant beeping of the monitors and a nurse sitting in a corner writing something in a file. I could feel someone holding my hand, a large loving hand that seemed so familiar to me, but one my muddled mind couldn't quite grasp.

The Haunted Reality by Sharon A. Gill & Dave R. Oester

Then, the smell of apples and Prince Albert pipe tobacco stunned my senses. I heard a voice, not really with my ears, but with my mind, and my eyes saw the man I had spent so many of my childhood days with. My grandpa told me not to be afraid that he had come to help me.

He stroked my hair as he told me I had a good life in front of me yet, and that as much as he missed me, it wasn't time for me to come live with him in Heaven. I recovered after that but I will never forget my Grandpa helping me to get my life together and become a responsible person.

Within a Circle

A friend living in England tells the following true story. Many of the terms used are English words common to the people of that country. I have tried to translate by using the American version of the word whenever possible.

Heavy rain pounded the tarmac sending ricochets of spray back into the air. A constant haze of moisture hovered above the road's surface. The water mingled with the fresh blood that seeped out of the rabbits mouth. Death had been instantaneous, the car driver oblivious. The pathetic corpse lay broken in the line of traffic whilst vehicles tore by. The rabbit was positioned on the road in such a way that the car's wheels ran either side, though it was only a matter of time before a vehicle pulled away from the curb and crushed the body beyond recognition.

The driving rain obscured most things and the solid clouds shut out the midday light, the rabbit's body was no more than a gray lump in an even grayer world, overlooked by all. All that is, but one pair of eyes. Eyes that hardly blinked even though the rain poured down and around them. Focused eyes, heedless to all else, concentrating on the tiny corpse, hawk like in their intensity. Nevertheless, these were not animal eyes, they were human.

The roundabout (intersection like road) was large. Once on, forgetting it was a roundabout at all was easy. More a dual carriage way (highway) that swung endlessly clockwise with wide feeder roads at regular intervals. The local council (highway department) had abandoned the center for the roundabout and nature had been quick to take back possession. The trees were well established and dense undergrowth bordered the inner circumference in an almost complete wall. The occasional break, had you been in a tall vehicle would have shown a steep incline leveling out to form an enormous basin in which a small stream ran through the center. The stream entered through a large storm drain, it meandered its way across the land, then left by the drain at the opposite end.

Few people ever saw into the center. The roundabout was notoriously dangerous, traffic never slowed. Most drivers maintained the speed of the motor ways (freeways) that feed from the south and east edges. There had been a long history of accidents on the roundabout and different road schemes (plans) had been attempted, but the accidents continued. After one particularly bloody pile up where several people had died in a horrendous fire, the councils had considered a complete rebuilding of the roundabout, but in the end, financial restraints prevented any major alterations and they built a token crash barrier on the inner circle to stop vehicles from crashing down the banking.

The figure in the undergrowth had not moved from the moment the rabbit had been hit. Patiently it watched, eyes' slit with concentration, they flicked from the body to the oncoming traffic, then back as the cars passed over the dead rabbit. The figure was tense, coiled and ready. The gaps were short lived. A break appeared and the figure leaned forward alert and poised. Then another car. The figure stayed ready.

Distant thunder sounded across the sky backed by a carrion bird near by. A sudden break in the stream of traffic and the figure darted forward, leaping with muscular grace and liquid movement, grabbed the dead rabbit and in the same movement turned to spring back.

The car headlights picked the figure out, an etching in the solid wall of rain, and was immediately upon the figure in the fraction of a heartbeat. The thunder rolled by.

Torrential rain beat endlessly on the windscreen of Luke Parker's Audi, the windscreen wipers set to top speed to keep the view ahead clear. Even this awful weather was not going to get his spirits down though. He smiled to himself and hummed along to the track on his car stereo. Things were looking good for Luke. He had graduated with his two-one degree (like 3.5 GPA) twelve months earlier. He had accepted the job of a sales trainee at Alias Micros (banking trainee) three months later and after only nine months, had just been made area manager. A very good twelve months all tolled.

He was driving to Oxford to break the news to his adoptive parents. Luke did not think of them as his adopted parents, they were simply mum and dad. His own parents and elder sister had died twenty years ago when he was only four years old. He could barely remember anything about them, least of all his sister. They had died in a car crash and that was as much as he knew. He had a couple of photographs but had never really wanted to know anything else. It occurred to him now that perhaps he would ask what had happened, but not today. Today, it would be champagne and smoked salmon. He could not wait to see his fathers face.

Summer storms were common but this particular downpour was very heavy and had maintained its strength for most of his journey. Luke was approaching the turnoff he needed to take that would connect him to the Oxford bypass. He squinted at the signs as they flashed by. He could never remember which turning it was traveling south instead of his usual northward route. The traffic was particularly heavy even for a bank holiday.

He saw the sign for the turn and took it. At the same time, a large van which had been traveling along side Luke, decided to turn at the last minute, running down the exit road in parallel. Luke speeded up to pull ahead of the van so he could cross over into the right-hand lane. He managed to get far enough in front, then he signaled and pulled across. He entered the roundabout faster than he would have liked but fortunately managed to slip into the circling traffic with only one horn being sounded at him. He stayed on the inside lane of the roundabout. The traffic was moving too fast for his liking and he contemplated pulling into the outside lane, but when he looked across the same van as before was along side him. Luke turned off the stereo and put all his attention on the road ahead. The van was moving ahead and signaling, wanting to pull into his lane. Luke started to slow when ahead of him a figure leaped directly into the path of his car.

Luke could not say with certainty what happened next. He braked hard which caused him to swerve into the tail end of the van. This bounced his car round and he hit the crash barrier heavily on the right-hand side. The car spun out of control, crashing back across both lanes of traffic.

Remarkably, he came to rest on the hard shoulder facing in the right direction, having avoided being hit by any other vehicle. Luke sat panting, he was vaguely aware of a shooting pain running down his right arm and he had hit his head which was already starting to throb. He also noted with detached interest that his gold ring had bitten into his finger causing it to bleed. The van had not even stopped, the traffic tore by oblivious to what had just occurred. The rain drummed heavily on the car roof.

Luke turned off the car engine and sat looking out at the rain laden sky. The image of the figure darting in front of him played in his mind. He turned and looked back at where he had hit the barrier, he could just about make the spot out through the downpour. Once out of the car, he let the rain fall on his face, hoping it would snap him back to reality. He glanced at the side of his car. the whole right side had a heavy dent running its length. The front wing was crumpled beyond repair, pulled back to revealing the wheel. Luke walked away quickly, stopping at the point opposite where he had hit the barrier. Pieces of debris were scattered across the length of the road. He half expected to see a prone figure by the barrier. He could not recall with any certainty whether he had missed or hit the person. He prayed hard that he had missed.

After several dangerous attempts he made it across the dual carriage way (highway) to the barrier. He quickly climbed behind the metal curtain when he realized how invisible he must have been to the cars. Luke pulled his jacket close and zipped it up. He then scoured the road edge looking for any signs of the figure that he had seen. His eyes came to rest on a stain a couple of yards away, he edged toward it. His heart stopped. The rain and spray had done a good job of washing the stain away but it was still quite clearly a pool of blood he was looking at.

Luke felt sick. His head was spinning and he staggered backwards. He sat on a stone, some way back behind the barrier. No matter how hard he tried, he could not remember hitting the person. Nevertheless, more obviously, he had. Why were none of the other cars stopping? He contemplated flagging one down but on seeing the blood again, he decided to search for the injured figure.

The tightly knotted trees were grown around with brambles and hawthorn preventing Luke from moving through, so he followed the barrier along carefully looking for any signs that someone had passed that way. He had covered some fifty yards and was thoroughly saturated by the unabated rain. His eyes were attracted to a darker patch in the undergrowth. When Luke came to a halt, he could see a low clearing which wound back into the thicket. He paused for a moment, glancing back at the traffic then crouched down and pushed forward.

In the heart of the young trees the rain ended abruptly, cut off by the many branches and leaves overhead. The constant drumming blocked out most of the traffic sounds and Luke was momentarily caught by the tranquility. He pressed on, following the path which wove its way into the center of the roundabout. The trees and undergrowth halted at the edge of the incline and Luke rested to take in the view ahead. From his elevated position he could see the whole inner circle stretching away from him in two great arcs.

Down the steep incline he saw the stream and a

small pool a short distance from him. The rain seemed much gentler on this side of the trees and the sky less oppressive. It looked as if the rain might stop. Luke wiped the loose leaves and brush from his coat then flicked his hair back and smoothed it against his temples.

He stood working his arm flexing and stretching it. The ache in his head was intensifying and a large lump just above his eye was forcing his eyelid down partially closing his eye. He looked at his hand, the blood from his finger had spread across his palm making it seem far worse an injury than it was. His mouth was dry.

Luke Parker stood some time on the banking looking around the circle but there was no movement, no injured figure in sight. The traffic noise was remarkably dulled, the only clear sound was the croaking call of a crow. He decided to go down to the stream and clean his hand. He would have a drink and than head back to the car and get help. If someone was injured down here, he would be no use to them any how. What had he been thinking of?

He would let himself slide down the slippery grass taking it steady so as not to jar his head or his aching arm. The blood pumping through his veins was making the ache in his temple throb in time with his heartbeat. By the time he had completed his careful descent the rain had stopped and the clouds showed signs of breaking up. His headache was beginning to feel like a migraine, he knew the signs in advance. Experience had taught him not to ignore the warning, if he were not careful, he would lose the right half of his vision then most probably throw up.

He made directly for the small pool he had seen. The going would have been difficult but he stumbled on what might have been an old track heading roughly in the same direction. The traffic sounds could hardly be discerned in the bottom of the basin. All he could hear was the sound of running water.

The pool was larger than it had looked from the embankment, about ten feet across at it widest and quite deep from the look of its stillness. In his eagerness to bathe his hand and take a drink Luke failed to notice the small poles he dislodged around the pool. The tiny animal skulls and pieces of ephemera that had been carefully attached to the sticks clattered to the ground. Luke stretched out on the sodden bank next to the pool, then dipped his head forward and drank deeply. He had not realized how thirsty he was.

When he sat up, he was dizzy but he tried to ignore it. He reached down with his injured hand and started to rinse the blood from it. Instead of clearing the blood, however more blood seems to appear. He examined his hand and only then did he discover the blood was not in fact emanating from his cut on his finger but was running down his arm. Luke's head started pounding again, as he exerted himself removing his coat.

His shirt was sodden with blood that was still flowing from a deep laceration running across the width of his elbow. Luke carefully touched the gash, then reeled with nausea as the flesh pealed back far enough for him to see the bone joint. He turned his face back to the pool to take another drink but froze in the act.

Directly across the pool from him was a woman. She was hunched down staring at him. She was dressed like nothing he had ever seen before. Luke's stomach contracted and as he knelt forward ready to vomit, he over balanced. His head spun and the dancing flecks of a migraine sprang into his vision. He was vaguely aware of the pain in his arm and of falling. As unconsciousness took him, his last image was of the woman moving swiftly toward him, a large knife clenched in her fist.

When Luke opened his eyes, he was staring into a grotesque face grinning at him, almost nose to nose. He pushed back, dragging himself away but came to a halt against a tree stump, after moving only a couple of feet. The face was made from a car hub cap with two holes punched through to form rough eye sockets and a ragged gash for a mouth. Leaves and twigs had been wound around it to form hair. Long trails of ivy hung out of either side of the serrated mouth. They suspended the mask on a short rough stick bound round with different colored plastic shreds which flapped in the breeze.

Luke let out his held breath. He had been placed in

a makeshift shelter. Above him was a slanted roof made from branches and corrugated metal sheeting, which was crudely held aloft with four wooden poles. Even though the shelter was ramshackle in appearance, it was doing an effective job of keeping him dry from the pouring rain. Luke looked at his watch, it was half past two. He had been unconscious for about three hours. He sat up to get a better look at his surroundings.

By his feet, a small campfire burned. The rocks around it were blackened from regular use. Next to the fire was a collection of objects. A car reflector, a wing mirror, an old bucket thick with hardened tar, a crushed traffic cone, pebbles of various sizes and colors. As Luke looked around, he saw other collections all carefully positioned, as it dawned on him that they formed shapes though what those shapes were, was hard to say.

Luke struggled to look at his elbow, mud and moss had been smeared onto the cut but at least the bleeding had stopped. He felt the bump on his forehead, again mud and moss had been smeared on the swelling.

"Come back, I see."

Luke jumped. The woman was squatting by the shelter, a small bramble bush had hidden her from him. Luke stared at her openly. She was clothed in strip upon strip of different textile mixed in with shards of plastic bags, some with the logos still intact, in and among them were large numbers of feathers tied with string and cord of a variety of colors. There did not appear to be a coat or jacket so how the fragments were held together was impossible to say.

Around her neck were many elaborate necklaces made with feathers, pieces of glass, small animal bones and skulls. Her hair was mostly black, tied with different colored feathers, saying which was growing hair was hard and which was ephemera. His scrutinization stopped, when he reaches her face. Her dark brown eyes looked straight into his. Gauging her age was difficult but he would have said she was older than him, her gaunt face was covered in grime. She moved closer, her face coming within six inches of his own.

"Come back at last?" Her speech was stilted and had an awkward accent, Luke at first felt sure she was not English. He was unable to speak. When the woman had moved, the strange clothing had flowed with her, attached but somehow detached. It weaved around her like a multicolored smoke. From the brief glimpses afforded by her movement, it was clear she was naked beneath. She pulled back from him, and went to sit by the fire.

"Fire still here." She spoke as if to herself in the strangely stunted way.

"I thought I had hit you, in the car, I mean." Luke said as he licked his lips, they felt dry and cracked.

"I thought I'd hit you, and when I saw the blood," he swallowed noisily, "I thought I'd better check, just in case."

She poked at the fire turning the larger pieces of wood.

"Are you roughing it here?" Luke asked since he had seen travelers in his local village and this woman had the same look. Dreadlocks tied in with beads and such, all looking under nourished and dirty. She was more bizarre than any traveler he had yet seen, but he had not really paid much attention to them. He looked at her again. She had no footwear but her feet were remarkably clean, small scars ran around her feet some obviously old, just pale lines.

Her legs were the same, covered in small cuts running all over. The strange cloak covered the rest of her body. As she moved, he caught glimpses of her torso. She was tanned and slender but her arms and legs were muscular. Again, there appeared to be the same scaring across her skin.

"My name is Luke," he paused hoping she would volunteer hers, she did not.

"What is yours?"

She raised an eyebrow at him.

"Luke?" She paused, "I'm Sara." She said as she looked him in the eyes.

"My sister was called Sara."

The statement was bland and he felt acutely embarrassed. It felt like a lame chat up line. He might as well have said Sara was his mother's name. Sara laughed briefly, then smiled exposing perfect white teeth.

"My brother was called Luke." She laughed again.

Luke felt his face flush. She did think he was lying. He decided to change the subject quickly. "How long have you been living here?"

Sara's face became serious and she looked back to the fire. Luke had the feeling he was intruding with every question he asked. Perhaps he should just go. His car was unlocked and he still had to work out how to get it and himself home. Yes, it would be best if he thanked her for dragging him out of the pool, then leave her to herself.

"I'm waiting." She said, "I don't live here."

Luke was less sure of her accent now, perhaps it was not foreign after all. He could not quite say. Her stunted way of speaking was more like a child's. He tried to stop himself from asking, but after a moment of silence asked, "Waiting for who?" There he was, asking questions again. "How long have you been waiting?" He could not stop himself.

Sara looked back at him, her head resting on its side. A smile bloomed lighting her eyes. "Don't know." Luke was not sure which question was being answered, but he was determined not to probe any further.

"I'll show you." Sara stood and moved away from the shelter. She halted and turned around. It was obvious she intended him to follow. Luke struggled to his feet, his legs had gone to sleep and it took a moment stamping and rubbing before they came back to life. Sara moved off toward the sound of the running water. It was very distracting the way gaps appeared in the weird cloak, revealing areas of flesh.

Luke looked around him. The rain had turned to a light drizzle and the air was pungent with the smell of earth and vegetation. Sara had come to a halt. In front of her was an ancient oak, it must have survived the roundabout excavations by being in the circle's center. Luke stared past the woman at the oak's branches. Every limb, every branch and virtually every twig had ribbons tied to them. On closer inspection, the ribbons were made from strips of plastic or cloth, all different shades of color. There were thousands flapping in the breeze.

"What's this?" He looked at Sara. She was tying another strip to a low branch.

"Waiting." She gestured to the tree branches.

Luke walked forward nearer to the tree's trunk, still looking at the ribbons. Sara was crouched down at the tree's roots with her back to him. She was brushing the wet leaves from a white object at the tree's base. If the ribbons represented a day of waiting then she must have been waiting for years, there had to be another explanation. He moved up close to her wanting to rationalize the events around him. He froze in a half formed question when he saw what she was clearing the leaves from.

A small human skull was propped against the tree roots, he moved so he could go around the woman's back. There was a full skeleton laid out there. The skeleton of a small child. The rags of clothes had nearly vanished but a few artifacts were laid out next to the body. Luke felt a wave of fear flood him. He stepped back. Sara turned to look at him, her eyes full of tears. His fear evaporated, compassion replacing the feeling of foreboding. He wanted to comfort her but was still apprehensive.

"Who is it?" His voice was shaky. He softened his tone. "Is it your daughter?" Sara shook her head without turning to look back at him.

"Is it your sister?" Luke could not stop himself from asking, the feeling of apprehension growing. Sara stopped the careful clearing and turned to fully face him.

"No, not my sister." The emphasis on "my" unnerved him. She repeated, "No, not my sister." Her tears filled eyes were riveted on his, watching, burning into him.

"Mr. Parker?" The sudden voice made Luke jump.

"Mr. Parker, are you Mr. Parker?" Luke spun round to face the source of the shout. A police constable was walking toward him. He was only fifty feet away.

"It is Mr. Parker, isn't it?" The policeman was getting closer not needing to shout. "We found your car abandoned. Headquarters said it belonged to a Mr. Luke Parker." He put away his notebook.

"Yes, that's me." Luke instantly felt guilty. He always felt guilty around the police and should not have left his car.

"I thought I had hit someone on the roundabout." It sounded like an excuse. "She's okay though, I didn't."

The policeman looked surprised.

"She?"

"Yes, Sara. She helped me." He touched the lump on his forehead. Luke turned to Sara for confirmation. She was gone. He quickly scanned the area, there was no sight of her.

"She was here a minute ago." He saw the doubtful expression on the constables face. Luke turned back.

"She put all the ribbons . . . " He stopped half way through his sentence. The tree was empty, no sign of any ribbons. Luke could feel panic climbing within him. What was happening? The policeman's attention had shifted from Luke to some thing past him. The constable moved past him to the base of the tree. Luke followed him.

"What the heck?" The policeman knelt next to the tiny skeleton. "Do you know anything about this?" His voice had turned cold. He obviously thought Luke did.

"No, there was a woman here, she said," Luke was unsure, what she had said. Not her sister. The constable had picked something up and was wiping the grime from it. It looked like a small plastic purse with a printed name on it.

"Sara Parker." The policeman turned to Luke repeating the name. "Sara Parker."

Not 'her' sister, but his sister. Sara was his sister, her spirit watching over her body until the earthly remains were found.

Luke and the constable walked without speaking back toward the outer turning circle. Luke's peripheral sight was plagued with elusive images of Sara's world. The ramshackle shelter and the many totems that lined the stream bank. He glanced back at the old oak and for the briefest of moments saw the fluttering ribbons.

When they reached the parameters incline, Luke stopped, letting the policeman move ahead, climbing the slippery bank. A gentle breeze moved Luke's fringe aside as carefully as a lover's touch. He blinked slowly and inhaled deeply, the faint smell of earth and human musk. A fragile voice caressed his ear. "Thank you, Brother."

Authors Notes:
The accident that had killed Luke Parker's family had taken place on this same roundabout some twenty-years previous. His sister's body had never been found. The authorities believed the body was lost in the wreckage and terrible fire that had occurred. Perhaps she had survived the crash, fatally injured but had crawled away from the fire to die unseen. They finally laid the body of Sara Parker to rest in the same graveyard as her parents, in Luke's village.

The Nurse Ghost

This is a true story because it happened to me. I was twenty-six at the time and just gotten a new job. Along with that job, I got a new apartment closer to my new job. My first night in the apartment, my best friend came over with a house warming gift. Jean did not like the place at all. She told me it gave her the creeps. I laughed it off because I loved my apartment. The next morning my alarm went off at six o'clock and I reached over and hit the snooze button. Then at 6:10, the alarm went off again and I lay in bed feeling that someone was watching me.

I snapped open my eyes and there at the foot of my bed was a young woman approximately 25-30 years old, long brown hair and dressed in white. I thought I was being robbed so I reached over to the night stand and grabbed my pistol which I always kept on my night stand when I slept. When I looked back, the woman was gone. I immediately got up and searched the apartment. There were no signs of a break-in, the woman was no where to be found and the alarm was still set.

I called my friend Jean and my boyfriend to tell them what had happened. I was afraid so I packed several days of clothes and stayed with my girlfriend for three nights. When I went back, everything was normal for a long time. My boyfriend says he never felt comfortable at the apartment. Once he was watching television and the lamp in the next room began to shake. My cat showed some strange behavior. The cat would get on top of my dresser and howl at night, scaring the heck out of me.

I saw the woman in white once more. This time, it was much briefer. She appeared in the same spot, at about the same time. This time, strangely, I wasn't scared. After I was there about four months, my two sisters came for a visit from Florida. The first night there, my sisters wanted to talk with and hoped to see the woman in white. We all sat around the kitchen table and we attempted to talk to this spirit. I was watching my sister and all of a sudden, her face went pale. I asked her what was wrong and she stated that she could see the ghost down the hall. I jumped up to see from her vantage point but the lady in white was gone.

Right after this experience, we went to bed. My older sister is a night owl and must have the television on to go to sleep. Not that night, she immediately went to sleep. It seemed weird to me and my younger sister. When I got up the next morning, my younger sister asked me why I woke her up in the middle of the night. I didn't know what she was talking about. My younger sister then explained that I woke her up and asked her if she were okay. Then my older sister said, "You did the same thing to me." I denied it all because I didn't do it. This really scared us.

Well, I moved out of the apartment the next month. The lady in white did not follow me to my new apartment. However, the next month, I found out I had cancer. I had to have surgery to have the cancer removed. My mother said that the first thing I said when I opened my eyes in the recovery room was, "The ghost was a nurse, she was in the operating room with me." I haven't seen her since, but I will never forget her.

Buried Treasure

This story was given to us by a lady named Elvie Marker who presently resides in Long Beach, Washington. It is actually a compilation of stories which have followed Elvie, no matter where she has been, since the 1940's.

It's been fifty-five years ago, Elvie was expecting her first baby. Elvie, her husband and her brother-in-law were in the San Joaquin Valley in California. They had found an old abandoned house sitting along the banks of the San Joaquin River and had moved in. That was a common thing to do in those days. After living there for a time, they learned the house had a history, quite an interesting one in fact.

It seems a man, whose name is not known, had built this beautiful home for his beloved bride to be. He was a man of great wealth so he spared no expense in building the home they were to share. The setting was perfect, as was the house, with the vast fields, tall trees and the beautiful river running close to the house. He must have been overjoyed at the thought of spending the rest of his life in the home he'd so specifically built for the woman he'd fallen so deeply in love with.

As he stood on the banks of the river, he saw his bride-to-be coming toward him, across the river. In his excitement, he jumped into the river to greet her and drowned. Everyone knew he was a man of wealth. It was also known he was not a man who trusted in banks to hold his money. Rumor had it, he had buried his wealth, somewhere on the property. No one knew where, but they suspected it was close to the place where he had built the house.

After moving into the house, Elvie's brother-in-law had a dream about where the money was buried. The two brothers went out to dig at the site he'd seen in his dream. Elvie was pregnant, remained seated at the kitchen table. The back door was open, only it was covered by a three to four-foot canvas sheet. "Canvas rubs, it makes a noise when you move it," Elvie explained.

Suddenly, Elvie heard the canvas rattle, like someone was coming in. She looked up and saw a man's hand and his feet coming through the canvas that covered the open doorway. She got up and went over to look and the man disappeared. She went back to the table and sat down. A moment later, Elvie decided to go out to where the men were digging. She was curious to see how far down they'd dug into the ground.

She observed they'd not dug down very far so she returned to the table and sat down. It wasn't long before the incident repeated itself. Upon investigating, once again the man disappeared. Elvie decided she should alert her husband to what had just happened in the kitchen, she wanted to see what he thought about it. Once again, she went out to where the two men were digging and told them both what had happened.

In response, both men scoffed at her story, so she invited one of them to come sit at the table with her and see if it happened again. Elvie's brother-in-law went back to the kitchen table and sat with her, only to hear someone coming through the canvas sheet. He turned and saw a man's hand on the edge of the sheet, ready to pull it aside to enter and his feet.

He jumped up quickly from the table and ran over to the doorway, pulling back the canvas, but no one was there. He turned and walked out to where his brother was still digging and told him to stop. Naturally, his brother asked why he wanted him to stop digging for the wealth they had anticipated finding in that spot. His brother responded, "We're not supposed to dig." Though the brothers did not agree, they ceased digging so of course they never did find the money.

Elvie's brother-in-law continued to dream where the money was buried but they would not dig for it. Not long after that, they moved from the house. Elvie said she never was frightened, but seeing a man coming through the canvas cover did startle her. It seems her brother-in-law was meant to know where the money was buried, but he was not meant to possess it. He must have felt a benevolent presence when they tried to dig down to find it, otherwise he would not have stopped their digging.

Elvie was one of seven children. When her Mother became seriously ill, Elvie was the only one available to move to Nyssa, Oregon to care for her Mother. Feeling like she needed to be close to her Mother but not live in the same house with her after so many years, after being there a while, Elvie bought the two lots, that were for sale, next door to her Mom and had a house built for her and her stepdaughter.

The stepdaughter became afraid to sleep in her bedroom alone. She wouldn't explain to Elvie why the room bothered her, so Elvie volunteered to trade rooms with her. After a few nights, Elvie found herself awakened between two and three in the morning, to the sound of someone coming through the back door. She listened as she heard footsteps walking across the linoleum floor. That struck her as strange since there was no linoleum in the entire house, it was all carpeted!

Elvie turned on her bedroom light and crawled out of bed to go investigate. She walked back to the utility room, where she'd heard the sounds of intrusion only to find the back door was still locked. There was no one there and no evidence that anyone had tried to break in. Elvie never mentioned the incident to her stepdaughter knowing she had already been frightened by probably the same sounds.

In December 1973, Elvie remarried. The couple moved into Elvies' home next door to her Mother. The third night after they were married, she and her new husband were sound asleep in their bedroom. Suddenly, her husband sat straight up in bed. Elvie asked him what was wrong, he responded by telling her he'd heard someone come in the back door.

Since Elvie had experienced these phenomena many times before, she knew what it was. She said, "Well, why don't you get up and go see who it is?" She chuckled to herself, she knew he wouldn't find anything there. She watched as her husband cautiously crept out of the room to confront, what he knew was an intruder. A few minutes later, her husband walked back into the bedroom and said, "The back door is locked, there's nothing there!" Elvie then related the story of what had been happening since she had moved into the house. Though her husband had heard these sounds distinctly himself, he told her, "That was silly!"

One year later, Elvie's Mother became terminal with cancer. Elvie moved her Mother into her house, with all her belongings. Elvie's sister came down from Washington to stay at the house and help care for her ailing Mother. One afternoon, as they were siting in the living room, her sister told Elvie she was going to have a visitor.

Elvie asked her why and her sister replied that she had just heard someone walk across the wooden back porch. Elvie suggested to her sister that she go look at her back porch. Her sister looked outside, only to discover the porch wasn't wood at all, but concrete! With shock on her face, she returned to ask Elvie, "What does it mean?"

Elvie's Mother was able to reveal a bit of history about previous owners of the property. It seems the previous neighbors had, at one time, built a home on that spot. It had burnt to the ground. It had a wooden back porch as well as a wooden front porch and presumably linoleum floors. The activity became a regular anomaly, footsteps walking across front and rear wooden porches, at all hours of the night and day. Doors sounded like they opened and closed but no one was ever there.

Elvie never felt frightened by these sounds, they just became a normal part of everyday life for her Nyssa home. She never determined who it was either, although she had her suspicions. It wasn't too long until Elvie lost her Mother to the cancer. This was when she felt, she knew for sure who the presence was in her home. Once Elvie's Mother had passed away, the sounds of walking and doors opening and closing stopped. She feels it was her Father, staying close, waiting around until the day when his wife would join him. He would be there to escort her into the realm beyond.

In the late 1970's, Elvie and her husband relocated to Harrisburg, Oregon. They were shown a big two-story house on Smith Street, in town, by a teenage boy, the son of one of the neighbors. The house being for sale, they liked it very much and decided to buy it. Elvie learned later that the house had been shown to several people by this young man, but until now no one had purchased it. His being a part of selling the house earned the young man a new bowling ball and bag.

Having settled into the house, Elvie was pleased with her large new home. She felt safe and very comfortable there. When her husband had to fly to Ontario for treatment for an ailing back, Elvie decided to stay home alone. The neighbor boy paid a visit one evening, asking where her husband was. Elvie explained he'd had to fly to Ontario.

The boy asked her if she were afraid to be alone in the house. Elvie, a bit surprised, responded that no she was not afraid and then asked him why he would be concerned she might be fearful. He told her the house was haunted! Elvie asked the boy why he had not told them it was haunted when he was showing them the house? Clearly, he knew if they didn't buy the house, he would not receive the new bowling ball and bag he'd wanted so badly. He knew first hand it was haunted as not only he but his Father as well had some eerie experiences in the house.

As history would have it, a man had died in the house, whom we'll call Mr. Mac. His spirit was said to have remained in the structure, roaming the premises. When Elvie heard strange sounds in the house, she'd call out, "Now Mr.Mac, you stop that!" The commotion would stop. Mr. Mac was never a malevolent spirit, therefore Elvie felt they could all live comfortably, accepting the invisible presence as part of their home. She was never frightened.

"You could lay in bed at night and listen to a party going on upstairs," she said. People walked across the floor, even the sounds of women wearing spiked heels were clearly heard. You could hear laughing and talking but could not distinguish words being said. Upon investigating the noise, the large room upstairs would be empty. The room was a place where Elvie kept her collection of dolls, all lined up against the walls. None of them were ever disturbed though the sounds of celebration were clearly heard, regularly.

After returning from the bowling alley one evening, Elvie and her husband, Percy, were preparing for bed. The lights were off, the room was in total darkness. The shades were drawn so no light was entering through the windows. There were no street lamps to light the dark street outside.

Elvie noticed a ball of light, about the size of a baseball, at the head of the bed. She pointed it out to Percy, asking what he thought it could be. Neither of them had any idea what this strange ball of luminescence could be. Suddenly, the ball of light separated and there were two balls of light. As suddenly as the phenomena had appeared, the two balls of light disappeared, never to return.

One July 4th, Elvie sent her children down to the banks of the Willamette River to watch the fireworks display. She had gone also, but they'd gotten separated in the crowd. When Elvie returned to the darkened house, she discovered her son, Forrest, outside under the big maple tree. She asked him why he had not gone inside. The boy appeared terrified and responded he would not go in, that there was a man standing in the window.

Elvie looked up at the second floor window and saw a figure standing there. She could not determine whether it was a man or a woman, but clearly there was a figure there. The white lace curtains were pulled aside as though being held by whomever was standing there, looking out the glass.

Elvie told her son they would go upstairs together and she would show him there was nothing there. The young boy was frightened, insisting, "But look, he's right there, look!" Yet finally on investigating, there was nothing there. Elvie admits she sometimes felt uneasy but never frightened. Feeling there was someone or something there made her uneasy, but she never felt threatened or endangered.

She expressed that had the ghosts she's encountered over the years been the kind that threw things across rooms, moved things around or intimidated her or her family, she would have felt differently. She probably would have left in fear.

Not feeling intimidated, she resigned herself to coexist with these spirits in peace. She never considered having them extracted from her homes by a religious ritual, or asking them to leave. I'm certain Elvie felt they remained on this plane of existence for a purpose unknown to her. She never felt it necessary to attempt to interfere with their unfinished business, therefore allowing them to find completeness and peace to move on.

The Ghostly Coffee Cup

Ida Norred has lived in the Saint Helens area of Oregon most of her life. She is a believer in the paranormal, and has a great curiosity as to the nature of ghosts. Ida, has herself had many of her own experiences with invisible presences in her home and has made the acquaintance of many others who have shared unexplained phenomenon with her.

Many of Ida's experiences took place in her home in Saint Helens. It was the dream home that she and her husband had built after their marriage many years ago. Her fondest memories are of the years they spent together in their home on Railroad Ave., where their children were raised and their most joyous times were spent together. Ida's husband has since passed on, her children are all grown, raising families of their own and the old house now sits empty. It has been condemned for safety reasons, Ida has relocated to the Portland area.

Several years ago, late at night I was preparing to go to bed. As usual one of our married children was living with us in our big home. They had already gone upstairs to bed and my husband was in his recliner ready to go to sleep. I was always the last one to retire, as I always checked all the stove burners, the door locks and all the other last minute things, so all would be safe. I took my gum out of my mouth and pressed it down on the edge of a coffee mug on the draining board. I walked about four feet away to the trash burner to throw in my last cigarette for safety.

I'd taken off my glasses so I couldn't see much, but as I lifted the lid from the trash burner, I heard something hit the floor between my feet. It hit hard as if someone had thrown something at me. Not being able to see very well, I reached down to pick up whatever it was that had landed at my feet. It was a wad of chewing gum. It looked like the gum I had just stuck to the side of my mug!

I thought, "Oh no." I didn't want to look to see if my gum was where I had placed it only moments before. Curiosity got the better of me, I had to know, so I reached for my glasses so I could check it out. Sure enough, the gum I had placed on the coffee mug was now laying between my feet. The strangest feeling came over me.

I had pushed the gum firmly to the side of the ceramic mug, if it had not stuck securely, it would have fallen down, most likely onto the draining board. But the gum had landed four feet away from where the mug was sitting. It had hit the floor hard enough that I heard it clearly. The first thought that came to mind as I once again looked down at my wad of gum, was my Father. He had passed away many years before.

I remembered when we were growing up, one thing he would not stand for was any of us kids parking our gum on something, to save it. He insisted that once we took gum out of our mouths, we throw it into the wood stove. It seems Father still feels that way, even on the other side. That night, he got my full attention, letting me know I needed to put my gum into the trash burner, and get rid of it.

One afternoon, some years ago, my husband and I were sitting at our kitchen table. He was reading a book. Directly to the right of him under a dish cupboard, I had fifteen mugs, hanging on cup hooks neatly in a row. Suddenly, my husband peered over the top of his reading glasses, as he often did, toward the mugs. He looked at me and said, "What's with that coffee mug over there?" I looked and one of the mugs, was swaying back and forth, all by itself. None of the other fourteen mugs were moving at all.

There had been no earthquake, no natural explanation for the mug to be moving. I looked at my husband and said, in answer to his question, "I don't know. What do you think I am, an authority on ghosts or something?" He just went back to reading his book and ignored it. I never could put it out of my mind as easily as he was able too.

About a year after my husband passed away, I saw him standing at the foot of my bed. It wasn't as if he walked in and walked out. It was as though he was suddenly there and then he wasn't. Our very short conversation was not talking, like we normally did. It was more as if he were transferring thoughts to me, like telepathy.

I was so surprised and sat straight up in bed at the sight of him. I thought for a moment he was really there in the flesh. I remember saying, "My God, I thought you weren't here anymore. I thought you were dead!" He said something to me and I knew as soon as he was gone that he had come especially to tell me something.

I never knew what it was that he said to me. I have tried many times to get him to return and tell me again what it was that he wanted me to know. I have had no success in bringing him back. I was so shocked at seeing him standing there and looking so good that I didn't hear a thing he said. I can only remember what I said.

The first Thanksgiving after my husband died, my youngest son and his family were living in our house. He and his wife were upstairs in bed. Traditionally, we left the turkey in the oven until the next day so anyone could snack on it when they wanted. My husband had always slept in a recliner in the living room of our home. When he would get up, he'd rear back and then push himself forward to get out of the chair. The sound of this process could be heard all over the house.

The night of that first Thanksgiving after his death, my son heard his father's chair, like his dad was getting up out of it. He then heard the oven door open and close and the sound of footsteps walking back to the recliner. The chair was no longer there! Right after my husband passed on, I had the chair removed from the house.

Authors Notes:

      It seemed even after leaving this physical realm, Ida's husband was never too far from his beloved family. He must have wanted to make certain that his dear wife was okay and still felt a need to let her know he wasn't far away and was overseeing things. He must have felt the need to protect her, in the only way he could, just by being there. It doesn't always have to be a tragedy that keeps a spirit earthbound. Sometimes all it takes is the strong bond of love and devotion between two people that keeps the spirit of the one departed close enough to just keep an eye on things.

Beware Underwear

      I am always at my wits ends trying to figure out what to buy my special friend, Nellie, for Christmas. When musical mugs came out and I discovered how unique they were, I bought five of them for gifts. I had them all gift wrapped, lined up with the proper name on the tags, on the back of my bookcase headboard. Every time I walked into the bedroom and turned the light on, the one I bought for Nellie would start playing music. None of the rest would do this.

      After I had given her the gift, she took it home with her. Every time someone would come for a visit, her Christmas mug would begin to play music. She finally shut it in the oven to make it be still.

      These are the same musical mugs that won't normally play their music until they are lifted up from a solid surface. The other four mugs responded they way they were meant to, but the one for my special friend, seemed to have a mind of its own.

      One year I found myself in the same predicament as to what gift to give my best friend. I found something unique this time. I bought Nellie a beautiful, crystal ball.

It was a gift not everyone had and it would make a great conversation piece.

We talked on the phone a lot, kidding about the crystal ball saying things like, "How about telling me my fortune?" One day she and I were talking on the phone and she saw a wisp of smoke. No one in their house smokes so she thought she was maybe imagining it. A few minutes later, she smelled smoke. The light shining through the crystal ball had set some papers on the table on fire.

Thank goodness there was no real damage done. But now the crystal ball, the lovely conversation piece, has been hidden away in her underwear drawer. Her husband, Merv, says he can't wait to see what they get for Christmas this year.

Focus on the Positive

The Howard's residence, in Camas Washington is as normal a family household as you could find. The grounds surrounding the house are lush green lawns, bright cheery flower beds and rock gardens. Outside the grassy yard are tall fir trees and a park-like setting. It is a peaceful atmosphere, no sounds of traffic filling the air, only sounds of the wind in the treetops.

The interior of the home is light and airy. Upon entering, we could sense the harmony within. It wasn't a home where you would enter expecting paranormal activity. It is a newer home with all the modern conveniences and a loving family place. While visiting with them, we found ourselves standing outside in the warm, morning sun, talking with Patricia. She was seated on a redwood bench out on the patio.

We asked her if she could tell us any more about the history of the house and of any experiences she's had there. She began recalling an event that took place prior to Mr. and Mrs. Howard purchasing the home. It seems some strange things had been happening that the Realtor felt he should reveal to the Howard's before they decided to buy the place.

A young teenage boy had lived here at one time, his name was David. In an act of desperation, he ended his young life by positioning a gun to his head and pulling the trigger. He committed this act in the garage, near the wall closest to the family room. The bullet hole can still be seen, even after having been patched and painted, if you know where to look in the ceiling of the garage. The details of David's reason for taking such drastic action are not known. Chad Howard, believes that David is one of many entities that have taken up residence in the home.

Friends of Chad and Patricia's have spent evenings with them in the family room on different occasions. They have seen the face of a boy in the window, looking in at them. He waves and then "flies off" into the darkness of night. On investigating, they find no one outside. The blinds covering the window remain closed, due to the insistence of visitors who have experienced David's phenomenon.

Danny Howard told us he has always had one policy that the family must abide by. When the kids come home from school or work, when he comes home from work, when family members come to visit, 'the anger and hostilities of the day are left out on the doorstep." This is understood by all as well as applied by all and it is amazing how smoothly it works in this household.

Even the entities within must also understand the house rules as their activity is of a nonviolent, non-threatening nature. They make their presences known in various ways, but none thus far, have been destructive. Playful bangs and bumps throughout the house are a normal part of the Howard's everyday life. Apparitions have been seen on the hallway stairs but most frequently in the family room.

The youngest son, Wyatt Howard has actually felt the presence touch his shoulder and grab his ankles. Every member of the Howard family has at one time or another experienced strange phenomena in the home. It has always been in the form of child-like pranks, never violent in nature. Cold spots have been felt in the family room in an area near the outside door which stands at the end of the far wall. This wall separates the family room and the garage.

Chad Howard described a flowery lamp that lights up and plays "It's a Small World" all by itself. The lamp came on and went out repetitively. The only way the lamp would operate was by turning on a wall switch. When the activity was occurring, the wall switch was in the off position!

An apparition has been observed throughout the house, more frequently walking up the stairs, roaming the upstairs bedrooms and down stairs in the family room. All of this activity takes place on the east side of the house, above and next to the garage.

Authors Notes:

Most often, we have found that when a violent death occurs, such as murder or suicide, the spirit entity which remains in that place is of more of a malevolent nature. The emotional energy which remains behind is of a negative pattern. The same negative pattern as the person who had died there.

Most poltergeist activity is reported in households in which there are teenaged people as their emotional and physical energy runs high. The emotional charge that young people experience can cause friction in a residence and can often draw negative energy patterns, such as poltergeist activity of a more destructive nature.

Lets face it, as teens get older, they want to be able to do more, feeling their independence. Parents are not always in agreement with this and the disputes begin. It's a normal part of the growing up process.

This also can draw in entities which feed off these negative emotions. We have all heard stories of malevolent paranormal activity portrayed on shows such as Sightings, Paranormal Borderline and in movie productions that are based on true stories. It was very refreshing to see a normal home in which teenagers reside where the

Father has established a policy that the negative emotions of the day be left outside the front door. This policy has demonstrated to us that this behavior can make a difference even in the actions of the resident ghost.

We sincerely believe that this has made a big difference in the Howard' household. By all rights, this ghostly entity would have every reason for acting in the manner he did in life. He was obviously very distraught, upset and feeling as though the only way out of his problems was to take his own life. The emotions leading to an action such as suicide are extremely negative. It seems the most serious of occurrences that could take place have been averted by positive behavior and loving family members.

Grandmother's Concerns

It was a dark and stormy night as we went out to the car to head for the outskirts of St. Helens. Rain was pounding on the windshield, visibility was limited as we crept our way toward town. We were the only car on the road, which in itself was eerie. We turned off of Highway 30 onto Sykes Road, heading west.

The headlights were of little value on this night as we proceeded slowly so as not to miss the mailbox with the house number we were searching for. There were no street lights to help guide us on our way, we had to depend on the headlights and sense of direction to find the location. We couldn't help but wonder what we would find on such a stormy night.

After driving for a time, we came to the mailbox with the house number we were searching for. Dave turned the car onto the gravel driveway and slowly drove toward the house lights we could see dimly in the distance. Trees lined the driveway which made it seem even darker and more ominous. As we approached the house, what we saw was not what we had anticipated. It was a beautiful modern home and didn't resemble a home that would possibly be haunted. We were very anxious to spend some time with the owners and learn what had been happening within these lovely walls.

We were greeted at the front door by Bob and Renee Chamberlain, their son Travis and daughter Heather. They had all experienced something strange going on in the house over quite a long period of time. None of them had mentioned to each other any of the strange phenomena, fearing they'd be laughed at. Explaining the things away rationally at the time they happened was easier than sharing the experience with other family members.

One afternoon, however, Heather mentioned to her Mom that something strange had occurred in the house. Very soon, all four family members were sharing experiences they'd been having and realized this was something very real since they were all having the same kinds of encounters. It soon began to seem like the invisible visitor could very possibly be Renee's Mother, Ursula, who had recently passed away. The activity gave every indication she had remained in the house.

Heather Chamberlain seemed to have the most encounters with this presence, perhaps because Heather had been a favorite of her Grandmother. Being very close, as they had been, it only seemed right her Grandmother would want Heather to be aware that she was still there. Heather told us she always went to bed late at night. While lying in bed, trying to fall to sleep, she'd feel something brush across her face, tenderly like that of an unseen hand.

When home alone, Heather would hear coughing coming from some place in the house. She remembers when her Grandmother would light up a cigarette, she'd cough or when she was done with a cigarette, she'd cough. Though she could not identify where the coughing was coming from, it was clearly a cough, like that of her Grandmother.

Some nights the seventeen-year-old would leave her radio playing. It had a green light that acted as a night light, which gave the room a dim green cast. At times, Heather would see a shadow on the wall, resembling the form of her dear departed grandmother. At other times, Heather just felt her Grandmother near her. She felt no fear, though at times hearing, seeing or feeling things abruptly would startle her for a moment.

Heathers Grandmother was very protective of her, watching over her, sticking up for her. Even when Heather and Renee would disagree over something, Grandmother always took the teenager's side. Even today, when Heather and her Mom argue, she feels her Grandmother nearby, still taking up for her.

One of Ursula's greatest wishes was for a peaceful existence among family members. She wished for Renee and Heather to be close as Mother and daughter and for the family to remain close, loving and supportive of each other. Her greatest desire was to see the birth of her first great-grandchild. Unfortunately she passed away before this happened.

Travis and his wife have since been blessed with a daughter whom they named Charity. Since our interview, they have moved to Belfair, Washington. How proud Great-Grandmother must be as we are certain that was one purpose in her spirit remaining close.

Each family member has caught movement out of the corners of their eyes, seen shadows which take the form of a woman, have smelled the odor of cigarette smoke and heard coughing in the home. For a while, they were receiving mysterious phone calls as well. The telephone would ring but there was never anyone on the other end of the line, just a strange windy sound. When they added Caller ID to their line, the same calls would come in, the phone number would appear, but could not be identified.

Ursula had some favorite articles in the house that even after her death, she could not resist touching or moving. One piece in particular was a porcelain rocking horse. At times it would be seen moved to the front of an end table, from its normal place closer to the lamp at the rear of the table. Many times it would begin rocking by itself and rock continuously for quite some time.

While she was ill, the family would gather for games

of Scrabble, which became a favorite. Bob, Renee's husband, would leave the game set up on the dining room table for convenience. After her death, the tiles would be found moved around. Both Bob and Renee felt she was letting them know she hadn't forgotten all the evenings they'd played her favorite game, though she never spelled out messages for them.

Ursula, departed this physical plane after the unexpected diagnosis of lung cancer. Her death came at an early age and her business here, was unfinished. Ursula had lived with her daughter and family until her passing.

Ursula's Mother, living in the house located in front of the Chamberlain home, was very disapproving of her daughter smoking. She was forbidden to smoke in her Mothers house, in fact it was a standing rule for anyone who smoked cigarettes that they not smoke on the premises.

As it was, Ursula's Mother experienced her daughters presence in a very distinct way. On occasion, she would smell the odor of cigarette smoke inside her home, the one thing she had forbidden her daughter to do. What better way to show that she was still around.

Now she could smoke in the house and get away with it! The things Ursula had loved in life have been found disturbed, the people she loved have clearly felt her presence, seen and heard her within the home. These days, she finds it easy to smoke freely in the home of her Mother without consequence.

Authors Note:

Since our visit with the Chamberlain family, we have learned there have been no signs that Renee's Mother is still in the house. All has been perfectly quiet, to the disappointment of all family members. Whether Ursula was awaiting the arrival of her Great-grandchild or whether she remained until she was sure the family clearly understood that she is okay and that there is life after life, we're not certain.

While transcribing the audio tape we made of our interview with each member of the family, we discovered most of the tape to be blank! The only voice that recorded was that of Heather. This is the first time that we have recorded an interview and the tape failed to record. It was almost as if someone didn't want the personal stories of Grandmother's visit made public. When we told Renee about the tape, she said she had chills suddenly flow over her body. Grandmother allowed some stories to be recorded and not others.

One thing is sure though, Grandmother felt like she had completed her task that made her earthbound. She was free now to move on knowing that her family was going to be okay. Once again we see how love transcends death.

Lost and Confused Ghosts

The following ghost tales have a common thread woven throughout them of individuals who have died, but became lost and confused, unable to progress further in the Spirit Realm. These spirits are earthbound, trapped to remain behind until they become free of the anchors that hold them here.

Alice in Wonderland

In 1990 they transferred my husband, David, from Seattle, Washington, to Hudson, Ohio, which is about thirty-five miles south of Cleveland. We decided to build a new house rather than buy one already built, so we could add a Pacific Northwest flavor to the design. After a long search, we found a parcel of land that had trees and a small creek, and behind it acres and acres of undeveloped land that is home to deer, raccoon, ground hogs, birds and all other forms of forest creatures. The site was perfect for us and our cats.

A contractor was found that was familiar with building the type of home we wanted and construction began in August. The lot had to be cleared of some of the trees. Nothing exceptional happened during the clearing, digging, building, and final grading. No dinosaur bones, no unmarked graves, nothing. Nothing but a couple modern arrow heads stuck in a couple of trees where someone had target-practiced, not too many years earlier.

February 1, 1991, we moved into our new home. What excitement to see all our belongings after ten months in storage. Living in a condo for that time was okay, but not having my own furniture and other belongings was torture! We had just started unpacking our boxes when the phone rang that first day. It was my husband's boss, from Allstate Insurance. The company needed him to fly to Denver for ten days to work on some computers. David had to leave the next day, leaving with a house full of boxes to be put away, but oh well, I had nothing better to do. Now, I could do it at my own pace and be sure everything got put into its rightful place.

On February 3, I was upstairs unpacking books and putting them away in the library when I heard a child crying. I stopped and listened thinking it was outside, but remembered, this is February in Ohio with the temperature about fifteen degrees below zero. No child would be out in this storm. The crying was really just a soft weeping carried up the stairs to me as I turned off the radio.

Walking to the top of the foyer and looking down, there at the bottom of the stairs was a little girl about ten or twelve years old. Her hair was brushed back held in place by a black headband. She wore a blue dress with a white dress-apron, white socks and black patent leather shoes, and no coat! She was looking down at the floor, sometimes covering her face with her hands as she cried. Thinking someone's child had gotten lost, I went down the stairs to comfort her and to see if she knew where she lived.

When I had gotten to the bottom of the stairs, I asked her who she was. She looked at me quizzically, then blink, she was gone. "No, No, No." I said to myself, this just didn't happen. I stood there stunned and then decided I must have been letting my imagination run away with me. I thought to myself, "Yea, everyone has been right all along, I am a little too dramatic."

I sighed and decided to just go back to work putting stuff away. I dismissed the little girl and forgot about her, at least, until 3:15 in the morning. I awoke to the sound of a child crying, the same soft weeping I had heard earlier. I honestly and truly pinched myself to see if I was awake, and I was. This time, I ran down the stairs. The little girl was standing in my foyer in the same blue dress and white apron as before, her posture and expressions identical as earlier.

I tried to talk to her but she wouldn't acknowledge me. I walked over to her and tried to touch her and blink, she was gone again. I sat on the bottom stair shaking my head in wonderment thinking I was going crazy. The little girl I nicknamed Alice as she reminded me so much of a picture of Alice in Wonderland from one of my childhood books. Alice came and went during the next three years. She never spoke to me or acknowledged my presence, except for one time when she said she had skinned her knee and needed a bandage.

About a year after Alice started visiting, a man dressed in Depression-era type clothing started visiting as well. He always came with Alice, though neither of them seemed to notice the other. The man was always well behaved, standing in a corner with his worn hat held in both hands in front of him. He wore the clothes of a farmer; Baggy overalls with a flannel shirt, work boots, and a hammer tucked into a loop at his side. His face was rather gaunt; His build suggested a slight man not weighing more than 160 pounds and about five foot seven or so. His eyes looked hungry in a quiet way, almost sad.

He never spoke to me in all the time he stayed. I tried to talk to him as I did with Alice, but he like Alice, never responded. The only time I got angry at my visitors was when they woke me one too many times by staring at me until I woke up. I told them they were no longer welcome in my bedroom and after that, they never came in the bedroom again.

I went to a psychiatrist about my visions, thinking I was really losing it. He did a lot of talking, but in the end he wrote me out a prescription for a couple of drugs. He told me that I was under stress from moving and that I probably had a difficult childhood and that these visions were unresolved problems from my past. Okay, I took the drugs and told my visitors they weren't real but a figment of my imagination. When we went for a ride in the car, my visitors came along. Nevertheless, I would tell myself, it wasn't happening but when my visitors turned up at a Christmas party, I excused myself and went home thinking I was going crazy.

At that time I had no understanding of the ghostly realm of the dead. My two friends didn't go away over night, they slowly quit coming around; Their images growing fainter and fainter when they did visit me. They haven't been back in over a year. I truly thought I was losing my marbles.

Then one day, my stepmother called and told me about a book written by my cousin about ghosts and haunted houses called, Twilight Visitors: Ghost Tales. I had my stepmother send me a copy of the book. It arrived and within a few hours, I had read every page in the book. I couldn't believe it. The book answered so many questions I had about my visions. I realized others have had similar experiences and that I was truly not losing my marbles.

Authors Notes:

The little girl and the depression-era man were lost and confused, forced to remain earthbound. The little girl may have died without her mother, such as in an accident or illness and felt lost and alone. She found brief relief with the depression-era man who appeared to be begging for food or a place to sleep as was so often the case during the Depression era. The constant need for food and shelter was so strong at death that the depression-era man felt compelled to continue searching for food and shelter.

The Last Drive Home

Jimmy grew up on his family farm in rural Union County, North Carolina that his family had owned for several generations. He had been gone from the farm for three years and coming home was like a breath of fresh air. After the bombing of Pearl Harbor, he had enlisted in the U.S. Army and was assigned to the European theater as an infantryman.

He would never forget the rain as he kneeled in the mud digging his foxhole so he might survive another night. Every night was the same, never knowing if the incoming mortars or artillery rounds would impact his foxhole. Jimmy was one of the fortunate ones who survived and returned home without injury.

After World War II, the economy was at its height and everyone was rushing out to buy the modern conveniences that were not available during the rationing period of the war. Jimmy had missed driving around in his red convertible while in Europe. Now, he had taken the red convertible out of storage in the barn and was looking forward to cruising down main street in town.

The future looked bright and Jimmy was making up for lost time dating the local gals. He worked hard on the farm during the week, but on Saturday night he would have a good bath and then drive to town to take in a picture show with Mary Lou. She had been his sweetheart during high school and now that he was home, he was rekindling the romance.

The long summer days were hot so after supper, the family would retire to the long front porch that faced West and watch the evening sun set. The evening sky would be full of radiant colors that slowly faded as the sky dimmed in the twilight. Elmer and his wife, Marge would sit on the front porch, rocking back and forth in their chairs each evening while listening to the big radio in the parlor room. Elmer would open the parlor window and the magic of radio would drift to the front porch as the white lace curtains fluttered in the evening breeze. Amy would sit next to her mother and help her darn work socks, mend coveralls or begin a knitting project. Amy was fifteen and was the baby of the family.

The family farm had a large barn in the rear of the house with corrals on each side. Behind the barn were open fields that held a variety of crops depending on the rotation period for the crops. The large barn had a large hayloft where they stacked the bales of hay for the animals to feed on during the winter. Elmer had his workbench in one corner of the barn. Farm equipment was always breaking down and needed repair. Sometimes bailing wire was not enough so Elmer stocked a good size inventory of nuts and bolts.

The farm had a straight mile-long dirt driveway to the hard surfaced road where Mr. Ashfork, the rural mail carrier, delivered mail to their mailbox. The dirt driveway started by the barn and went along the side the house directly west toward the hard surfaced road.

During the day, they could easily spot anyone approaching the farm since they would kick up a dust trail on the dirt road long before they arrived. In the evening, the approaching headlights would tell them when someone was visiting them. They could hear no road traffic from the hard surface road because of the distance from the farm house.

After supper, Jimmy had taken a bath and left for a date with Mary Lou, as Elmer, Marge and Amy gathered on the front porch to watch the evening sunset. Elmer was reading the newspaper and smoking his pipe. Marge and Amy were darning some socks and carrying on in a light conversation about the upcoming church social. Tonight was their special time as they always listened to the Grand Ole Opry from Nashville on Saturday nights. The radio program would be over at 11:00 P.M. and then they would retire to bed.

The Grand Ole Opry radio program had just finished as Marge spotted headlights coming down the mile-long dirt road.

"Jimmy is on time. He is such a good boy." Marge

said.

"He sure is sweet on Mary Lou." Elmer smiled as he looked at Marge.

"Well, I don't know what Jimmy sees in Mary Lou." Amy said with a disgusted look on her face.

"Honey, when you are older, you will understand." Marge said as she picked up her needles.

Since it was their bedtime, they got up from their chairs and went into the house to get ready for bed. Elmer and Marge's bedroom was on the driveway side of the house. Their bedroom window was open for some fresh air. They were looking out the window as the red convertible drove by their window. Instead of stopping at the rear of the house, the red convertible drove past and into the barn and out of sight. This was unusual since Jimmy normally left the car by the back door.

They could not figure out why he would drive into the barn since beyond the back of the barn was only an open field. After a few minutes, Jimmy had not come into the house and Marge became worried. Elmer said he would go out to the barn and see if Jimmy was having a problem. Elmer walked to the back porch, grabbed the kerosene lantern and lit it. He then walked over to the barn and to his astonishment found no car in or behind the barn. The tracks led into the barn, but suddenly vanished once inside.

Everyone was, needless to say, unnerved by this ghostly apparition and no one was able to go to sleep. They all huddled around the wood stove in the kitchen and talked about the incident until about midnight when they heard someone knocking on the front door. Elmer went to see who would be out at this time of night.

Marge told Amy that nothing good comes at a late hour. Elmer opened the door and saw the Union County Sheriff standing at the door with his hat in his hands. He asked to come in because he had some terrible news for the family.

The Sheriff walked over to the kitchen stove and held out his hands to warm them. Marge could sense something was wrong so she stood next to Elmer waiting for the reason for the Sheriff's visit. He explained that he had some bad news. Jimmy had apparently fallen asleep at the wheel of his car, crashing into a bridge abutment instantly killing himself at about 10:45 P.M.. Now if Jimmy had not crashed that night, he would have arrived home at about the same time as his family saw him. The crash site was only about fifteen minutes from the farm and Jimmy would have arrived home just as Grand Ole Opry was going off the air.

Authors Notes:

For some reason, after the crash, this young man became lost and confused, thinking he still had to drive home. The reality of death had not yet registered with him as he drove home. Apparently, after he drove his car into the barn, he vanished, never to return again.

Pets

Frequently people speak to us about their beloved pets and life after life by asking the following question: "Do they have a spirit that lives on after death?" We have experienced and recorded paranormal events suggesting that our pets have a spirit that survives the death process and continues in their life after life transformation. This belief that pets have a spirit that transcends death is based on our studies and empirical evidence gathered from our paranormal investigations. We have included some ghost stories about pets who have died and have returned to remain with their masters as a departed animal spirit or ghost pet. The following short stories are told by people who have deeply loved their pets and have treated them as if they were actual members of their family.

It is a very comforting thought to know that our beloved pets will live on after death. The bond of love welded in this life will not be broken in death. Our own pet is a fourteen-year-old Yorkshire Terrier, named "Shadow." Each day "Shadow" trots into the computer room and climbs into her bed next to the computer and oversees our literary project. "Shadow" has a personality of her own that is special and loving and is as much a part of this book as is the authors.

The authors have had their own experiences with pet ghosts. The house we were living in at the time of this book being published had such a ghost pet. We suspected it was a small dog or a large cat based on the activities and physical imprints of this spirit. Several times we have heard what sounds like the rustling of a dog or cat collar, but no such dog or cat has been observed. We suspect the former occupants of our home had such a pet and since we have a Yorkshire Terrier, the lonely ghost pets may be drawn to us.

The former occupant of the house was an elderly widowed lady who moved into the house after the death of her husband many years before. She loved the home very much and had lovely garden of both flowers and vegetables. Upon her death they interred her body in the cemetery behind the house. Her physical body may have been buried in the cemetery, but her spirit still roams the hallways of her house.

Several times we have been reading in bed late at night when all of a sudden the bed will rock as if a small dog or a large cat has jumped up onto the bed. The movement is not an earthquake or a house tremor due to a passing vehicle. The impression is immediately of a pet who jumped up onto the bed. This physical manifestation is eerie, especially when you look and see nothing on the bed.

This photograph reveals a ghostly dog!

Credit: Anil Harjani, Hong Kong

The Haunted Reality by Sharon A. Gill & Dave R. Oester

The following stories are tales about ghost pets that have returned to be with their Masters. The first tale is about two cats and then we have included a series of tales that are shorter, but still reinforce the concept that the spirits of our beloved pets live on after death. At the end of the chapter is a photograph of a ghostly dog proving that pets have life after life.

The Return of Two Cats

I don't know if you had any experiences with the ghosts of deceased pets, but my friend and I have had quite a few, one of which I stumbled into myself. I had a cat that my family had saved from near-death and my friend Sharon took the cat and gave it a home. The cat's name is Vincent and was continually plagued with health problems. Sharon spent amazing amounts of money on Vincent in vet bills, but he was definitely a special cat. He was the kind of cat that just flopped into your lap and purred away forever. When Sharon's father passed away, Vincent would seem to be constantly near her, as if he could sense her lost and was trying to comfort her.

It got to the point where Vincent was healthy and happy. He was running around the house in good spirits until one day he turned up missing. Sharon feared the worst, perhaps run over by a car or killed by raccoons that roamed the woods behind her house. She searched for him without success and when he didn't return in a couple days, she knew he was dead. A few days later she found part of a cat skull and a collar in her back yard and knew it was his. The racoons must have cornered him and torn him apart.

Sharon was very hurt by his loss and I felt grief at his passing. We had both loved that cat very much and it had come to mean something to each of us. In time, Sharon had various house guests including myself stay at her place. Once I was laying upstairs on a couch resting, not having gone to sleep yet. The house was dark and quiet and I wasn't anywhere near sleepy. As I lay there, I felt something moving at the foot of the couch, on top of the covers. I waited a moment and felt it a little more.

Now, anyone who has a cat, knows the feelings of a cat kneading the covers with one paw, then the other back and forth continuously. I recognized it immediately and looked down expecting to find a cat, but there wasn't anything. A series of vibrations occurred like that of a purr, which I also recognized. It wasn't a sound, just something you could feel. It was the strangest thing, feeling something that took up weight, yet wasn't visible! Then, it moved to my side and lay purring.

I was scared at first but then realized that it wasn't anything really harmful, just too bizarre for words. I felt the area of the cover with my hand, and could feel nothing although the actual spot on the covers was warm. Eventually it stopped and I went to sleep after a long while. In the morning I mentioned it cautiously to Sharon who seemed surprised and delighted at the same time. She said a mutual friend who had stayed as a house guest at different times had mentioned a similar experience in a downstairs bedroom.

When I had described that it had laid next to my side and purred, Sharon beamed and said that it was one of Vincents favorite spots. Now, I would probably have dismissed this whole thing as a freak incident, but it happened a few times after that in my own house where Vincent originally lived during his first recovery.

The second time I was startled, but not scared. The third time, it was like any other cat on your bed. The oddest instance was when Sharon went to London for two weeks and was in the middle of a performance of "Phantom of the Opera." She looked down at her feet and saw her cat, Vincent, which then disappeared in front of her eyes. This time corresponded to the same time that I had seen Vincent for the last time.

My own cat was named Susie, a Siamese that was eighteen years old when she passed on. On one occasion, both Vincent and Susie had come back to me. Now one cat is odd, but two cats are just really bizarre! Suzie had breathing difficulties in her last year or so of life, so I recognized the off-kilter purr and short breathing. Vincent had brought Susie back to see me. Since that time I have had no more personal experiences with my deceased pets. Sharon, on the other hand, has had an occasional rare visit from Vincent, but not so often.

Now, Sharon has gotten a new cat. She is not new to ghostly visitors. She could tell an interesting tale of her own. It seems that when she moved into her home in Mukilteo, Washington which is just off the waterfront where Indians had lived, an old Indian woman standing in her staircase greeted her. When she went to talk to this old Indian woman, she vanished.

Kitty Haunting

My family rented a small house in Castro Valley, California from 1980 to 1982. After a few months we found a small orange tabby kitten about six months old and adopted it, but a month later the cat died of distemper. Two months later we got another kitten. Now, I should say at this point, that when we moved into the house, an adult male cat already occupied it who adopted us.

After a few weeks my mother complained of little incidences of small items disappearing. She kept finding them tucked in a dark corner under the kitchen sink. We figured the new kitten was doing it but soon noted that both cats avoided the area. However, this was the preferred hiding place of the kitten who had died. Soon after my mother began laughingly talking about the "ghost" cat. It seems that she would feel a pressure on her legs at night but there was no cat present. Another time we found the throw blanket slightly moved and a depression formed, as if a cat was kneading the area before settling down in a curled-up-ball.

My grandmother was visiting and complained of a

kitten bothering her all night. By this time our living cats were both over a year old. A friend of mine spent the night and complained of the same thing. Neither of them was told about the ghost before their complaints. Just prior to our moving, everything was boxed up for the move. I was laying in bed, on my back, having just finished a book. I turned off the light, closed my eyes and stretched, preparing to roll over on my stomach, when I felt a cat jump onto my chest.

Immediately, I realized this was not either of the adult cats. I opened my eyes and my heart lurched and played a rapid rumba. I saw through an ectoplasmic image shaped like a fuzzy six-month-old kitten. It was grayish white and definitely see-through, but had the impression of color and stripes. I was startled at the time, but knew quickly that this creature was friendly. I shut my eyes tight, and held my breath until the animal moved. Without opening my eyes, I turned on the lights and then opened my eyes. Nothing appeared to be in the room.

Fluffy, the Ghost Cat

My wife is one of those people who have a special place in their hearts for stray animals. I, on the other hand, am one of those people who don't like cats. So I was less than pleased one evening when my wife came home with a stray cat, which she named Fluffy. Well, Fluffy and I didn't hit it off. I have a habit of hanging my neckties over the door handle of my closet door.

It just so happened that Fluffy quickly turned my ties into hanging pieces of exercise equipment. He would work off his feline love handles by jumping up and clawing my ties. Too stubborn and too stupid to simply fold my ties and put them into my dresser drawer, I used my shredded ties as a tangible argument why Fluffy had to go.

After about six weeks and three or four ties destroyed, our landlord received a mysterious anonymous note saying that the couple in apartment 9-A were keeping a pet cat. Since having the cat violated the terms of our lease, we shipped Fluffy off to live at my in-law's farm. Unfortunately, a pickup truck hit Fluffy three weeks later. My wife took it quite hard. My grieving period was a bit shorter.

Weeks passed and I was enjoying a pleasant night's sleep, not battling my wife for control of the blankets as she was out of town for a few days on business. I had a brand-new tie hanging on my closet door, and all was right with the world. Suddenly, the familiar scratching sound on the closet door awakened me, just as I had been so many times before. Seconds later, reality struck, and I sat straight up in my bed. Fluffy was now residing in kitty heaven, so what was making the noise? Just then, and I swear to this day, that I saw that familiar white tail dash out of the bedroom.

My heart began to pound. I turned on the lights and ran to the closet. I grabbed the four-iron out of my golf bag and searched the entire apartment, feeling like I was in the middle of a Stephen King novel. As I bent down to look under the sofa, golf club firmly in my grip, I expected a crazed wildcat to dart out and sink its claws into my throat. After finding absolutely nothing, I sat on the edge of the bed and laughed at myself. A grown man allowing his imagination to run wild, like a teenager staying alone for the first time. The next morning, I laughed again at myself as I got dressed for work. I was standing in front of the mirror as I put on my tie. Suddenly, the reflection in the mirror couldn't be true. I looked down at my tie and saw it had been shredded at the bottom!

The Warning

I was saddened when my beloved pet dog passed away. She had been with me for many years and had been a constant companion. Her name was "Buffy" and she had the most loving heart I have ever encountered. She would sort of whine when she wanted something from me. Her whine was different than other dogs. It was her personal voice pattern that I came to recognize after many years.

After her death, I would often get the strange feeling that "Buffy" was still hanging around the house. I never saw her but I had the distinct feelings at times that she was near. Once, I could almost believe that she would come trotting around the corner from the kitchen like she did for so many years. Other times, it felt like she was near, waiting for me. Finally, I was able to let go of her passing and get on with my life.

Nine months later, I was in the bathroom fixing my hair and running late for work when I heard a dog whine that sounded so familiar to me. I walked into the living room and again heard the same dog whine. This time the sound came from the same room that I was standing in. I knew who was making that sound. I called "Buffy's" name and the dog whined again. Now, this whine was the same pitch that my "Buffy" would make when she didn't want me to leave home without her. Immediately, I felt an overwhelming sense of danger encompass my entire being.

I didn't understand what it could mean as the feeling lasted only for a few minutes. I dismissed the danger and turned to go back to the bathroom when I saw my "Buffy" standing in the bathroom doorway. She was in full form, looking like she did when she was alive. She was wagging her tail like she wanted to play, then suddenly she vanished. I had to finish getting ready for work as I was going to be late so I had to put the incident out of my mind until I had some time to think about it without being under pressure.

My car had to be filled with gas if I were going to make it to work so I had to stop at the only gas station close to my home. I left home and drove to the gas station situated along a very busy intersection. After filling the gas tank, I entered the busy intersection. The highways leading into the intersection, each had four lanes. I pulled into a lane that I thought was empty.

Wrong! A large diesel 18-wheeler carrying a full load

had decided to occupy that same empty space on the busy road at the same time that I had moved into it. I still don't know how I survived or how I avoided the collision that should have followed. I remember other people staring at me, but I can't recall any other details of that near-fatal accident. Now, I think back and wonder if "Buffy" had been trying to warn me about this danger. She must really have loved me to come back and warn me.

I Want You Back

I'm sure there are people out there who don't realize animals feel the same way we do and hurt for the same reasons. Years ago my Mother had a small dog named Mickey who was very love spoiled and very much a part of the family. One day my stepfather got sick. A neighbor lady came and took him to the hospital where he was admitted.

Several times that same neighbor came to see how Mother was doing and if she needed anything. Each time she came, Mickey would hide her face in the corner and refuse to look at the neighbor who had taken her master away.

In our own family we had another incident occur which convinced us that animals do have feelings, as we do. We had a wire-haired terrier named Lady, who was very smart. One day my young son brought home a poodle in his shirt pocket. We named her Tink Pot for obvious reasons. She had to learn everything from scratch.

When Lady was seven years old, she got sick. I wrapped her in a blanket and my husband and son rushed her to the vet, where she died. After a time I took away the box bed she had slept in and disposed of it. Soon after that, Tink Pot started putting bits of food in the spot where the box had once been. Each day when I went into the room, I would find small pieces of bread or anything else she could carry and leave at the spot where she had last seen Lady.

The Technology

This section will deal with a discussion of the technology used for the detection and recording of ghostly EMF energy anomalies. The electronic equipment employed is not unique or of special manufacture or design. All of the electronic equipment is considered to be "off-the-shelf" variety and purchased in most electronic stores or ordered through the mail from electronic supply companies. Radio Shack stocks many of the meters that we use. We have included the catalog number where appropriate.

The authors are using the portable electromagnetic field tester produced by A.W. Sperry Instruments, Inc., Model EMF-200A. This unit has a range of zero to 199.9-milligauss and comes with a large LCD display. The unit operates on a nine-volt battery and is small enough to fit inside the shirt pocket. EMF meters can also be acquired from Davis Instruments. Their model #480822, catalog number EH11948056, is similar to the EMF-200A. Davis Instruments has a budget EMF Detector, catalog number SY2110011 called Electro-Sensor EMF Detector ES9000.

If we employ the hand-held electromagnetic field tester in the detection of EMF energy anomalies, then the operator must be aware that many appliances generate an EMF field. Large appliances such as refrigerators, microwave ovens, television sets, fish tanks, etc., will generate a very strong EMF field that will affect the EMF meter. Therefore, we disregard readings greater than 10-milligauss. If the EMF sensor is placed near a potential

EMF source and the LCD display numbers rapidly increase as we shorten the distance between the EMF sensor and the object, then disregard the false readings. When scanning with this sensor common sense must be used, as not all readings will show the presence of an energy anomaly or departed spirit. Always verify that a hidden source of EMF is not generating the reading, such as junction boxes on the outside wall of the house or building.

Actual field scans seem to suggest that whenever a reading is obtained greater than 1.0-milligauss, then the operator has a potential ghost target. However, a spike could give a reading greater than 1.0-milligauss, but the reading will immediately drop below the 1.0-milligauss level. If this happens, then the operator may have scanned across a departed spirit that is moving about the room. It has been our experience that when we have discovered the target, its parameter is about the size of a football. The outside edges of the football-like energy anomaly are weaker while the center would yield the strongest reading. The target may be stationary or it may be in motion within an area after the initial contact. We must continuously scan the EMF sensor probe to find the target if it is moving.

This unit may lack some bells and whistles of the more sophisticated and expensive EMF units but the circuitry is sufficient for the detection of the various shifts in the electromagnetic fields. As stated earlier, we could employ a simple compass if an EMF meter was not available. The operator would scan with the compass until they observe a deviation in magnetic North, as shown by the needle swinging off magnetic North. When this occurs, simply follow the direction the needle is pointing. The needle would be pulled from the North position toward the source of the electromagnetic energy. The compass would point to the EMF energy anomaly. Once the target has been identified, then start photographing the area.

The phantom voice phenomena are events where a ghost or departed spirit speaks to us and we hear this voice with our ears or on audio tape recordings made at the time. Often the ghostly voice is below or above the human range of hearing which is one reason that an animal such as a dog or cat can "hear" their voices. During our investigations, we employ an analog sound level meter that is available through Radio Shack, catalog number 33-2050, to monitor sounds emitted above or below our human range of hearing. The analog sound level meter can detect sounds below or above this range and display an intensity level for them. The room has to be absolutely quiet or the sound level meter will be ineffective.

The analog sound level meter is hand-held with selectable range scales of intensities. A nine-volt battery powers the meter and includes a battery checker that is build into the unit. We employ the analog sound level meter like the EMF sensor for scanning. If ghostly sounds are present, the sound level meter will detect them and by shifting the direction of the meter, we can learn the location of the target. Watch the intensity meter for minor needle movement while the analog sound level meter is set on the lowest scale. Once we discover needle movements, slowly scan the meter around the room until the signal is increased. The needle will flutter lightly when ghostly sounds are detected then photographs should be taken of the area. A tape recorder could tape these sounds for future evaluation.

Another method of detecting these energy anomalies is with a digital thermometer. Investigators have documented many cases where a narrow column of cold air is rising from the floor to the ceiling. The investigator can pass their hands through this column of cold air that appears always to be very narrow. Could this cold spot be the chills that people have reported on the backs of their necks as their hair stood on end? Could their hair be standing on end be due to the electrostatic charge of the swirling energy vortex?

Perhaps this swirling energy vortex is the source of the column that produces the cold air and the electrostatic discharge. It is interesting that our photograph of this swirling energy vortex apparently has density because it reflects light and casts a shadow. Sometimes, the temperature has not been cold but hot. A good example is at the Liberty Theater in Astoria, Oregon. There is one seat with a wooden arm rest that becomes hot to the touch.

The authors are using a Micronta, which is a digital thermometer produced by Tandy Corporation, Radio Shack catalog number 63-844. This unit has the combination LCD twin display for both temperature and humidity. The unit records temperature changes in tenths of a degree which is sufficient. Any such piece of equipment that can register rapid minor changes in temperature would be acceptable to work with for the detection of cold or hot spots.

We recommend any 35mm camera for photograph-ing ghostly apparitions. This can range from the simple point-and-shoot 35mm cameras to the more complex cameras with automatic focusing and automatic shutter speeds. We recommend that the 35mm camera be set on manual mode and the aperture at the lowest f-stop as the aperture needs to be wide open to allow the maximum amount of light to enter through the lens. Shooting with flash is okay but remember that the camera will be operating at 1/60th of a second speed so be sure the camera is steady in your hands before snapping the shutter, otherwise the picture may be blurry. Where possible, use a tripod!

The authors are using two 35mm cameras for their ghost photography work. The first camera is the Pentax PZ-20 with a 28-80mm lens at 1:3.5-4.7 that can operate in both the manual and automatic settings. The second camera is the small Pentax UC1 with a 32mm lens at 1:3.5. We have obtained good ghostly images from both 35mm cameras. Friends have sent us some photographs of ghostly images obtained with an inexpensive point-and-shoot 35mm camera. The key to photographically capturing ghostly apparitions may be in the brand of film used.

We have concluded that Kodak produces the best color film to capture these apparitions or energy anomalies. Film produced by Kodak is more responsive to the reds then other films. Kodak films respond to the higher end of the visible light spectrum where we find that we can capture ghostly images. The authors prefer to use a high speed Kodak film of 400 ASA or higher during their investigations. We have shot and developed hundreds of rolls of other film brands without recording any ghostly images. All of the ghostly apparitions we have captured on film have been with Kodak film.

Polaroid film is a transparent material containing embedded crystals that can polarize light. Perhaps this polarization of light allows the energy anomaly to become visible. Polaroid film will often capture images from the infrared regions of the electromagnetic spectrum. Polaroid film has an advantage over conventional film, such as the photograph being developed immediately, thus allowing the viewer to see if they have captured any ghostly apparitions on film. Any kind of Polaroid film can be used for photographing ghostly images. The authors use a Polaroid Captiva for instant access to photo prints.

Some consider infrared film to be the best. This film is also the most difficult and expensive to use and to have developed since the film must be sent to a special infrared processing lab. The film must be loaded and unloaded in absolute darkness within a black bag. For example, a light source the size of a pin hole would ruin the unexposed infrared film rendering it useless. In addition, infrared film requires an 87C-filter or a red filter to block out all light completely. The 35mm camera must have the infrared setting so check your manual before attempting to use infrared film.

Someone interested in trying their luck at becoming a ghost hunter could start building their ghost hunting tool bag with simple yet effective tools. We would suggest the following two items to be considered for your initial ghost hunting bag of tools. First, a 35mm camera with Kodak 400 ASA film. The second piece of equipment is a standard magnetic compass for detecting the ghostly energy anomalies. The compass should be used as a directional finder, using the needle to point to the energy anomaly. With these two tools, you are ready to begin as ghost hunters. Good luck and good hunting.

The Contributors

We wish to thank the following individuals for taking the time to send us their ghost story either by snail mail (letter), in person, or by E-mail. Some of the contributors requested that we list their story under the name, Anonymous.

Contributor	**Name of Ghost Tale**
Anonymous	Friend Returns From the Dead
	The Girl in the Nightgown
	The Return of Two Cats
	Kitty Haunting
	Fluffy, the Ghost Cat
	The Warning
Anthony, Adrian D.	The Substation
	White House with Red Trim
Barton, David	The Ghost Biker
Briggs, Sean	Within a Circle
	The Lost Sheep
	Shadows in the Mist
Burdick, Joyce	Wedding Day Photograph
Burgh, Virginia	Mirror Reflection Photograph
Carver, Susan	The Nurse Ghost
Cassinelli, Bill	A True Story
Chamberlain, Bob/Renee Travis & Heather	Grandmother's Concerns
Conlin, Tisa	The Ghost of Connor Hotel
Cook, Azarina	The Ghostly Party
Dahner, Sara	Returning for the Rosary

Wanted:

Ghost Stories

and

Ghost Photographs

We are busy collecting stories for our third book. If you have had an experience and would like us to consider it for our next book, please send it to us. If you have an interesting photograph of something strange or ghostly, please send it to us.

Send your stories and/or photographs to:

StarWest Images

P.O. Box 976

St. Helens, OR 97051

Thank you,

Sharon A. Gill
Dave R. Oester